SNIPER VS SPOTTER

CARI Z
L.A. WITT

Copyright Information

This is a work of fiction. Names, characters, places, and incidents are either the product of the author's imagination or are used fictitiously. Any resemblance to actual persons living or dead, business establishments, events, or locales is entirely coincidental.

Sniper vs Spotter

First edition

Copyright © 2021 Cari Z & L.A. Witt

Edited by Leta Blake

Cover Art by Lori Witt

All rights reserved. No part of this book may be reproduced or transmitted in any form or by any means, electronic or mechanical, including photocopying, recording, or by any information storage and retrieval system without the written permission of the publisher, and where permitted by law. Reviewers may quote brief passages in a review. To request permission and all other inquiries, contact L.A. Witt at gallagherwitt@gmail.com

ISBN: 979-8-47268-975-5

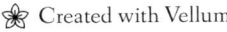 Created with Vellum

ABOUT SNIPER VS SPOTTER

Mortal-enemies-turned-furniture-breaking-lovers August Morrison and Ricardo Torralba have found a groove that suits them both. They've teamed up as hired guns, they live together, and by some miracle, they haven't killed each other. It's the closest to normal they'll ever have, and they love it.

But their guns-and-roses future is thrown into chaos when Ricardo's past comes crashing into their present. What begins as a favor for an old friend—well, "friend," but don't tell August—quickly spirals into something far bigger than they anticipated. Now they're in way over their heads with powerful people on both sides of the law, and it's going to take more than snark and explosions to see them through.

Nevertheless, there *will* be plenty of snark and explosions, because this is August and Ricardo, and no one would expect any less. In between the smoke and sarcasm, though, they are determined to bring an evil operation crashing down... no matter who they have to work with to get the job done.

And no matter who they have to kill.

Sniper vs Spotter is the sequel to the apparently-it-doesn't-want-to-be-a-standalone *Hitman vs Hitman*, which absolutely *was* supposed to be a standalone, but August and Ricardo (predictably) refused to be contained. Our audiobook narrator also shares some of the blame, *Michael*. So here we are.

CHAPTER 1

"UGH." AUGUST GROANED THEATRICALLY AND slammed the car's passenger side door with his hip. "I swear sometimes it's like I don't even *know* you."

Ricardo shut his own door with less force, though the sound still echoed through August's cavernous garage, and he hid a grin as he casually said, "You *don't* know me."

August shot him a look, then tsked and came around to the trunk. "I'm just saying—what kind of Philistine sees something *that* sexy and doesn't pick it up for his boyfriend?"

"August." Ricardo joined him behind the car and slid a hand over the small of August's back. "I'm an assassin, not a thief."

"So, what?" August glared at him. "You just told me about that sexy pair of platinum-set diamond-and-tanzanite cufflinks you saw in the mark's house to tease me?"

Ricardo let the grin come to life. "See? You *do* know me!"

He got maybe a little too much enjoyment out of the

exasperated groan that followed. "You are the worst, Ricardo!"

"Mmhmm." Ricardo popped the trunk, then reached in to get his bag. "So then you don't want to join me for that shower?"

The petulance in August's expression vanished. "I didn't say that."

"But you just said—"

August cut him off with a long kiss, then murmured, "Get upstairs and take off your pants."

Ricardo snorted. "Anyone ever tell you what a romantic you are?"

"Says the man who passed up a free pair of overpriced cufflinks for the man who gave him an entire closet." August jabbed Ricardo's chest. "A *closet*, Ricardo!"

Ricardo just laughed, and they collected their gear from the trunk and headed inside. The job had been a straightforward one. Well, as straightforward as any job was when the client hired two people to do it, anyway. Ricardo had been tasked with snuffing out the billionaire ass clown who aggressively engaged in overseas labor exploitation (read: slavery) to keep his production costs down, and August had simultaneously made sure the man's arguably *more* evil adult sons didn't inherit the family business. In fact, the business itself was the other reason Ricardo hadn't taken the cufflinks; theft wasn't something he did, but given some of the industries these assholes were involved in, the odds of those diamonds and tanzanite being sourced responsibly were... slim at best.

Upstairs, he and August went into their respective closets to put away their clothes, guns, and other tools of the trade. And he had to admit—when August said he'd given him a closet, he hadn't been kidding. While Ricardo had been reluctant to give other partners (what few he'd had) so much as a drawer or some hanger space, August had given him this gigantic thing. In fact, the entire guest suite was Ricardo's, including its labyrinthine closet with hidden biometrically accessed places to stash illegal weapons. Though Ricardo never slept in here—that was what August's bed was for—it was nice to have some space of his own. And God knew August's ridiculously huge mansion had plenty of space, especially now that the months-long construction project was over. August had basically blown up the place so he and Ricardo could escape a bunch of goons trying to kill them, and fixing it had been no small task.

"Such a shame to see all that go away," August had mused as a crew had begun tearing out charred, shattered, splintered, and otherwise destroyed chunks of his house. *"All we'll have left is the memories of you showing up to valiantly save me."* Then he'd touched Ricardo's arm and solemnly added, *"At least the closet where we had our first kiss won't have to be renovated. That's sacred ground."*

Rolling his eyes had left Ricardo with a hell of a headache after that.

Today, he went about the usual tasks of putting away his weapons. They'd cleaned their guns last night (*"Ooh, foreplay!"* August had exclaimed upon seeing the cleaning kits, and he hadn't been joking), so there was nothing left to do now except stash it all and then do laundry. Well, and take a shower. Not that either of them really needed it—all they'd done today was drive a few hundred miles—but Ricardo had used "if we leave now, I'll fuck you in the shower at home" to hustle August out the door when he'd been dawdling this morning. And he was, if nothing else, a man of his word.

After he'd put everything away and put clothes into the hamper, he took his personal cell phone—the one he *didn't* take with him on jobs—out of one of the safes. Checking his messages always helped him return to the mundane world where crosshairs and sightlines weren't at the front of his mind.

Most of the messages in his voicemail box were the usual—his mother asking when he'd visit (hopefully soon), if he'd been to confession recently (no), and when they'd meet his new boyfriend (hahahaha never). The dry cleaner was reminding him he still needed to pick up a few things. There was also a woman who sounded very concerned about his car's extended warranty.

But there was one message he definitely didn't expect.

"Hello, Mr. Torralba. This is Andi Caldwell at Brinkman & Caldwell. I... have kind of an unusual request, and I need to speak to you as soon as possible. Please call me back at your earliest convenience."

Following that was one message from her, reiterating that it was unusual and urgent.

Ricardo eyed his phone. Why in God's name was his ex-wife's divorce lawyer calling him? Their divorce had been finalized... what, eight years ago now? His own lawyer had gone to prison for something and the firm had closed, which was probably why she hadn't bothered calling him first, but still, why in the world...

"Ricky, darling?" August swanned into the closet doorway and struck a pose. He was completely naked, resting one hand on the door frame while the other stroked his prominent erection, and he met Ricardo's eyes with a smarmy grin. "Are you going to come out of the closet and join me or not?"

Ricardo huffed a quiet laugh, the sight of his naked and

eager boyfriend momentarily distracting him from the weird messages. "Just let me make a quick call." He gestured with his phone. "Go get ready for me."

August eyed the phone, his grin turning to a pout. "A quick call? Are you going to leave me in there getting all wrinkly with blue balls while you—"

"It'll be quick. I promise." Ricard touched August's chin and brushed a kiss across his mouth. "Go."

August scowled, but then he gave Ricardo's hardening cock a stroke through his pants, the grin returning when Ricardo gasped. "Five minutes, or I'm taking care of it without you."

"Don't you dare," Ricardo growled.

August quirked a brow in a challenging look. "Then don't keep me waiting, hmm?"

With that, he turned to go, and Ricardo gave that perfect ass a sharp slap, which earned him a saucy wink.

Goddamn. His ex's lawyer was notoriously long-winded, but come hell or high water, this would be a brief call.

Fortunately, some stars had aligned in his favor for once—Andi wasn't available. In fact, it was late enough in the day that she'd probably already gone home for the evening. Ricardo left her a quick message, and then he headed for the bathroom, unbuttoning his shirt as he went.

Ricardo didn't expect to hear back from Andi that night. When his phone lit up with her number at almost ten thirty, alarm shot through him, and he immediately thought the worst. If his ex-wife's divorce lawyer was chasing him down after eight years and calling him at this hour, something had to be wrong.

He put the phone to his ear. "Hold on a second." Without waiting for a response, he turned to August, who was lounging on the giant sofa in those Madagascar Penguin boxers he loved. "I'll be right back."

"Hmm?" August looked up at him, then at the phone. With a nod, he went back to scrolling through something on his own screen. For as obnoxious as he could be, he understood like few others that some calls required serious privacy. That, and Ricardo had fucked him in the shower and then into the mattress, and August was still a little too dazed to be his usual self. Ricardo considered that something of an achievement.

He stepped outside onto the back deck and put the phone to his ear. "Sorry. What's going on?"

"Oh, I'm so glad I got in touch with you." Andi sounded genuinely relieved.

"Yeah? What's wrong? Is Eve all right?"

"She's..." The hesitation made his blood turn cold.

Gripping the phone tighter, Ricardo straightened. "Is she or isn't she?"

"She's fine. Sort of. I..." Andi exhaled. "Look, she needs to speak to you, ideally face to face. She's got a situation and she thinks you're the only one who can help her."

Ricardo cocked a brow for no one's benefit but his own. "What kind of situation?"

"She didn't give me details. But she said it's urgent that she see you."

He swallowed. "All right. Tell her to call me."

"Can I give her this number, then?" The answer seemed obvious, but being a lawyer, she probably had to ask.

"Yes."

"Perfect. Thanks, Ricardo."

"Don't mention it."

They ended the call, and he stared at his phone. He wasn't sure what he'd been expecting when he'd contacted Andi, but his ex-wife needing help? Being in a jam where she couldn't think to ask anyone else? He couldn't begin to guess what the situation was or how he could help. It wasn't like she knew about his job. He'd carefully hidden it from her and was still paying alimony because he'd falsely admitted to cheating on her in order to avoid telling her (or the judge) that the real reason for his second phone and evasive behavior was that he was a hired gun. As far as he knew, she still thought he was a cheating son of a bitch, which meant she probably hadn't somehow found out about his primary source of income.

So then what the hell was—

The phone rang again, this time with an unknown number.

Ricardo swallowed. Then he cleared his throat and answered. "Hello?"

"Oh, thank God." That was a voice he hadn't heard in a long time. "It's Eve. You talked to Andi?"

"Yeah. She said you have a situation."

"I do." Eve pushed out a breath. "I'd... I think this is better discussed in person."

He furrowed his brow. She sounded nervous. Downright paranoid. Swallowing, he glanced over his shoulder into the house. August's sock-covered feet were still hanging over the couch's armrest.

Facing the yard again, he said, "I'm going to give you an address. Meet me here." Ricardo glanced back at the house again, then added, "But I need you to do something for me."

"What's that?" Now she sounded suspicious.

"I'm... There's someone else here. Just... Do me a favor, and do *not* mention that we were married, all right?"

Silence hung on the line. Sounding even more suspicious, she asked, "Why?" But before he could explain himself, she quickly said, "You know what? I'm not going to worry about it. I'm asking you to do me a huge favor, so if you don't want her to know we're divorced... fine. It's none of my business, and I really need your help."

"All right. Here's the address."

Eve didn't let the grass grow.

Less than an hour after they'd spoken, Ricardo motioned for her to park in the garage between his car and August's many. Apparently she'd done well for herself since their divorce—that shiny blue Porsche was a hell of an upgrade from the Charger she'd been driving back then. Beautiful car, though he was more than a little disconcerted by the prominent dent in the passenger side door. The paint hadn't been damaged, so it likely wasn't a metal-on-metal impact. In fact, if he had to guess by its height, size, and shape, that was from someone's foot. Likely with a lot of force behind it.

He gritted his teeth. *If you're here to ask me to off an abusive ex-boyfriend, I won't even charge you.*

The engine quieted. When Eve stepped out, he stole a second to take her in. She had on a bespoke gray pantsuit whose designer August would probably be able to name at a glance, and her red hair had some white along the edges that hadn't been there before. She'd always been striking, and that hadn't changed. She was... What was she now, forty-three? Forty-four? Whatever. She looked as good now as she had back then.

Tired, though. She looked incredibly tired. Dark circles were almost hidden beneath some makeup, but she couldn't mask the fatigue in her eyes. Eve was not someone who let life beat her down, so between the dent on her Porsche and the exhaustion in her expression, Ricardo was even more alarmed now about what had brought her here.

Unaware of him scrutinizing her, Eve looked around the immense garage and its array of sparkly toys. August had insisted on upgrading Ricardo's decrepit sedan to something a little classier, but even the silver Mercedes looked somewhat junior varsity parked alongside August's fleet of vehicles, including the new Ferrari, the Aston Martin, and the Escalade. And that was to say nothing of the gleaming Ducati Desmosedici, a motorcycle that Ricardo was pretty sure had set August back around a quarter of a million. Basically pocket change for a billionaire. Now Eve's Porsche 911 had been added to the mix.

Speaking of, Eve turned her wide-eyed stare on him. "This is, um..." She gestured at the various vehicles. "Did you win the lottery?"

Ricardo opened his mouth to speak, but—

"He most certainly did." August sounded spectacularly pleased with himself. Even more than usual, which said something. Appearing beside Ricardo, he extended his hand. "Augustus Mason. And you are?"

She blinked a couple of times, glancing at Ricardo, then shook August's hand. "Eve T—" Her eyes flicked toward Ricardo, but she recovered quickly and smiled. "Just Eve is fine."

Ricardo's teeth snapped shut. Fuck. She hadn't gotten around to changing her last name, had she? Good thing she'd remembered herself and hadn't said it. Dear God, August would be insufferable if he knew he was in the company of Ricardo's ex-wife.

"It's lovely to meet you, just Eve." August looked her up and down in a way that was conspicuously not the leer of a straight man. Not that anyone would ever mistake August for straight anyway. "Is that Stella McCartney?" He put a hand to his chest. "My goodness, that's amazing. And why haven't you invited her in, Ricardo? Do you want some wine, Eve? I have coffee and a million other things too, but I also have a lovely bottle of Pinot Grigio if you're—"

"Just some coffee would be fine." Eve offered a tight smile. "Thank you."

August turned to Ricardo. "You?" There was a question in his eyes beyond the drink preference, and Ricardo recognized it for what it was—was this someone who could know they were together? Or should they be "roommates"?

Ricardo answered with a hand on August's waist and a light kiss on his cheek. "Coffee. Thanks."

August brightened, relief replacing the uncertainty. Then he disappeared into the house, leaving Eve and Ricardo in the garage full of luxury on wheels.

When Ricardo turned to her, she was staring in the direction August had gone, her eyebrows higher than he'd ever seen them.

The door shut, and she looked at Ricardo, eyes still wide. "Well, then. You found yourself a hot, young, rich man." She squeezed his arm and smiled. "Nicely done."

"Yeah, yeah. But I meant what I said—do *not* tell him you're my ex-wife."

Amusement quirked her lips. "Why not?" she asked with faux innocence. "Don't want your new boyfriend to know you've been married?" The playful teasing in her voice made him suddenly wonder if he did, in fact, have a type. Because while Eve was subdued right now, she could be very... not. God help him if she and August ever drank together.

"Oh, he knows I've been married." Ricardo gestured for her to head inside. "He'll just be insufferable about it if he finds out *we* were married."

"Why's that? Is there something wrong with being married to me?"

"No, but he's..." Ricardo paused. "You know what? Go ahead. See what happens."

She looked over her shoulder at him. "Hmm. Yeah, how about we keep that between us?"

"That's what I thought."

In the kitchen, August had poured everyone coffee, and once the coffee had been duly polluted, the three of them sat down in his recently reconstructed living room. There was still a part of Ricardo that felt weird about lounging in here, watching movies, or fucking (which August *loved* to do on that damn couch) when he could still vividly remember burnt wood, shattered glass, and pieces of dead goons littering the floor. Sitting in here with his boyfriend and ex-wife to discuss what had prompted the call didn't go down very easily either.

"So." Ricardo sat back in one of the armchairs. "You said you have a situation."

He half-expected August to make a snarky comment about *"Jesus, Ricky, let the girl drink her coffee and chat for a bit,"* but he didn't. More and more, Ricardo was coming to realize that August did, in fact, possess some understanding of when it was prudent to keep his damn mouth shut. He appreciated that.

Eve sipped her coffee, then set it on a saucer on the

ultramodern glass and metal coffee table. "I do, yes. And you're the only one I can think of who can help."

"Why's that?"

She crossed her legs, clasped her long fingers around her knee, and took a deep breath. "Because my ex-boyfriend is stalking me. He won't leave me alone, and he's decided if he can't have me, no one can." She shuddered, looking right in Ricardo's eyes. "And I don't know of anyone else who might be able to stop him, because no one else knows him as well as you do."

Something curdled in the pit of Ricardo's stomach. The way she said *him*. The dent in the Porsche. The fact that she couldn't think of anyone else.

Oh, fuck. Eve. Tell me it isn't...

She held his gaze.

He held hers.

Ricardo could feel August glancing back and forth between them, question marks floating above his confused face, but he wisely stayed quiet.

Ricardo swallowed. "Don't make me guess."

She shifted with obvious discomfort.

Groaning, he rubbed a hand over his face. "Please tell me you didn't date him."

"I can't change it now," she snapped. "It doesn't matter why I did anything in the past. It matters what he's doing now, and—"

"And I could have fucking told you that dating a goddamned sociopath would—"

"Yeah, well, I was hurt and pissed off and it turned out a good way to get back at my cheating asshole of an ex-husband was to date one his Army buddies, okay?" Her voice shook, and not just with anger. "I'm not proud of it, and I'm definitely not proud of being with him for *so* long, but it happened. When I finally got smart and tried to leave him, he went psycho, so can it with the *I told you so* and just figure out how to fucking stop him, okay?"

Ricardo blinked, as startled by the tirade as the revelation. Deflating a little, he put up his hands. "All right. All right. I'm sorry." He sighed, and he wanted to choke that motherfucker because how many times had he made comments about Ricardo's hot wife? How many times had he and Ricardo gotten into fights—a few of which had involved fists—because the asshole had shamelessly let it slip what he'd do to Eve if he ever got her into bed? And the minute she was single, he'd swooped in like a—

August cleared his throat. "Um." He put up his hand like a timid schoolboy in class. "Quick question... When you say 'cheating asshole ex-husband,' do you mean...?" He gestured at Ricardo.

Eve sucked in a sharp breath. Ricardo's stomach dropped. Goddammit.

"Whoa." August's eyes flicked back and forth between them. "And the asshole stalker boyfriend—"

"*Ex*-boyfriend," Eve interjected.

"Ex-boyfriend, excuse me." August turned to Ricardo. "He's one of your Army buddies?"

"'Buddy' is being generous," Ricardo said through his teeth.

"Wow," August breathed. "Dude doesn't respect women *or* bro code." Shaking his head, he brought his coffee up. "I can already tell he's a dick."

Ricardo eyed him, fully expecting more snark. Oh, it was coming. August would absolutely make sure to be an insufferable pill, but again, he did seem to be more capable of reading a room than Ricardo had previously given him credit for.

Slouching back in the chair, Ricardo sighed. "He's a dick, all right. Because this isn't just any asshole from my Army days."

August's eyebrows climbed. "Oh?" Then he stiffened, his lips parting. "Oh, *fuck*. Not your ex-spotter?"

"The one and only," Ricardo muttered.

Eve smirked. "So you've told him about Matt."

"Yeah," Ricardo said. "I have."

"Whoa." August whistled. "I see why you came to Ricky."

Ricardo didn't even mind the antagonistic nickname. Not this time.

He was much more concerned with what to do about his ex-wife being stalked by motherfucking *Sandman*.

CHAPTER 2

If there was a word for a state that vacillated between childish delight and adult gravitas like an Italian soprano on vibrato, that was August right now. It took almost everything he had not to break down into hysterical laughter right here in his own living room as he watched the interplay between Ricardo and Eve. It was like watching two cats who'd never met before walk into a room at the same time. Tails were bristling, whiskers were twitching, but there was an underlying level of comfort between them that said, *"Hey, at least you're not a dog. I hate those fucking assholes."*

It wasn't that what was happening to Eve was funny—far from it. August loathed stalkers, who were one small step away from kidnappers as far as he was concerned. Seeing how concerned Ricardo was about his former spotter's involvement, and the fact that Eve was downright shaky over the whole thing, reinforced to him that this was a Very Serious Matter. And he, despite all evidence to the contrary, was frequently capable of being a Very Serious Person. But...

No. Stop thinking about it.

If he kept thinking about the look on Ricardo's face as he'd watched August put two and two together and come up with "ex-wife," he'd start laughing no matter how hard he tried not to. Ricardo Torralba, the number one professional on Rate Your Hit.com, August's strong, silent partner in crime, a gun-wielding badass who not twenty-four hours ago had killed a man so cold-bloodedly he might as well have been on ice, was getting ready to march off and be his ex-wife's knight in shining armor.

It was just so *cute!*

"It took me a long time to realize that something wasn't right with Matt," Eve said, keeping her eyes on her coffee as she spoke. "He was very...attentive, for a while. There were stretches where he traveled for work, but he was good about calling and he always seemed happy to see me when he got back." She shrugged, a frown twisting her mouth. "It was nice to have someone around who let me know he cared."

August would have missed Ricardo's wince if he hadn't been looking for it. It didn't matter how genially you and your ex called it quits, every interaction was bound to be studded with landmines from there on out. Of course, some people were better at avoiding them than others, and Eve at least realized—too late—that she'd stepped right into one.

"That's not... I'm not talking about you and me, none of this is about us," she said firmly. "This is about Matt, and what he made me believe."

"What *did* he make you believe?" Ricardo's voice was one note above a growl. August loved that voice—it was so close to the *pin you down and fuck you* voice that he practically got hard just hearing it, like a freaky kind of Pavlovian conditioning.

"He made me think it was about love, and not about

control," Eve replied, looking Ricardo in the eyes. She was a fighter, for sure—not the kind of person who backed down from a confrontation.

She was probably lucky to be alive, if Matt was as bad as she and Ricardo were making him out to be.

Eve took a deep breath. "Look, we ran into each other a few years after the divorce. He laid on the charm because that's what he fucking does."

Ricardo grunted in unhappy agreement.

"I was still hurting even after that much time had passed, so he pulled me right in, and..." She sighed miserably. "We dated for ages before we moved in together, but once we did, it didn't take me long to figure out that that just wasn't going to work. He got very intense, always wanting to know where I was and what I was doing when I wasn't with him. I actually caught him following me to work one day, and when I confronted him about it he said he was just checking to make sure I made it to the office okay." She rolled her eyes. "I told him he needed to back off. He said he wasn't going anywhere. Finally I threatened to call the cops if he didn't get out of my house, and he..." She looked down again, like the depths of her coffee cup might have some kind of answer for her.

Poor thing, not even August's Black Ivory-brand brew—five hundred dollars a pound and worth every penny—could act as her oracle. Not unless he spiked it with some really excellent whiskey. Then it might serve up some truth bombs straight from her subconscious.

Shit, he should *definitely* do that. Preferably while Ricardo was out of the house. They could—

"Matt just laughed," Eve said a moment later, and August's gleeful internal monologue faded away at the sound of the fear in her voice. "And he told me to try calling the police, and see what that got me."

"Son of a bitch."

August snapped his focus to Ricardo. He knew that voice, knew it too well. That was the voice that heralded him putting away his sniper rifle, holstering his sidearm, and dispensing some indiscriminate justice with his fists, and maybe a knife if he felt like putting up with more screams. August hadn't heard that voice very often since they'd gotten together, but it was scary every single time. It meant action was imminent.

Shit, would August be able to keep Ricardo from running out of here without frightening Eve?

Turned out, Eve recognized that voice too, and she wasn't having it. "Don't you dare take off like some big fucking hero before I even get a chance to finish telling you what's going on." She set her coffee cup down on the table with a brittle *clink* and pointed a finger at her ex-husband. "You've always been shit at listening to people, Ricardo, but this time you're going to sit there and hear me out before you take one damn step toward the door. You're going to show me *that* much respect, do you understand me?"

August could see Ricardo's teeth grinding, and winced internally—he was going to need *so* much dental work at this rate, crowns might not be able to cover it all. August took a gamble, reached out and put his hand on the back of Ricardo's. Not on his wrist, because that might make him think August was trying to pin him down in a non-sexy way, but the back of the hand should be neutral enough...

After a moment, Ricardo relaxed and sat back into the couch. "Fine. Keep going."

Eve looked at August and smiled, her aplomb entirely

back. "So you're rich, pretty, *and* a dragon tamer, huh? Are you sure this guy deserves you?"

"Oh honey, no one deserves me," August replied with a wink.

"You can say that again," Ricardo muttered. August turned his gentle touch into a brisk pound of his knuckles against the small bones of Ricardo's hand, making him swear.

"Rude," he snapped.

"You said it first!"

"I said it *differently* and you know it," August said with an exaggerated huff, and Eve chuckled. Good. It was way better for her to focus on how Ricardo's new lover was a drama queen than on the man who'd scared her so badly. She picked up her coffee again and took a sip, then continued.

"Anyway, if Matt had the police on his side there was no way I was going to call them. I thought about throwing his stuff out while he wasn't at home and letting him pick it up off the lawn, but I didn't trust that he wouldn't lose his mind. He...*hovered* over me for more than a month after that, almost never letting me out of his sight even when he was on the phone for work." She grimaced. "I was starting to get really desperate. I even hid a knife under my pillow, in case... I mean, I told him we were done, but *you* try kicking a guy like that out of your home without backup. I was afraid he'd try to..."

"Eve." Ricardo sounded pained. "You should have called me sooner."

"I couldn't call anyone without him listening in," Eve said sadly. "He bugged my phone. I think he bugged my office at work, too, and my car. I made an appointment to get the car detailed the other day, and when I got home

Matt was there, and he was *very* displeased that whatever he'd put in there wasn't working anymore. That's when the dent happened. It was... It's been a lot. Anyway," she said more briskly, "he finally got called away for a work trip, and I got in touch with Andi on a friend's phone and asked her to contact you immediately. And now..." She shrugged and forced a smile. "Here we are."

Here we are. Jesus fucking Christ, August wanted to hunt down her skeezy won't-take-*it's-over*-for-an-answer ex and skin him alive after hearing all this. How much worse would it have been to live it?

At least when August was kidnapped as a child, he'd never been under the impression that any of the people who'd stolen him and hurt him so badly cared about him. They'd always been terrible people in his mind, and that had made it easier to handle the aftermath, in a way. They were the enemy. He was allowed to hate them. But when it was someone you'd welcomed into your home, someone you loved and trusted until one day you realized they weren't the person you thought they were...

Well, that was the definition of his first nanny, but the point was that this wasn't about *him*, it was about Eve and her fuckhead ex-boyfriend.

Eve was silent, looking at them expectantly. Ricardo was still turning his teeth into powder, so it fell to August to be the sociable one.

That's probably for the best.

"Obviously, you're invited to stay here until this is all worked out," he said, smiling brightly. "If that's what you want, of course. I can promise you that absolutely no one can get into this house without running a very protracted and, um, *inconvenient* gauntlet." *I've got landmines, I've got landmines!* Or the closest thing he could get that was still largely non-fatal. After all, he didn't want to blow up the groundskeeper, but his home improvements after the last invasion had been...thorough. Millions of dollars' worth of thorough.

"Thank you, I'd really appreciate that," Eve said with a faint air of self-deprecation. "I don't like thinking about him being in my home when I'm not there, but I don't have the resources to keep him out. I mean, I guess I could have bought a gun, but—"

"No," Ricardo said, his voice cold. "Pulling a gun on Matt wouldn't end well."

"Clearly I figured that out all on my own," Eve retorted, and *oookay*, it was time for August to step in again.

"Did you bring a bag?" he asked. "Not that I don't have some ladies' clothes lying around here and there, but you don't look like a hot-pink lace thong kind of lady to me."

Eve's shoulders relaxed. "I might surprise you. But yes, I did bring a bag, it's in the car. Let me—"

"I'll get it." Ricardo got up from the couch and stalked out of the living room at the kind of speed usually reserved for ramming barriers. August watched him go with a smile. There was something so reassuring about a man who moved like nothing in the world could stop him, and August had seen for himself that in Ricardo's case, short of a bullet to the gut, it was true. And even then, a smart person wouldn't bet against him.

"He's hardly changed at all." Eve watched him go, a similar smile on her face. "Always a man of action. You know we dated for less than a month before he proposed?"

"No, I know next to nothing and I want to know *everything*." August ignored the discarded coffee mugs for the moment and stood. "You can regale me as I show you the way to a guest suite!"

"Guest *suite*?" Eve also rose. "Not guest room?"

"I think I would qualify as the stingiest person in the world if I relegated someone spending the night in a ten-thousand square foot mansion to a single room," August replied. "I mean, honestly, am I going to complain about someone else taking up space?" He gestured toward the stairs. "It's this way! Unless you want to take the elevator instead?"

Eve laughed. "Elevator? Really? I have to say, the lifestyles of the rich and famous doesn't disappoint, but who needs an elevator for a single story?"

Me, sometimes, when my feet are killing me and I can't walk another step without wanting to shoot myself in the head.

"You never know," was all August said as he led the way to the second floor. "I like to be prepared to host all kinds of guests." Not that many people other than Ricardo and his sister, Elodie, made it through the front door most days, but the point was, he was *prepared* to be a good host, even if he didn't want to.

He guided her left at the top of the stairs, down a short hallway, and into the sole door on the left. He flicked on the light, and Eve gasped. "Oh my God," she said, stepping a few feet in and looking around with wide eyes. "This room might be bigger than my entire house."

"Really?" August glanced around. "I mean, it's pretty good-sized, but that's accentuated by the open-concept look. I would have preferred more walls, personally—" *They add a level of defensibility, for starters.* "—but my interior decorator told me that more walls means more art, and *ugh*, opinions about art are so subjective, and I would hate to put someone in here only for them to suffer through my cubism obsession."

He kept babbling about art as he showed her around the private living room and kitchen, only pausing to point out amenities and, very subtly, reinforce that this was a safe place.

"You would literally need a rocket launcher to get through these windows," he said, tapping the glass after he showed off the view of his garden. "Or at least that's what the salesperson told me. And they're tinted so that no one outside can see in, so there's no need to worry about peeping toms." Unless someone was spying on her with an infrared camera or thermal imaging weapons site or something like that, but they'd have bigger problems to worry about if someone got that close to the house. Like cleaning up body parts, or better yet, throwing them into the fish pond and letting his totally legal, not-at-all-suspicious alligator snapping turtles clean things up.

Eve smiled, but there was a knowing edge to it that August wasn't completely comfortable with. "A rocket launcher, huh? You aren't military too, are you?"

August had to laugh. "Oh my God, no! What? *No.* Look at me. Do you think I could stand to wear those awful uniforms, much less run around all day following someone else's orders? Hell no. C'mon, let me show you the Jacuzzi."

His attempt at deflection didn't work. Well, it kind of worked—who didn't like a Jacuzzi that could fit six people with room to spare?—but it didn't last long enough for him to escape.

Eve ran one hand idly along the edge of the white marble countertop in the bathroom. "So how did you and Ricardo meet?"

"At a party," August said with perfect honesty. "At a really terrible party thrown by a man with even more money and less sense than me."

"Seriously?" She raised her eyebrows. "What was Ricardo doing at a party like that?"

"He was on someone's protection detail."

Kind of. Insofar as he protected Baldwin from...himself. And me, I guess.

"And the two of you locked eyes and decided, what, it was fate?"

It was a good thing August wasn't drinking, because that question definitely warranted a spit-take. Why was Eve interrogating him right now? What was she getting out of it?

Information. Comfort. Hot gossip. Who cares? Don't be a dick.

"Honestly, we hated each other at first." August hoisted himself onto the counter beside the sink so he could give his feet a break. He'd had to run one of that enormous shit's sons down, and the guy must have just done an upper, because he was goddamn *fast*. "I thought he was a stick-in-the-mud asshole, and he thought I was a frivolous idiot, but we got to know each other a little bit, and..." August shrugged. "Our opinions changed. It doesn't hurt that he's ridiculously hot," he added.

"God, I know, where the hell does he get off being so hot?" Eve asked in disgust, and August grinned at her. "I can't tell you how many arguments ended in sex just because he's never looked so good as when he's mad enough to spit nails."

"Ooh, I know that look." August knew it well.

"Some people might have been scared, but..." Eve looked down, her gaze distant. "I never worried about Ricardo hurting me. Never. Not even when I found out about the cheating, and you better believe I chewed him the fuck out over that. I still never, ever worried about him harming me." She paused, thoughtful. "Maybe that's part of what got me in so deep with Matt—I wasn't used to being afraid of a man."

"That's not something you should be used to," August pointed out gently. "No one should be afraid of their partner for any reason, but especially because you think they could hurt you. You had every right to expect more from the person you loved."

Eve chuckled, and it sounded just a little bit damp around the edges. "You sound like a therapist."

"I've been to so many therapists I should have an honorary degree at this point," August said. "I'm serious, though. You have nothing to feel guilty about. Some people are horrible for reasons that have nothing to do with you, and if he made you feel unsafe around him? The person who's supposed to be *your* person? Then he's extra assholistic, and I can't imagine anything Ricardo will enjoy more than having a very detailed conversation about that with him, man to man."

And I'll stand by with a shovel, just in case.

"Hmm, probably." Eve was smiling again. "You know, I never liked to picture what kind of person Ricardo would choose to be with who wasn't me, but now that I've met you... I have to say, he's lucky to have you."

"I agree, I'm fantastic," August said with a wink. "And you should tell him that in fulsome detail, but being lucky goes both ways."

"I can see that. I—oh." She turned to the bathroom door, where Ricardo was standing with a slightly hunted expression on his face. "Hi!" she said brightly. "We were just talking about you!"

Ricardo looked between August and Eve like he wasn't sure whether to demand answers or run screaming. "Ah...

your bag is on the bed," he said at last. "Do you...need anything else?"

"August has me set up nicely, thanks." She walked over and patted Ricardo's arm. "He's *great*, by the way. I'm so glad to get the chance to meet him, even under these circumstances. We have *so* much to talk about."

August had to clap a hand over his mouth at the look on Ricardo's face. Had he ever looked so much like prey in his entire life?

"Well, we'll get out of your hair," August said, eventually having mercy on his partner. "Your kitchen is fully stocked, but if you can't find something, the one downstairs will probably have it—unless it's Limburger, because I draw the line at cheese that smells so much like feet. We'll talk again tomorrow."

"All right. Thank you." She gave Ricardo a hug, then gave one to August as well. Shit, Eve gave good hugs, warm and strong without making you feel like your back was about to crack. He was a little sad when she let go. "I really appreciate your help."

"It's nothing," Ricardo insisted.

"No, it's a lot," she argued. "It's a *lot*, but the fact that you're here for me even after eight years..."

It was time to go, before Eve lost the composure she was so desperately holding onto. "Use that tub," August said, gently tugging Ricardo toward the door. "Put it through its paces and tell me if the massage jets work or not in the morning, okay? Sleep well!"

"Thanks, guys."

August got Ricardo into the hall and shut the door, then turned to look at him. "She's awesome. I wish we could keep her. Can we keep her? Can I introduce her to my sister? Elodie could use a new gal pal."

Ricardo rolled his eyes and headed for the stairs. "I regret everything."

"Aw, I know. You're so beset." August caught up with him and walked down by his side, ignoring the grinding pain in the ball of his right foot. "So, shall we gear up and go have a chat with Matt-the-stalker?"

"*I'm* going to talk with him. *You're* going to stay here and rest."

"Um, no."

"August."

"Ricky."

"*August.* You're tired; you can barely walk, and this isn't your business anyway."

Just like that, August flipped from Teasing Playboy to Serious Person again. "You're my business. Now that she's staying in our house and relying on our protection, your ex-wife is my business too. And anyone who makes you look like you want to rip their spine out through their mouth is *definitely* my business, because when you get angry you get sloppy, and I do *not* want to have to break you out of prison." Ricardo had plenty of emotions, and a lot of them made for some very fun times, but his fury came in two flavors—torturously cold and blazingly fierce, and neither of them led to good decision-making by himself.

August could see Ricardo try to tone it down, and fail. "August, really, I've got this."

"I know," he replied. "But let me help you with it anyway."

Ricardo took a long, slow inhale and let it out again. "Fine," he said after a moment. "But we're taking my car."

August groaned. "But it's *so boring!*"

"Deal with it," Ricardo snapped. "Get dressed. We're leaving in five minutes."

"Whatever you say, Ricky." The scowl was back, and better than any false reassurances. August walked toward the bedroom, already mentally picking out the perfect suit for the job. Something black, with a bit of a shine to the fabric—his new Givenchy was just the thing. Beautiful, and it would hide the appearance of blood, just in case some happened to get splashed around.

August whistled as he pushed open the bedroom door and headed for his closet. Hopefully one heartfelt, personal visit to Matt was all it would take to convince him of the best course of action—namely, leaving Eve the hell alone.

And if it wasn't?

That was a problem for future them, including Future Matt, who would be learning how to eat through a straw at that point.

CHAPTER 3

Ricardo was going to kill him.

No contract needed. He didn't even care if his ass got arrested. Avoiding prison was usually a priority, especially for a hired gun, since there would be a lot of people highly motivated to kill him before he had a chance to *"Hey, I've got dirt on some people..."* his way into a plea bargain.

But tonight, they could send him to Gitmo or to goddamned Siberia. Whatever. As long as one Staff Sergeant Matt "Sandman" Ashford ended up with more blood outside his body than in it, Ricardo didn't really care what else happened afterward.

"Ricardo." August's voice was firm and unusually serious, which was probably how it cut through the rage-fogged mental tirade. "Look at me."

Ricardo slammed the magazine into the rifle, then glared at August in the low light of the closet-slash-armory. "What?"

The growl didn't intimidate August. Ricardo was pretty sure he was incapable of intimidating him anymore. Which was generally a good thing—intimidation wasn't really conducive to healthy relationships, even between a couple of dysfunctional hitmen.

August held his gaze, expression surprisingly subdued but with a hard edge. "I know you're pissed. So am I, and I'm not half as invested in her as you are and I don't know Sandman from Adam." He put a hand over Ricardo's on top of the rifle. "But I *am* invested in *you*, and I would appreciate it if you went into this with your head together so I didn't have to kill him for blowing it apart. You feel me?"

Ricardo blinked.

"You go in there with your nostrils flaring," August went on, his tone sharper, "you're going to get yourself killed, and that's going to piss me off. Now take a deep breath, pull it together, and let's make a plan that doesn't involve me going full vigilante to avenge your stupid murdered ass."

Ricardo's lips parted, and he shook himself. "Since when are you the one telling me to calm the fuck—"

"Since you turned into el toro loco at the thought of your ex-spotter making your ex-wife's life hell. *Now*." August gripped the gun firmly and tugged it. Ricardo was so off guard, he let go of the weapon. August dropped the magazine, cleared the chamber, and put the rifle aside. When he faced Ricardo again, he stepped closer, putting his hands on Ricardo's chest and looking him right in the eye. "I know you're pissed, and I get it. But you need to be Ricardo Torralba the cold-blooded hitman right now, not Eve's ex-husband or that asshole's ex-BFF."

"Who said anything about hitman? I'm just going to go tell him to leave her alone."

August looked pointedly at the rifle, then back at Ricardo. Gesturing at himself, he asked, "Is this the face of a man who's going to buy that bullshit? Cut the crap. How are we doing this? We don't even know where he lives, the lay of the land, if he has anyone there with him..." Shaking his head, he said, "*No.* You wouldn't go into a job without doing recon first, so you're not going into this like that either." Ricardo opened his mouth to speak, but August put up a hand: "Eve is safely here in my Fortress of Fuckery, as you insist on calling it, so we have time to take care of this. We have time to do it *right*."

Ricardo desperately wanted to argue, but damn it, he couldn't. August was usually the one who needed to be talked back to earth when he had some outrageous idea. Then again, August had a much shorter fuse. Ricardo didn't lose his temper often, and he was hardly on a hair trigger, but it took a *lot* to send him into a rage. Sometimes he still wondered what he was thinking, partnering up with a former rival, but right now... Hell, right now, August was the calm, level-headed one in a more rational frame of mind.

Closing his eyes, Ricardo sighed. "Fine. Fine. Let's... Let's make a plan."

And then he cringed, because August was not one to miss an opportunity to gloat that he was right.

Surprisingly, though, August moved right past it. "For starters, we need Eve to tell us where this asshole lives."

"HAVE I MENTIONED LATELY THAT STAKEOUTS ARE SO boring, they make me want to piss on a high voltage line just to end it all?"

Ricardo snorted. "Only half a dozen times in the last four hours."

August groaned so theatrically, it made the Bluetooth earpiece vibrate in Ricardo's ear. "This is *bullshit*."

"You're the one who didn't want to go in guns blazing."

There was a huff on the other end. "Rude."

Ricardo let go of a quiet laugh, mostly because he knew it annoyed the shit out of August when he laughed at his expense. From the barely audible grumbling, he'd hit his mark.

He understood. This was one of his least favorite parts of any job—staking out the mark to get an idea of their habits, their security, and anything else that might create an obstacle or an advantage. It was excruciatingly boring, but necessary. Admittedly, it had also allowed him to pull his temper under control. He was still ready to rip Matt to shreds with his bare hands, but he was composed now. He could be careful and methodical about this, knowing that increased the odds of his ex-spotter ending up duly dead while August and Ricardo walked away.

But first...surveillance.

Boring, monotonous surveillance.

This was one of those areas where having a partner came in handy. Prior to teaming up with August, Ricardo had to handle all the recon himself. Some of that was easy enough—cameras, GPS trackers, and other spy toys (as August called them) weren't difficult to unobtrusively plant and remotely monitor. It was especially easy these days when so many people had various forms of home security but were woefully lax when it came to securing that security. It never took long for Ricardo to find a few doorbell cameras that he could hack.

Word to the wise, kids—don't use the default username and password on your home security.

Neighbors inevitably had dashcams, and Ricardo was damn good at slipping in and replacing a camera with one that had a transmitter. People would be amazed at just how much intel he could gather from a dashcam passively recording from a car in a driveway.

But there really was no substitute for in-person recon. A person physically watching a scene could turn their head if something caught their peripheral vision. If they saw or heard something, they could try to investigate.

And that was why August was currently sitting in the upstairs bedroom of an abandoned house kitty-corner to Matt's, watching the street, the house, and what he could see of the yard. Not that there'd been much activity, especially since it was three-thirty in the morning. A couple of stray cats had apparently had an amorous encounter in a nearby yard. August had made sure to fill Ricardo in on every detail he could hear "in the name of thorough surveillance." Or more likely, in the name of exploiting the fact that Ricardo had no choice but to listen to whatever came out of August's mouth until it was time for them to switch.

Ricardo was downstairs in the same house with a couple of laptops set up so he could monitor the feed on cameras they'd planted or he'd hacked. This room was boarded up, so no one from the street would see the light from the computers. Otherwise, he'd be upstairs with August, who was watching out one of the few intact windows.

So far, neither of them had seen or heard a thing besides, as August had called it, a "poorly-executed and disturbingly pornographic off-Broadway rendition of *CATS*."

Ricardo sat back in the folding chair he'd brought in from the car, which was tucked into the house's garage. Stretching his arms, he glanced toward the boarded-up front window.

It was great for him and August that Matt lived in a rundown neighborhood like this. Areas with abandoned buildings and regular criminal activity (or at least, lots of activity that cops considered criminal, even if it was just people trying to survive in poverty) made it easy for the real criminal elements like him and August to blend in. Especially after Ricardo had talked August out of his high-dollar suit and into something a little less conspicuous. The black turtleneck was apparently by some fancy designer and ran five grand or something, but along with the equally overpriced jeans and sneakers, he didn't stand out like the idiot he could sometimes be.

So the location was convenient as hell for August and Ricardo, but it was weird to be here. What in the fuck had gone so wrong in Matt's life that he'd wound up living like this? As brutal and cutthroat as he'd always been, Ricardo had always expected him to wind up in law enforcement. Matt had commented more than once that he wanted to wear a badge, and the thought still made Ricardo shudder.

Now, Ricardo knew cops didn't make a ton of money, but this city paid them decently. More than enough to afford better than a house on this street. It was possible he'd put himself into serious debt. Gambling had been a vice of his back in the day. There was nothing he wouldn't bet on, and his response to losing was to bet bigger the next time around. Had he gotten himself into a hole?

But he was also a misogynist, and he'd been adamant forever that he'd never allow "his woman" to make more than him. Eve had been making good money since before the divorce, and she was driving a Porsche. She'd never in a million years have lived in a neighborhood like this. Hell, she and Ricardo had fought a few times about her elitism and snobbishness. There was no way Matt lived in a place like this while Eve made money like that, and Ricardo couldn't imagine Matt hitting rock bottom and Eve making it big in the short period since she'd tried to leave him.

So why in the world was he living in—

"Why do you call him Sandman?" August, clearly bored, pulled Ricardo out of his thoughts. "Is it because he puts people to sleep by being so dull that watching him is like..." He snored.

Ricardo chuckled as a bittersweet memory came to him. "No. It's like any nickname in the military—because he did something stupid and none of us were going to let him forget it."

"Oh, really?" He could practically hear August's ears perking up. "What was your nickname?"

"Don't change the subject." Ricardo rolled his eyes. "Do you want to know why we call him Sandman or not?"

"Yes. But someday I want to know your nickname and the story behind it."

Ricardo huffed a laugh. A CIA interrogation squad would never get *that* nickname *or* its origin story out of him, at least not within earshot of August. "We were on a deployment in the desert. Just got there. A sandstorm was coming in, and Matt thought everyone was a bunch of pussies for going inside, closing everything up..."

"What did he think you should do? Just sit outside during a sandstorm?"

"Something like that. Anyway, we were a bunch of bored spec ops idiots, he was talking shit, and long story short, if he was willing to stand outside in the sandstorm for five minutes in his skivvies, he'd get a hundred bucks and a carton of cigarettes."

"A hundred bucks and a carton of cigarettes?" August made a haughty sound. "I'd at least have asked someone to throw in a blowjob."

"That much money and smokes is a lot when you're out there. Cigarettes are basically currency."

"Was this war or prison?"

"Eh, they're not much different sometimes." Ricardo scratched the back of his neck and stared up at the hole where a light fixture had probably been at one time. "Anyway, that was the price. Five minutes in his skivvies in the sandstorm. He goes out. The storm comes in." Snickering, he added, "And the, um... The lock on the door stuck."

"The lock on the door stuck? What does that mean?"

Voice full of innocence, Ricardo said, "It means we couldn't let him in. We *tried*, but I don't know if it got sand in it, or—"

August guffawed. "Oh, you assholes. You locked him out there, didn't you? In the sandstorm?" He was laughing so hard now he could barely speak. "Oh, that's glorious. I love it. Love. It. Was he mad? Tell me everything, Ricky. Everything."

Ricardo couldn't help chuckling. "There was a guy in our unit from Alabama who said Matt was madder than a wet hen."

August was howling. There was a rhythmic thumping that Ricardo thought was him hitting his hand on the windowsill or something. "That's *amazing*. How long did you make him stay out there?"

"Oh, it wasn't that long. The storm didn't even last all that long. When we let him in..." Ricardo snorted. "Christ. He's probably still getting sand out of his ass crack to this day."

"Oh my God. Oh. Wow. That's..." August was nearly wheezing with laughter, and as he managed to pull himself together, he cleared his throat. "Oh, fuck, that's amazing.

No wonder he's such a dick—he's had sand in his ass for the last... how many years?"

"Twelve, thirteen, I think?"

"See, if I'd had sand in my ass for that long, I'd probably be a dick too."

"You *are* a dick, August."

"Rude."

Ricardo chuckled, and they fell back into their silent surveillance. For a while, anyway.

"He's back." August's voice was completely serious. "Car just pulled into the garage, and it matches Eve's description."

Ricardo leaned forward, peering at the various monitors. A camera he'd planted beneath the mailbox at the end of Matt's driveway caught the license plate, and that was definitely Matt striding past in—

In a suit? The fuck? Matt hated suits more than August hated generic coffee.

"Good Lord," August mused. "That suit—that's a Canali!"

"What?" Ricardo squinted at the screen. "How the fuck can you tell?"

August tsked. "I can tell, okay?"

Ricardo rolled his eyes. Didn't matter how long he lived with August—he would never understand high society.

"Ricky." Something in August's tone made Ricardo ignore the nickname and sit up. The earlier joking was long gone.

"What's wrong?"

"I think..." August was silent for a moment. "Hold on." There was some movement. Then, above Ricardo's head, footsteps.

As August strode into the living room, Ricardo stood. "What are you doing? You're supposed to be—"

"The camera's still rolling." August gestured at the plywood front door. "But I think one of us—namely, me—needs to go over there."

Ricardo stared at him. "What? Why? Are you insane?"

"Probably, but don't change the subject. Listen." August folded his arms. "That suit..." He shook his head. "It doesn't match that house. Not even close."

Ricardo raised his eyebrows. "He isn't coordinating his suit to his house? What does—"

"No. *Listen*." August pointed sharply across the street. "No one who can afford *that* suit is going to drive *that* car or buy *that* house."

"So, what are you thinking?"

"I'm thinking that house is like my meth lab safehouse—it's a base of operations or something, given that he spends enough time here that Eve knows about it, but it's not *his* house. Not his main house, anyway." August swallowed. "I think he's involved in something."

"Something? Like..." Ricardo gestured at himself and August. "Like what we do?"

August's lips quirked, and then he shook his head. "I feel like we'd have heard of him by now. At the very least, some sort of gossip about someone who fits his description. Something. But maybe. The point is that he's involved in something."

"But this is the house Eve knew about. Why would he keep her at his safehouse?"

"He lived with her, remember? She kicked him out."

Ricardo thought back to the conversation. Shit. August was right. Exhaling, he raked a hand through his hair. "Oh, fuck. So he could be... Hell, he could be working with one of the cartels, selling meth... Anything."

"Mmhmm, exactly." August shifted his weight. "So I think we need to do a little more recon before we engage."

"Maybe we need to ask Eve some more questions."

"Do you think she'd know much about what he does?" He eyed Ricardo. "Did she know what you were into?"

Ricardo scowled. "All right, you have a point, but it wouldn't hurt to ask. And maybe we need to get some sleep, let the cameras follow him a little more, and come at him fresh."

August's eyes lit up. "Ooh, I could go strutting over with a casserole and tell him I'm a new neighbor who wants to introduce—"

"Not a chance."

"What?" August looked affronted. "Why not? Don't you think I can pull off genial and neighborly?"

"I'm sure you can, but I'm pretty sure you can't pull off *straight*."

"Straight? Why would—" Confusion shifted to offense. "For fuck's sake. Do you mean to tell me that asshole is a homophobe, too? How the hell did you not shoot him?"

"Because I didn't want a dishonorable discharge?"

"If I go over there right now, there's going to be some discharge coming out the back of his dishonorable head..."

Ricardo chuckled as he wrapped an arm around August's shoulders and pressed a kiss to his temple. "Calm down. We'll get him."

"Hey." August elbowed him playfully. "That's my line."

"Uh-huh. Let's get out of here. We'll come back when we have a better idea what we're walking into."

August wriggled out of his grasp and grinned at him.

"So, what you're saying is, I was right earlier? When I said we should make a plan instead of rushing in guns blazing?"

Ricardo rolled his eyes. "I'm not going to hear the end of that, am I?"

August cackled. "Not in this lifetime, darling. Not in this lifetime."

CHAPTER 4

Ricardo slept in the next morning, which after the day—and night—they'd had was perfectly understandable. It was *unusual*, for sure; Ricardo was the sort of guy who found a zone that worked for him and stayed there. August could set a clock by Ricardo's habits: up by six, coffee—or occasionally espresso now that he had access to August's superior kitchen, thank you very much—and a quick check of his email, and then...ugh, probably exercise. Running or something. Pushups. Pullups. Things that made him sweaty and disgusting and unreasonably attractive. Swimming or free weights if August was lucky, since he could join Ricardo for those. Then breakfast, then on with the day's work.

Today it was August who got up to make the coffee, August who whipped up some batter for German apple pancakes, August who greeted their guest when she ambled down the stairs a little after eight, wearing an old ARMY T-shirt and a pair of sleep shorts.

"Hi," she said when she caught sight of August.

"Good morning." He indicated the sideboard. "Coffee?

It's amazing, I'm not going to lie. Your tastebuds might be ruined for regular coffee after this."

"I think I'll risk it." She poured some into one of the mugs he'd set out. She ignored the cream and sugar—Jesus, she and Ricardo were alike in some ways—and took a sip. Then she groaned and grasped the mug with both hands. August was as queer as a three-dollar bill, but even he could appreciate the sheer sensuality of a noise like that.

Maybe he should be taking notes.

"That is *really* good."

"Is it your ruination?" he asked cheekily.

"I think my ex is in the top running for that spot, but it's damn close." She leaned her hip against the kitchen island and took another sip, looking at him over the rim of the mug. "So, did you find Matt?"

"We did," August confirmed, grabbing his own coffee. "Care to go someplace more comfortable to talk? We can—"

"I care to get the whole story from you right now without distractions, actually."

August smiled with all his teeth showing. "Did Ricardo get his terseness and propensity for interruption from you, or was it the other way around?"

Eve paused, then nodded. "Right. Sorry. That was bitchy of me."

"You can be bitchy," August assured her. "Just don't think I won't sling it right back. Seriously though, couch?" His foot was better today, but he still preferred not to push it when he didn't have to.

"Sure." They resettled in the living room, and he took another sip of his appropriately creamed-and-sugared coffee, then got down to business. "We did find Matt, but the house was a little...incongruous. Are you sure he lives there?"

"I mean, it's the address he gave me." She shrugged. "He told me that I should drop anything I found of his off there. I actually went there once, back when I thought he was really going to leave me alone, to leave some of his clothes for him. He didn't answer the door, though, and I wasn't comfortable abandoning a bag full of his stuff on the porch, so I mailed it to him."

"Mm." She would have done better just setting that man's shit on fire. Maybe it wasn't too late for that... Arson had never been August's thing—it was too hard to control who died as a result of it—but for *Matt*...

Actually...now there was a thought.

"What's that look?"

"Excuse me?" August refocused on Eve and smiled, but it was too late to dissemble—she was staring at him with laser-like intensity.

"That look. I've seen that kind of look before." She narrowed her eyes. "It's the sort of look that gets people into trouble. You're not going to drag Ricardo into trouble, right?"

"Eve," August said patiently, "in this case, and I mean this in the best way possible, *you're* the one showing up and handing him a heap of trouble on a silver platter. You asked him to help you, and he's going to do that. You know he is. You wouldn't seek out your ex-husband after eight years if there wasn't some serious faith going on."

"That's true," she admitted. "But I don't want him to... I don't know, end up in jail just because I fell for an abusive asshole and made him feel guilty about it."

"Pssht, please." August waved one hand. "You think I'd let him languish in jail? Do you have any idea the amount of bail I've posted over the years?"

Eve shook her head. "I bet it would boggle my mind."

"We're talking more than the GDPs of some countries, and I would spend a hundred times as much to keep Ricardo where I can see him."

"Uh-huh." She leaned back against the couch and crossed her legs. "I don't exactly understand the two of you as a couple, but I'm not dumb enough to think I need to, either. Ricardo doesn't do anything he doesn't want to. Which makes the fact that he cheated on me especially galling," she added, "but you guys seem to...fit."

August winked. "Well, I mean, with the right foreplay and some half-decent lube a motivated man like Ricardo can fit a *lot* in there, an—"

"Oh my God, stop!" Eve shrieked with laughter. "Stop, Jesus, I don't want to know!"

"Are you sure?" He scooted a little closer. "I mean, maybe you can give me some pointers on what he really likes. I'm always trying to broaden my horizons and I assume *he's* always been flexible about giving and receiving, so if you ever tried pegging and want to compare notes about—"

"Holy shit, I really am going to kill you this time."

August turned a bright smile toward the stairs, where Ricardo was standing with his most potent murderface on. "Oh hi, honey! We were just talking about you."

"I figured you were."

The *you fucking asshole* went unsaid, but August heard it all the same. And...yeah, nobody wanted to wake up first thing in the morning to their ex and their significant other comparing sex notes. "I'll make you an espresso," he said by way of apology, and headed for the kitchen.

"Don't be mad," he heard Eve say. "Most of our conversation was about Matt, not you. You were just thrown in there to lighten the mood."

"Ha-ha."

"See? You're so good at it."

August snickered as he found Ricardo's favorite blend and added it to the machine, tamping it down and grimacing a little at the strong smell. Coffee that could take the veneer off your teeth wasn't his personal favorite, but he tried to do little things here and there to make Ricardo feel at home.

Living together wasn't easy—it was fun, it was frustrating, it was sometimes sexy as hell, but it was very rarely easy. August wasn't about to start changing his personality to make someone else happy, but he could soften the blow a little bit.

A hand gripped his waist firmly as the machine warmed up, and August jumped, then rounded on Ricardo.

"Jesus, don't ninja me this early in the morning," he snapped, thrusting an elbow against Ricardo's sternum and driving him half a foot back before reaching out and reeling him in close again. "Jackass."

"Maybe I woke up on the wrong side of the bed," Ricardo said, accepting both the hit and the hug with a straight face.

"Maybe I should put you back in it," August suggested.

"I wish you could, but..." He sighed and tilted his head toward the living room.

"Right. Yes." August thought about that for a moment. "I've got an idea about Matt, but I don't want to leave Eve here with nothing to do." The last thing they needed was her getting curious and finding the closets, but he wasn't about to engage his internal security system and zap Eve with ten thousand volts if she turned the handle to their room either. "You know, I wasn't kidding about introducing her to my sister," he went on, warming to the idea. "And there's an on-site spa at Elodie's offices, which incidentally have *excellent* security."

"You want to encourage my ex to spend the day getting spa treatments with your sister?" Ricardo pulled back and stared at him for a moment. "What sort of world do you live in where this is normal?"

"The kind where family sticks together, no matter how fucked up they are," August replied. The machine hissed, signaling it was finished, and he picked up the espresso cup, set it on a matching gold-rimmed china saucer because he wasn't a goddamn Philistine, then handed it over to Ricardo. "You go chat her up, I'll make some calls, and we can make a plan for the day. Sound good?"

Ricardo hummed contemplatively as he took his first sip of espresso. "Do these plans involve breaking a few bones? Because if they do, I'm in."

"I promise we'll get to the bone-breaking portion of the program before you know it," August said. "But first we increase our level of surveillance."

And he had just the right thing in his closet to sell it, too.

THREE HOURS AND AN ACCIDENTAL SPILL OF SOME sulfurous-smelling mercaptan later, and August was in Utility Worker Costume Take 2, the slightly-shorter version that Ricardo had had on hand, with the pants tucked into the tops of his boots to hide the length issue.

"Congratulations," August said sourly as he pulled on the dingy brown uniform jacket and slammed a generic ballcap on his head. "You've made me into a fashion monstrosity. I hope you're happy."

"Delighted," Ricardo said, his voice coming through the earpiece loud and clear. "Are you ready for this?"

"Has the aerosol run out?'

"Almost. Maybe just a minute left." Ricardo was running backup and support for this part of things, which left him with the job of getting a good stink wafting through the neighborhood. Not *too* much of a stink, though; they didn't want someone from the actual utility company to show up while August was putting on his act, after all. Ricardo had a backup plan to stall them if that happened, and it only involved a slight amount of collision damage, but August was hoping to avoid that. He sat back in the truck—almost identical to the beater Ricardo had used in the Baldwin job, ah, such fun, frenzied memories—and waited for the all-clear before driving onto Sandman's block.

"It's done. You should be good to go."

"Finally." He started up the engine, blasting the air conditioner as soon as it was on. God, polyester did *terrible* things to his skin. The other outfit had been made of beautiful, breathable cotton, with reinforced seams and a special pocket for his favorite knife and—

"I can hear you sulking. Get over it."

"Shut up, you can't hear that," August snapped as he turned the corner and got his eyes on the house in question. God, what a run-down piece of shit. And he was going to go in there. If he came out with fleas, he was definitely making sure some jumped off onto Ricardo.

"All right." He parked the truck in front of the house and turned off the engine, then grabbed his utility bag and headed for the front door.

Security cameras by the door, the hidden one in the bush over there, what looks like a setup for a...tripwire?

Cautious fucker.

August plastered a smile on his face and knocked briskly on the door. No answer. He knocked again. Sandman was in there—they'd verified it before heading out.

Still no answer.

"Sir?" he tried, calling through the door. "Or ma'am? If there's anyone home here, please open the door. I'm not trying to sell you anything, I promise! Just trying to keep you all from a potentially fatal accident with your—"

The door jerked open a second later, and Matt Ashford, the infamous spotter and asshole ex himself, stood in the doorway with a gun in one hand. He had a cranky glare and a severe high-and-tight haircut that suggested no one had ever told him he'd been discharged from the Army.

"Fatal accident?" he demanded in a cold voice. "What the hell is that supposed to mean?"

"Whoa, sir!" August chuckled nervously, holding his clipboard up like a shield. "I'm here with city utilities, just checking on whether or not you've noticed the smell of a natural gas leak in the vicinity! One of your neighbors complained about it, and there was no number listed for this house for us to call. I promise, there's no need for violence."

"Why the fuck would there be a need for violence?" Ricardo demanded over their open connection. "What's he doing?"

"Please put the gun away, sir, I'm just trying to do my job," August went on, and a stream of Catalan curse words erupted in his ear. He tried not to wince. "If you have a gas leak, it could be very dangerous. It won't take me long to check, though."

"I don't smell any..." Leaving the door open apparently did the trick, though, because Matt's nose suddenly wrinkled. "Shit."

"Exactly," August said sympathetically. "I promise, I'll be out of your hair soon."

Matt was frowning. He might have been considered attractive—August could see the sharp-jawed appeal, from a certain angle—but the frown completely spoiled his face. "If the smell is coming from outside, why do you need to check in here?"

August thought fast. "All of the pipe fittings in your home were likely installed at the same time," he said. "If one of them has started to fail, it's likely that the other fittings are close to it as well." He tried on a tremulous smile. "I, um, I certainly wouldn't like to have to come bother you a second time, sir. If we can get the inspection knocked out right now, that would save you some trouble."

Matt stared at him for a long moment, his eyes slightly squinted, before finally nodding. "Fine. But I watch you the whole time."

"Of course, sir." *Fuckity-fuck-fuck.* "That's perfectly reasonable." *You paranoid piece of shit.*

"You're going to have to get him to leave you alone," Ricardo warned over the earpiece. "He's too sharp-eyed to try and slip something by him while he's standing there."

"Thank you!" August said brightly, hoping that Ricardo would read the "not goddamn helpful" in it that he'd intended for him, and stepped inside of the house. He had to work not to wrinkle his nose. The whole place smelled like mildew—there were water marks on the ceiling, and the carpet had probably not *started* life as gray but had stopped fighting the color-changing grime long ago. It was *gritty* underfoot. Jesus, did this man not know what a vacuum cleaner was?

"You going to get started or what?" Matt demanded.

"Of course, sir, right. Right, right." August clutched his

clipboard to his chest like a teddy bear, and saw a flare of contempt cross Matt's face. *Yes, I'm just a simple little coward who's intimidated by your Big Man, alpha energy. Shiver, tremble, gasp.* "Um, is your stove a gas range?"

"No."

"Oh. Okay, great, one less place to leak, right?" He chuckled nervously. "Um, can you take me to your utility room, then?" Getting some space wasn't going to be easy.

When in doubt, fall back on incompetency to get the job done.

August kept up a patter of meaningless small talk as Matt led him to the utility room. There was a washer and dryer combo in it that had probably never earned its keep, and in the corner was a scattering of dark specks that were probably mouse droppings. Delightful.

"—people say that Dawn works better than Palmolive, but I've always gotten good results with the generic brand of dish soap," he chattered, one hand in his bag as he knelt down by where the natural gas was piped into the house. "I mean, a bubble is a bubble, right? It doesn't care what it's made of."

He unscrewed the top of his spray bottle of soapy water, a cheap and effective way of checking for gas leaks, and tipped it over, silently grateful that their surveillance equipment was safely secured on his own body, then—"Oh, whoops!" He pulled out a mostly-empty bottle and a damp, sudsy hand. "Gosh, I thought I screwed that on tighter," he mused, looking at the two parts and then looking up at Matt, whose scowl had taken on an incredulous tinge. "Do you have any dish soap?" he asked sheepishly. "Um, generic is fine."

"You..." Without finishing the sentence, probably

because it ended with something like "fucking idiot," Matt stalked out of the room.

August immediately got to his feet, shoving a hand down his overalls for the pair of tiny bugs he'd stowed by the seam at his waist. There was no internal surveillance in this place—which wasn't surprising, since it was probably a drug den—so he didn't have to worry about being seen, but he did need to be fast. He glanced out into the hall as he heard cabinets start to slam open and closed in the kitchen.

"They need to be somewhere high up," Ricardo said in his ear.

"Right, I know," August muttered.

"The living room and bedroom are safe bets."

"No, really?" August took two long steps down the hall and stopped outside two closed wooden doors. Both bedrooms, probably, or maybe one was an office. He removed the backing on the bug and placed it above one of the doors, then immediately turned and hustled back into the utility room as he tucked the second bug into the end of his sleeve.

Just in time, too—a few seconds later Matt came back in with a bottle of generic, store-brand liquid dish soap. It was radioactive orange in color, and had a thin film of dust along the top of it.

"Thanks so much!" August poured some of it into his little spray bottle. He had a water bottle with him—a point of verisimilitude for a guy out working jobs all day, according to Ricardo, and it hadn't been worth arguing about. He was glad he had it now, because if he'd sent Matt back to the kitchen for water after this, it might have ended in a murder.

Matt's murder, obviously, because August wasn't about

to be taken out by an asshole whose nickname was *Sandman*, of all people.

"Mkay, now we just shake it like we're booty poppin'..." August snickered as he agitated the bottle, then looked up at Matt, who was even more stone-faced. "Twerking? No? Okay then."

He made sure to look intent as he sprayed all the pipe connections, checking for burgeoning bubbles. There were none, of course. "Gosh, I'm not seeing anything here." He tapped his cheek thoughtfully, also tapping his earpiece at the same time. "Maybe if I check the—"

As he expected, his phone rang. August tapped his earpiece. "Yello?" he said brightly. "Oh, really? That's great, I'm glad you found it. I'll go ahead and get out of this guy's hair now." He ended the "call" and looked up at Matt. "My colleague found the leak at one of your neighbors' houses. Looks like you're good to go, Mister..."

"Smith."

"Okay, great. Um. So. I'll just..." He held up the bottle of soap in his slightly sticky hand. "There you go."

Matt actually rolled his eyes as he took it. August counted that as a personal victory. "Get up and get out." The man looked two seconds away from grabbing August's arm and heaving him out of there bouncer-style. That wouldn't do; he still had a bug to place.

"You got it," August said. He picked up his bag and clipboard and let Matt lead him toward the door. Halfway across the living room, though, he balked. "Oh! Um, could you sign here?" He shoved the clipboard in Matt's direction and pointed to a line. "It indicates I was really here and performed my job satisfactorily. We, uh, we don't get our holiday bonuses if we don't get signatures." He smiled meekly. "Workin' for the man, you know?"

"Jesus fucking Christ, are you serious?" Matt muttered, but he took the clipboard and scrawled a name—John Smith, really? *Really?*—across the line.

August palmed the bug and pressed it under the edge of the coffee table as he rearranged his grip on his bag, then staggered as Matt shoved the clipboard back into his chest and literally pushed him out the door.

"Thank you so much, Mr. Smi—"

Slam!

August turned and scurried away down the walk, hustling back to the van like a scared little bunny of a human being. He started it up quickly and did an awkward U-Turn in the middle of the street, an apologetic look plastered across his face the whole time, before making it around the corner and onto a larger road. Ricardo met him another few blocks down.

"You get them set?" he asked as he settled in the passenger seat.

"As if there was any doubt," August said with a sniff, and he turned them toward home. "So...how much do you think it would upset Eve if we just disappeared Matt completely?"

Ricardo laughed. "As charming as ever, I take it."

"I would happily kill him for five dollars—no, five cents!" Not for free, because that was unprofessional and could get you kicked off *Rate Your Hit*, but in Matt's case August was willing to work for a deep discount.

"Let's see what information we get out of him first."

Right, right. August was kind of curious about that. "Let's."

CHAPTER 5

"So?" Eve watched the two of them over the island in August's sleekly appointed kitchen. "What now?"

"Now, we wait." August poured a few glasses of some wine that probably cost more than Eve and Ricardo's divorce, and as he distributed them, he said, "The bug has a transmitter that will ping our phones if it starts picking up any sounds." He brought his own glass to his lips but paused. "Of course, it's a sensitive device, so there might be some false readings, like... I don't know. Doors closing or a mouse orgy."

"Ugh, so much for smart devices," Ricardo muttered into his glass.

"Hey!" August shot him a look. "I told you, the device is *sensitive*. Be nice."

Eve choked on her wine.

"It's also right outside the laundry room." Ricardo put his glass down. "What happens if he decides to use the washing machine while—"

In unison, his ex-wife scoffed and his boyfriend barked a laugh.

"Oh, I don't think we have to worry about that," August said.

Eve smothered a giggle. "The day that man does laundry..."

"Ugh. God." August rolled his eyes with theatrical exasperation. "After seeing the state of that house, especially the disgusting laundry room, I was genuinely amazed he even *owned* dish soap."

"He does?" Eve touched her chest. "My, my. Wonders never cease."

Ricardo eyed both of them. "Are you two finished?"

August pressed his lips together, apparently trying (sort of) to suppress more smartass commentary. Eve put her hand to her mouth, but she was clearly doing the same thing.

Oh God. I do have a type, don't I?

"Anyway." Ricardo tried to suppress his annoyance. "I'm not suggesting Matt has suddenly evolved past the asshole our buddies had to shower with a hose. I am, however, suggesting that if I were involved in something shady, and I were doing it in a house with working appliances, I might do all my incriminating talking in the vicinity of a loud appliance. Such as, say, a dryer with a pair of shoes in it."

Eve immediately sobered.

August rolled his eyes. "He can try."

They both turned to him.

"What does that mean?" Eve asked.

"It means I guarantee that washer and dryer are about as functional as the stove in my old meth house."

Eve suddenly looked confused. "Your old meth house?"

August opened his mouth to speak, no doubt planning to regale her with a lengthy story about the safehouse he'd built beneath a meth lab—and even less doubt planning to include the part where that was where he and Ricardo had fucked for the first time.

"It's a long story," Ricardo said quickly.

August shut his mouth again, but he narrowed his eyes at Ricardo. "Rude."

Eve hid another laugh behind her glass.

"Don't encourage him," Ricardo said. "*Anyway*. August, how do you know that washer and dryer are out of commission?"

He braced for another smartass retort—August did, after all, have an audience—but for once in his goddamned life, he took the moment seriously. "Because the dryer's door was hanging off one hinge, the knobs on both machines were all missing, and there was a black mark that looked suspiciously like something had caught on fire at one point." He absently swirled his wine as he added a casual, "I'm not kidding, Ricky—they'd have looked right at home in my meth house."

Ricardo couldn't recall the last time he'd seen Eve's eyes that big or her face filled with that much "what the fuck?" He was pretty sure he'd made the same face at August a few times in the beginning. Hell, he still made it sometimes.

"Okay, so." Ricardo flattened his palms on the island. "The appliances won't cause any noise interference for the bug. I guess now we just... wait."

"But what if they're in another room?" Eve asked. "Or outside? How do we guarantee we'll hear anything?"

"We don't," August said simply. "But at the very least, it'll give us a feel for when people are coming and going. If we can't get a bead on what they're saying or what they're doing, we can probably still pin down a pattern of when people come and go, how many people come and go...

Things like that. From there, we can keep enhancing our surveillance until we get something we can use."

"That sounds like it could take a while."

He nodded. "It could. But if he's using the house regularly, it probably won't take as long as you think." He looked at Ricardo, then did a double take. "What?"

"Nothing." Ricardo shrugged and picked up his wine. "It just catches me by surprise whenever you give someone a straight answer instead of—"

"Ugh." August rolled his eyes. "Rude."

Ricardo chuckled, but quickly sobered. "So for now, we wait."

"Good idea." August smiled sweetly. "And in the meantime, you can explain to Eve why we're pawning her off on my sister."

Eve whirled on Ricardo. "You're *what?*"

August cackled with glee and strutted out of the kitchen with the wine bottle, leaving Ricardo doing something he had never been good at doing: trying to encourage Eve to calm the hell down.

"Oh look." August glared at his phone, which had pinged for the fortieth time in the past five hours. "The bug heard something." Lounging in his chair in the living room, he jabbed the screen. "Wonder what it is this time. A neighbor's dog barking again? Or maybe another heaping spoonful of nothing?"

"August," Ricardo teased from the couch, nudging August's knee with his foot. "Didn't you say we should be nice to the sensitive equip—"

"I'll be nice when the little bastard does its job."

At the opposite end of the couch, Eve laughed. She'd been livid earlier, but she had actually calmed down once Ricardo had explained that, no, they weren't pawning her off. They were trying to keep her as safe as possible, and it would basically be like a spa day with a femme fatale who took shit from no one. Especially not August.

"Oh," Eve had said. "Well why didn't you just lead with that?"

"Because my idiot boyfriend didn't give me a chance to."

To that, she'd laughed. "Oh, Ricardo. You're the one who's head over heels in love with him." She'd given his face a patronizing pat. "I think that makes you the idiot."

Well, she was no longer eying the knife block, and she was giving playful barbs like she had when they were married, so he'd decided the situation was duly defused. He was going to get August back, though.

Unaware of Ricardo mentally figuring out a suitable punishment, August suddenly stiffened. "Whoa." His expression turned serious, and as he straightened, he cranked up the volume on his phone so Eve and Ricardo could hear.

"—visas are still hung up," an unfamiliar male voice was saying. "We're working as fast as we can, but the system's all jammed up."

"Yeah, you keep saying that," Matt snapped, his voice farther away, but still clear. "They don't need *real* visas. Just something that'll get them past TSA and customs."

"I know, I know. But that's just it—they keep changing the rules about what they want, and if the girls don't have the right paperwork, they're not getting past TSA, and they're sure as shit not leaving the country."

Matt groaned with obvious frustration. "For fuck's sake.

What's the problem, anyway? They've all got legit contracts *and* notarized parental consent."

"Yeah, they do," the other man growled. "But the feds are getting smart about it. All these organizations protesting about—anyway, maybe we need to start signing the girls to different gigs. Contracts like these are basically red flags now."

Ricardo's heart dropped as the pieces began falling together.

Matt huffed an irritated breath. "Then how do we recruit the pretty ones, huh? Tell them they're going to Dubai on, what? Humanitarian missions?" He laughed humorlessly. "That'll just get us the ones who got turned down by the Peace Corps. *Not* what our clients are looking for, Dave. Look, I don't want your fucking excuses. I've got four girls who are ready to get on planes ten days from now. I've got their passports, tickets, parental consent—all I need is those goddamned work visas." Something thumped, as if he'd smacked his knuckled on a counter or a wall. "Make it happen, or *you* can explain to the boss why one of his best clients is unhappy."

Then there was movement, as if the men were walking out, and their voices faded until the bug wasn't picking it up anymore.

As Eve, Ricardo, and August stared at the phone, silence descended in the living room, but it only lasted a couple of seconds.

"He's a *human trafficker?*" August bellowed, flailing so hard he nearly threw his phone. "Are you fucking *kidding* me?"

"Is he?" Eve asked. "Is that... Oh my God, is that what—"

"He's shipping girls out of the country," Ricardo said,

stunned. "If I'm hearing him right—if I'm understanding what he means about work visas and contracts—they lure in teenage girls with promises of modeling jobs or pop careers, then traffic them to wealthy men in other countries."

Eve's jaw fell open. "Are you serious?"

Ricardo nodded numbly. He'd known for a long time that Matt was a sociopath—their time together in combat had left nothing to the imagination about his lack of regard for human life—but this was a depth of fuckery he hadn't envisioned.

I should have shot him when I had the chance.

He'd had the opportunity. He could have killed Matt and prevented... Christ, what wouldn't he have prevented? But he hadn't been able to take the shot. And now...

"That son of a bitch." August, who had been fuming quietly for a moment, got up, nearly cracking his shin on the coffee table, and he started pacing, gesticulating wildly as he did. "Holy shit. Human trafficking? Really? *Seriously?* That's right up there with kidnapping! It's... Fuck, it's *worse* than kidnapping because they don't just hold someone for a little while to get a ransom. They sell them into—Augh!" He flailed again, and this time the phone did fly out of his hand.

Ricardo reached for it, but Eve was faster, and she caught it before it would have slammed onto the coffee table.

August didn't even seem to notice. He kept pacing, limping as he did. "That fucking—I will kill him. I won't even charge. I'll kill him for fucking *free*, Ricardo. Do you hear me? Do you? Fuck my rating, because I will go straight medieval on him. Do you know what drawing and quartering is? So help me God I am going to bring back drawing and quartering just for this asshole. Hell, I will full-on bring back the goddamned Spanish Inquisition and burn off his—"

"August." Ricardo got up and came around the table because August was still rambling, and at any moment, he was going to say something to make Eve realize he wasn't joking and might actually murder Matt. "August. *Hey.*"

His boyfriend flailed again, but Ricardo caught his wrist, and August froze mid-rant, staring at him as if he'd forgotten Ricardo was there at all.

"Breathe, August." Ricardo gently reeled him in. "We're going to stop him, all right?"

"I..." August's shoulders slumped as if all the fight had gone out of him, and his eyes suddenly went from murderous to almost childlike. In a shaky whisper, he said, "It's worse than *kidnapping*, Ricardo."

Ricardo's heart actually hurt. This was a man who'd survived three kidnappings as a child, including one that had cost him a few toes and a brother. "Worse than kidnapping" in August's mind was as bad as it got. That warranted no less than a one-way ticket to the ninth circle of Hell as far as he was concerned.

"We're going to stop him," Ricardo repeated. "We have to make a plan and figure it out, but we will."

August swallowed hard. "We only have ten days."

"Ten—" But then Ricardo remembered what Matt had said. "Because of the girls."

August nodded. "Once he leaves the country with them..."

He didn't have to finish that. If Matt got these girls off US soil, then there was no telling where they'd go or how to find them.

Ricardo moistened his lips and nodded sharply. "Ten days. We've done more in less time. But this means we have to pull it together so we can figure out our next move."

Mute, August nodded again. Ricardo didn't like how simultaneously raw and serious August was right then. As much as his partner's unbridled snark and penchant for button-pushing could drive Ricardo up a wall, he missed it in that moment. A solemn August meant shit was real, and Ricardo didn't like that one bit.

He squeezed August's shoulder. "You still with me?"

"Yeah." August inhaled deeply through his nose as he looked right into Ricardo's eyes. "Let me get another bottle of wine, and then we figure out how to fuck this guy's world."

"I hope the two of you aren't still planning on sending me out for a spa day." Eve's tone was one Ricardo knew well —flat and absolutely non-negotiable. When he looked at her, she was on her feet, and her expression doubled down on the *don't even try to argue with me* in her voice. "If that son of a bitch is hurting and selling kids, then I want a piece of him too."

"Uh..." August glanced back and forth between the ex-spouses. Then he put up his hands and stepped away. "I'm gonna go get that bottle of wine." With that, he hurried out of the living room.

For the second time today, Ricardo faced down his ex-wife. "Eve, we—"

"Don't '*Eve*' me, Ricardo Alcàntara Torralba." Oh, shit. She was using his full name now. That was even scarier than when his mother did it. Stabbing a finger at him, she growled, "I am not sitting on the bench while my asshole ex-boyfriend is smuggling children to fucking *Dubai*, and I am sure as shit not taking a goddamned *spa day* If August's sister is the femme fatale badass you say she is, then bring her in so we have more boots to put in more asses."

Ricardo stared at her, but she wasn't done yet.

"You're not the only one with military training." She sat down emphatically on the couch and crossed one knee over the other. "I'm part of this. Accept it, and work with it."

Okay, she did have a point. Though she didn't have spec ops training like he did, she *had* been a combat medic during her eight years in the Army. Given his time in spec ops, not to mention how August's brother-in-law the doctor had bought Ricardo enough time to get to the hospital after an inconveniently catastrophic bullet hole, Ricardo had a healthy respect for keeping medically trained personnel at the ready during operations. Especially medically trained personnel who were fearless under fire, which was kind of a job requirement for a combat medic.

Like it or not—he did not—he couldn't justify sending Eve to chill with Elodie right now.

With a resigned sigh, he took his own seat on the couch again. "Fine."

"That's what I thought."

"What did I miss?" August swept into the room with another bottle of wine in hand. "Besides someone explaining to me exactly what it was you called him." He arched an eyebrow at Eve as he filled her glass. "Was that some kind of Spanish insult I don't know about?"

"No, not at all." She smiled sweetly. "You don't know his full name?"

He tsked and narrowed his eyes at Ricardo. "Apparently I do not, Ricardo Alca... Alk... Alpaca? Was that it?"

Ricardo kicked August hard enough to make him yelp, though he was smirking even as he rubbed his shin. "Alcàntara, idiot. Now are you going to sit down so we can make a plan?"

"Yeah, yeah." August topped off their glasses, then took his seat and swirled his wine. "An army of alpacas could be—"

Ricardo glared at him. "Would you focus?"

August sobered—sort of—and sipped his wine.

As much as it annoyed Ricardo, he was relieved that August was back in his customary smartass form. That meant he'd rallied and pulled himself together. If he was cracking jokes, then he was thinking sharply, and sharp August was what the situation demanded right now.

Good to have you back, Ricardo thought even as he imagined stuffing a gym sock into August's mouth to shut him up.

"All right. So." Eve put her glass down and clasped her hands around her knee. "Where do we start?"

August blinked. "We?"

"Don't argue, darling." She gave Ricardo's leg a firm pat. "We've already discussed it."

August cut his eyes toward Ricardo. "Oh, did 'we'?"

Ricardo sighed. "She's an Army-trained combat medic, and she's more stubborn than the two of us combined. So let's not bother wasting time, and just figure out our next move, all right?"

From the way August eyed him, Ricardo would hear about this later.

CHAPTER 6

"Sooo."

"No."

August rolled his eyes from where he sat on the edge of their bed. "You didn't even know what I was going to ask."

"I'm sure I did." Ricardo paused in the process of taking his shirt off to hold up a finger. "Either it was a) a question about my name, b) a question about my ex-wife, or c) a question about *sex* with my ex-wife, none of which I want to get into with you."

"Okay, first of all, I would never ask *you* about sex with Eve," August said, ogling Ricardo's bare chest and not even bothering to hide it. "And I don't plan to ask her for more details either, because as fun as it is to see you get all flustered, it turns out I don't really care to think about you having sex with other people." He'd been a little startled with how vehemently he'd latched on to Ricardo at the beginning of this whatever-it-was between them, but he'd come to terms with it equally fast. "The name thing, nah, I'm done razzing you about that for now."

"Then what's—"

"But Eve joining us in this op? I thought you wanted to keep what we do secret from her. How secret do you think we're going to manage to keep things if she's right there with us while we take down a pack of human traffickers with extreme prejudice?" Because there was no room for leeway here: these fuckers were dying. The only possible exception to that blanket statement was Matt, and then only because August figured that Eve might prefer for him to go to prison for the rest of his natural, and probably unnaturally short, life. But that was as much leeway as he was prepared to offer.

Kidnappers. Human traffickers. Absolute fucking scum, and August wouldn't—he *couldn't*—change his mind about that. It might make him a little bit of a psychopath—his therapist might say a *lot* of a psychopath, but whatever, he didn't pay the man for his eloquence, just his honesty—but August had absolutely no sense of perspective when it came to kidnapping. Any rational distance and ability to have a calm, reasonable discourse about the topic had literally been beaten out of him as a child. The way his feet, equally trapped and protected inside his padded orthopedic socks, throbbed in time with his heartbeat was a constant reminder of his history. It wasn't a reminder he could fully escape without more drugs than were good for him, and August was fine with that. Someone needed to be ready to straight up murder a bitch when the situation called for it, and that someone was him.

August put on a good show ninety-five percent of the time. He was always blithe and unconcerned, a billionaire playboy who had fallen into a ridiculous lifestyle that, whether he was killing people for bounties or showing up at a country club soiree in a ludicrously expensive car, displayed what an arrogant jackass he was. It was perfect.

Very few people respected him, almost no one took him seriously, and he couldn't think of a better way to go through life.

But that last five percent of the time...that was when appearances stopped mattering. Those moments were reserved for when he finally pulled the trigger, for when he met with his therapist, for his sister and parents and now, for Ricardo. Some of the time, at least.

"I know. I get it." Ricardo's voice broke through August's dark musings, and he met August's eyes and didn't look away, no hint of discomfort in him even though he had to know August wasn't quite sane in moments like this. "We're not going to let them get away. I promise. We just have to be a little more careful with Eve in the mix."

"Careful." August rolled the word around on his tongue. "Careful how?"

"Careful not to let her see things we don't want her to see," Ricardo said. "Careful to do what has to be done in the dark. Your sister might still be able to help us there."

"As a distraction?" August sighed. "A spa day is one thing, but she can't ride herd on Eve while we go hunt people down. She *does* have a multi-billion dollar company to oversee on a daily basis, and my parents are coming to visit at the beginning of next month, which means Elodie will be in a *mood*." God love his parents, because August certainly did, but it was a lot easier for him to get along with them than it was for his elder sister. He was the weird, damaged child they were just happy was still alive, while she was the successful one who'd taken over their family's company at the age of thirty-one. It made their relationship uniquely stressful at times.

Ricardo shrugged, throwing his shirt into the nearby

hamper. "Maybe just help putting together an ops center, someplace to work on connecting the dots."

"Aww, you want the girls to bond over the big picture?" August smiled cheekily. "That's so sweet."

"It's that or we put up with Eve on stakeouts."

Oh, hell to the no.

"Command center it is! Elodie can bring over some toys for them to play with here, *and* they can do a spa day." August tilted his head and watched Ricardo keep stripping down, no hint of either self-consciousness or self-awareness in it. He got naked with the briskness of a soldier, which was a shame, because he had the body of a god, and August was more than willing to worship it for a while.

As Ricardo took off his pants, the light caught on one of the scars from the gunshot wound to his side that had nearly killed him. He hadn't been pleased with that addition to his many scars; it was larger and more gnarled than the others he'd accumulated over time.

The sight of it made August's blood heat up. Not because it was a turn-on, but because it made him possessive. It made him viscerally aware of how close he'd come to losing Ricardo forever. It reminded him that Ricardo had survived, that he was alive, and that August had every intention of making both of them *feel* alive.

Like... right now.

"You should strip slower next time," August said when Ricardo was done, letting a hint of petulance enter his voice. "It's not much of a show when you're moving so fast that all the good parts are a blur."

Ricardo raised an eyebrow. "I didn't think you liked anything slow," he said as he walked over to the bed. He didn't stop when he got to August, just pressed his shoulders back onto the Lånan eiderdown duvet and knelt over the top of him, one knee on either side of his chest, pinning his arms to his torso.

August grinned. "You're right, fuck slow. Or even better, fuck me. Just let me—"

"No."

Oh, there was the voice. The *voice*, the one that August usually had to be an incredible brat to get. It probably meant Ricardo was feeling sorry for him, but August genuinely didn't care to fight about that right now, not if he got the voice. It was somewhere between drill sergeant and Dom, flat and expectant and ever so slightly shouty, and it was almost enough to make August ruin his pants without a single touch.

"What do you want?" August asked, his ever-present sass falling away as he indulged in the luxury of being concerned about just one thing.

"Suck me off."

August was moving almost before Ricardo stopped speaking, craning his neck to reach whatever he could of Ricardo's dick with his mouth and tongue. His lover made it easy on him a moment later, leaning forward and fucking August's face, slow enough so that he could still breathe but rough enough that he had to work at it.

It was everything August had always wanted out of the play sessions he used to get at clubs, but rarely ever got. There was a line when it came to sex with him, a line between crass and cruel, and Ricardo knew how to walk it to perfection.

August didn't touch Ricardo with anything other than his mouth, no matter how badly he wanted to. He did try touching himself, just because his pants really were tight and it would feel so goddamn good right now, but Ricardo felt it the moment he began to move and stopped moving himself. "You can either have me fuck your face, or you can give yourself a handjob. Otherwise, no touching yourself."

"Ugh, *rude*. You're such a bitch when you get like this," August whined, but he put his hands back down. "Were you always this rude in bed?"

Ricardo's eyes narrowed. "Are you actually bringing my ex-wife into this right now? I thought you didn't want to talk about her."

"You're the one who brought her up, not me." Truth be told, August was a *little* bit curious, because the pair of them had that dueling-top energy that made him wonder if their prelude to fucking had been more of a negotiation or a fistfight. But now really, really wasn't the time to be thinking about where else this dick had been. "What else do you want?"

"To shut you up." And he did, very thoroughly, until August was on the verge of choking and loving every second of it. No drink was more intoxicating, no drug gave a better high than being fucked by Ricardo, however they went about it.

"Christ." Ricardo pulled back and manhandled August up the bed. He had the patience for exactly three buttons before he ripped the rest of the shirt open.

August moaned. "You are a sartorial menace."

Ricardo scoffed, his hands busy peeling the fabric back from August's chest, short nails scratching red lines into his skin. "You have half a dozen just like it less than ten feet away."

"I'm begging you, just take it out on me, leave my clothes alo—" August gasped as Ricardo pinched his nipple so hard it burned, arching into the contact.

"Like this?" he asked with a smirk.

"Just like that," August said, then hissed as Ricardo

twisted before he let go. "God, you're such an asshole. I'm going to bury you in the backyard. Fuck." Ricardo was taking August's pants off, but August was too blissed out on endorphins to pay much attention at the moment. "Like a pet hamster."

"You must have been a very odd child," Ricardo said, whipping his pants over his feet, then tugging his underwear—Calvin Klein, stretch-silk boxer briefs—off as well. He left the socks alone, didn't even touch August's feet, and August was suddenly blindsided by a swell of affection for the idiot above him. Ricardo drove August absolutely batshit crazy more than half the time, but he never fucked up the important things.

"Let's table all conversation of me as a child, and get back to putting your dick inside of me," August purred. "Where do you want me?"

Ricardo, in true-to-him fashion, didn't bother to use his words to reply. He just manhandled August over onto his front, hiked his hips up, and began to rub the tip of his wet cock over August's hole.

It felt amazing, and also terrible, because August knew that Ricardo wasn't going to fuck him without lube, but that didn't mean he wouldn't fuck *with* him. "Backyard," he said with a groan as Ricardo pressed in just hard enough to make him think he had a chance, then pulled away again. "In a fucking shoebox, I swear to God—"

"You talk way too much," Ricardo said, leaning over August's back and pressing a kiss to the top of his spine as he grabbed the lube.

"That's a problem you made for yourself," August pointed out breathlessly. "You could have kept fucking my mouth, but *nooo*, you had to—" Then he shut up on his own, because all of his attention had to go to making absolutely sure he didn't come on the bed like it was his first time being fingered. Ricardo was just the right side of rough, his calloused touch fast but thorough, and true to his sniper abilities, highly accurate.

"You need to fuck me," August said. "Right now."

"You're needy tonight," Ricardo mocked, but he sounded just as bad as August, and moved twice as fast to get behind him. The teasing had finally gotten to him, then.

Good. There was nothing like Ricardo when he let go and finally gave into his baser urges. His hands were like vise-grips on August's hips, holding him steady as he slowly pushed inside. August bit his lip and reminded himself not to curl his toes, because that was just asking for trouble, and then Ricardo was in, and moving, and August forgot to do anything with his body other than move to Ricardo's rhythm.

It was just what he needed, enough to distract him from the clusterfuck of the day and the horrors of the past and just be in his body, right where he wanted to be, right where *he* was wanted. Being alive and in bed with this man was a miracle—he'd thought he had a better chance of getting shot in the head by Ricardo than getting him into bed. Now they were here every night, together, and spent many nights just like this, on top of each other and inside of each other and giving each other everything they had, everything they could want. August was good at being greedy; he excelled at wanting more than he could have, but this... He didn't know how to want more than what he was getting, because it was already so much better than he'd ever thought possible.

"Harder," he said, or begged—or fuck it, cried, because that had happened more than once. Ricardo went harder, enough that August had to brace his hand against the wall to keep from being pushed through it. The pleasure ached like a broken bone, sharp and insistent and just one movement away from being totally overwhelming. "Oh, fuck—I need to—"

"No."

"I *hate* you."

Ricardo slowed down, then stopped. He bent over August's back, heavy and slick and perfect, and stroked his fingers down August's chest and across his thigh, feeling the tremors that followed his touch and chuckling. "No, you don't." He kissed the knob of his spine again, pulled back just a little and ground back in, hard and deep, not percussive but persistent, omnipresent—it was impossible not to feel on the verge of overwhelmed. "Because I take care of you." He finally touched August's cock, his hand loose, barely there, but that was all it was going to take. "Go on. Come."

If the wait had been excruciating, the orgasm was even more so. His whole body was an extension of his pleasure, throbbing in his blood, surging along with his heartbeat. It was the farthest thing from dissociative he'd ever known, the opposite of an out-of-body experience. He felt every second of it, knew exactly when Ricardo lost it and came himself, knew when he was about to collapse and let it happen, because he knew Ricardo would go with him. Which he did.

The silence between them after sex never lasted long, but while it did it was about as tranquil as August ever felt. His version of meditating. He thought about getting freaky with some Gregorian chants or singing bowls going in the background and started to laugh.

"That was fast," Ricardo said dryly before pulling them over onto their sides. He didn't pull out, though.

"It's not you, it's me," he managed between chuckles.

"No, actually, it is kind of you." The image of Ricardo glaring angrily at a flickering candle, trying to fuck August so hard they knocked the damn thing over and set fire to the bedroom—

"I'm glad sex is so amusing for you." Now he *did* pull out, but not away. Instead he wrapped August up in his arms and held him through the mild hysterics that his mental detour had caused.

"It's really not you," August said once he finally had control of himself again. "I'm just a little weird tonight, I think."

"You're weird every night."

"Aw, Ricky, you care so much," August simpered, snuggling back against his chest. Ricardo scoffed under his breath but didn't say anything.

Tomorrow could be another day of plotting and revenge. The rest of tonight was for this, for quiet company and easy, unspoken affection.

August had the feeling that moments like this were going to be in short supply in the near future, so he was damn well going to make the most of this one.

CHAPTER 7

"My God, Ricardo." Eve tsked and gave an exasperated but good-natured sigh. "When will you learn the art of sleeping in?"

He looked up from his phone as she came into the living room with a cup of coffee. With a shrug, he put the phone aside and picked up his own cup. "I like mornings."

Sitting on the other end of the couch, she wrinkled her nose. "People aren't supposed to like mornings. They're things that exist, like traffic and colonoscopies, but no one is supposed to *like* them."

He chuckled. Eve had always been a night owl. Her mother had even joked that she'd brought it on herself by giving her that name. *"Should've named her Dawn,"* she'd mused.

The thought made him admittedly nostalgic for their happier days. There was a lot they needed to focus on today —a lot of time-sensitive plans to formulate and execute— and anyway, he was happy with August and had no desire to go back in time. But there had been good times.

It hadn't exactly been love at first sight, but it was the

closest Ricardo had ever experienced. He'd been at a shitty bar near the base where his Green Beret unit was assigned, and some of his buddies were getting predictably rowdy. One—a Texan who'd earned the nickname Haymaker—had set his sights on Eve.

Prior to that night, Haymaker had never been one of those assholes who got pushy with women, but looking back, Ricardo had to wonder if it was just because no one had ever told him no. He was hot and always had women hanging off him. When Eve rejected him, he'd gone full Mr. Hyde.

As soon as the other Green Berets had realized what was happening, they'd collectively said, "oh, *hell* no," and tried to intervene, but before they could react—and they were spec ops, so they reacted *fast*—Eve neutralized him with a pool cue to the crotch and across his incredibly startled face. He'd tried to rally, but the team had gotten to him and dragged him outside. That was where Ricardo had wound up with a black eye before someone shoved Haymaker into a car to take him home, where he'd promptly had his ass kicked and been warned never to pull that shit again.

Ricardo, meanwhile, had gone inside to make sure Eve was all right. She'd snarked about his black eye, he'd offered to buy her a drink to make up for his friend being an asshole, and (at least in the version they'd told their mothers), they'd hit it off, fallen in love, and eloped three months later. That last part was true, of course. They'd just omitted the part where they'd gone back to her place and... Well, there was a reason they didn't tell their mothers.

In the end, they hadn't been good for each other, and he was pretty sure Eve knew that as well as he did. Even without his mythical cheating, they'd have split up sooner or later. He was too closed off. She was too in-your-face. They'd loved each other—and he supposed he'd always love her—but they were about as good together as alcohol and a rocket-propelled grenade launcher: It might be fun for a little while, but something was inevitably going to explode.

It occurred to him now that August wasn't that different from Eve. Arguing with him could be like trying to talk a brick wall into moving. But he and Ricardo complemented each other, too. Ricardo took things way too seriously, August hardly took anything seriously, but somehow Ricardo knew just when to lighten up with August, just like August always seemed to know just when to come back to earth. Ricardo had never found that balance with Eve, but he and August—they were each other's lightning rods. They shouldn't have worked, but they did, and having Eve here to remind him of his past made Ricardo more possessive of August than ever.

Except maybe "possessive" wasn't the right word. He had no desire to own August or to suffocate him. He just didn't want to *lose* him. He'd gotten over losing her—though he still regretted losing her as a friend—but he didn't want to face the prospect of getting over *him*.

Watching Eve drink her coffee, he was struck by a sense of urgency and determination about his relationship with August.

Don't let me fuck things up with him like I fucked them up with you.

So the question was, where did "pull him into an incredibly dangerous plan that might get him killed" fall into that?

Ricardo suppressed a sigh as he sipped his mostly cooled coffee. August could handle himself. It was Ricardo, after all, who'd rudely almost gotten himself killed while trying to rescue August, and August hadn't let him forget that. Ricardo just really, really didn't want him returning the favor. And knowing him, he would do it just for spite.

Upstairs, a floorboard creaked.

Eve looked up. "Sounds like the other half is awake."

"Early for him, too," Ricardo mused into his coffee. "He must be ready to go fuck up some human traffickers."

She turned to him, eyebrows quirked. "That's a tender nerve for him, isn't it?"

"Yes, it is." He didn't elaborate further. She didn't ask, which could have been because she figured it was better to get the answers straight from the horse's mouth, or because she knew Ricardo wouldn't tell her more than he'd already volunteered. Probably both.

August stayed upstairs for a few minutes, then came down and rattled around in the kitchen. A moment later, he shuffled into the living room with a steaming cup in his hand. In lieu of any grumbled greetings, he announced, "I had a thought."

Eve's eyes widened. She looked at Ricardo again. "Should I be worried? I feel like I should be worried.'

"Probably. I am."

August scowled, but then he rolled his eyes and somehow managed to throw himself unceremoniously into his favorite chair without losing so much as a single drop of his espresso in the process. After taking a sip, he said, ' I think we might need to keep Matt alive. At least for a little while."

Ricardo's eyebrows had to be in his hair by now. "Leave him alive? This from the man who wanted to go Inquisition on him?"

"Oh, I do, and I have all kinds of *glorious* plans for his transformation from irredeemable chucklefuck to mutilated corpse." August turned to Eve. "Trust me—you'll *love* them, and we'll get there. *But*—" He put up a finger. "There is a very large and ugly fly in the lube."

"In the—" Eve cocked her head. "Don't you mean fly in the ointment?"

"Eh, either way." August shrugged. "I don't want flies in my lube *or* my ointment. Or oh God, my *face cream*." He shuddered and made a horrified sound.

Under any other circumstances, the utter bemusement on his ex-wife's face would have had Ricardo howling with laughter. She was usually unflappable, but August had her... flapped.

"Okay, forget the substance," she said. "What's the fly? What are you talking about?"

August took a deep breath and sat up straighter, balancing his coffee cup on his knee. "Here's the thing—in that conversation we overheard, Matt makes a direct reference to 'the boss.' Which makes sense, because there is no way Matt is running this entire operation. Human trafficking organizations aren't all that different from drug rings, and if he's on a level where he's actually transporting the—" He wrinkled his nose. "Ugh, I feel gross calling human beings 'merchandise,' but bear with me here. If he's actually transporting them to the client, then he's definitely not the top dog."

"So, he's equivalent to a drug dealer?" Eve made a face. "Except with people?"

"I'd say he's..." August pursed his lips. "If I had to guess, he meets someone else when he gets to Dubai or wherever else he's going. Another middleman, you could say. So he's not the same as the guy who's actually swapping drugs for money on the street."

"More like the guy who's running the supply house," Ricardo said.

"Exactly." August leaned forward to put his cup on a coaster. "So he's got some clout, but he's not the top dog. And the thought I had is that taking him out will be like taking out a drug dealer—it'll temporarily inconvenience the clients and the organization, but he'll be replaced in short order. There are probably even failsafes in place for that, since it's a high-risk business."

"Because he could be apprehended at an airport." Ricardo nodded along, definitely catching August's train of thought. "There are probably other operatives who travel with him, too. Not with the girls directly, but on the same flights, so they can take over if Matt is detained."

"Oh my God." Eve shuddered. "Are these organizations really that... Well, that organized?"

August and Ricardo both nodded.

"They're transporting people across international borders for criminal purposes," August said. "They have to have *all* their ducks in a *very* tidy row if they're going to pull it off successfully."

"Which also means they have a lot of people on their payroll," Ricardo whispered. "Which is expensive. Which means..."

"It means they need a lot of money to keep this rolling." August swallowed. "Which means that, at the risk of sounding incredibly crass, they have to move a lot of product just to break even."

"Never mind to make a profit." The horror crawling up Ricardo's throat threatened to bring his coffee with it. On some level, he'd known this, but now that August was spelling it out, the true breadth of what Matt was involved in made his stomach turn. He looked at Eve. "Didn't you say Matt was traveling a lot? While you were together?"

She nodded slowly, losing some color. "Yeah. He was out of town on... On business. A lot. Oh my God, I can't believe he was involved in..." Abruptly, her expression shifted from horrified to the same level of murderous rage she'd had in her eyes the night she'd nearly gelded Haymaker with a pool cue. "August, what was it you were saying about the Spanish Inquisition?"

Normally, August would have perked up and begun regaling her with all his detailed plans for slowly dismembering Matt dick-first. Before Ricardo could step in and keep the conversation on the rails, though, August calmly said, "I think we need to put a pin in that."

Ricardo blinked.

Eve cocked her head.

August exhaled as he picked up his coffee again. "I want to do all kinds of colorful things to Matt. I want to use his screams as my ringtone. But there's no telling how many kids they've already sold, or how many more they'll sell if we don't do something about it."

"So... hand them over to the authorities?" Eve glanced back and forth between August and Ricardo. "You can't be suggesting we"—she gestured at the three of them—"take down what sounds like an organized crime ring."

"Actually, he is." Ricardo sighed. "And I think he's right."

August's eyebrows shot up. "I am?"

"Yes, and you can rub it in later. But right now, I think we are the best bet for quickly and completely taking down that kind of operation."

"What?" Eve sputtered. "*How?* How in the world can you do it faster and cleaner than—"

"Than the *government?*" August guffawed. "How can we do it faster and cleaner than *them?* Oh, my sweet summer child, let me count the ways."

She narrowed her eyes at him, and from the way her jaw worked, August was about to get a lesson in what happened if you insulted Eve's intelligence.

"It's quite simple," Ricardo broke in. "The FBI or the police or... Well, whoever is involved, they have to abide by laws and rules, and they have to collect evidence so they can convict these fuckers and send them to prison."

Eve looked at him, eyes wide. "And you guys...?"

"We can just kill them," August said casually.

Her lips parted.

Ricardo shrugged. "He's right."

"Kill... Whoa. Whoa." She showed her palms. "You guys are talking about going in, guns blazing, and just... What? Slaughtering everyone?"

"It's not quite that messy." August delicately sipped his coffee. "I was thinking we get them to turn on each other, and then *they* can slaughter everyone."

She blinked a few times. Then she faced Ricardo. "Is he joking? I can't tell if he's joking."

"No, he's not." Ricardo blew out a breath. "And as much as I know I'll regret admitting it, he's right. Again." From the bratty wink, he was right about regretting it, but he ignored August for now. "We're not constrained by rules about interrogations or detainment. If we can get our hands on Matt and a few other players, dig some answers out of them, and then convince them they're all turning on each other, they'll solve a lot of problems for us. Then we just tip off law enforcement to go in and clean up the rest."

She stared at him. Then August. Then him again.

"Constrained by... When you say 'rules of interrogations,' I mean, what are you planning to do? Waterboard them?"

August sat up so fast he nearly dropped his coffee. "Ooh! We just finished renovating the pool! We could totally—"

"Oh my God." Ricardo pinched the bridge of his nose. "Focus, August." He dropped his hand, and when he looked at his ex-wife, she still had a bemused expression, but then she shook her head and put up her hands.

"Okay, I'm not going to keep asking questions, because I feel like I'm going to learn more than I want to. Let's just..." She lowered her hands and folded them in her lap. "I don't want to know anything I might have to lie about under oath."

"Aww, you hear that, Ricky?" August touched his chest. "She'll lie for us in court!"

"No, sweetheart." Eve smiled sweetly. "I'll lie in court so I don't have to admit that I knew about all this fuckery and didn't go to the authorities when I had the chance."

August actually looked startled by the deadpanned response, and Ricardo indulged in a quiet snort of amusement before he spoke.

"*Anyway*," he said. "I think we should make a move quickly. We've only got ten days—nine, now—to intervene before he takes those girls out of the country."

"So what do you think our next move should be?" August had shifted into strategy mode—completely serious and ready for action.

Ricardo thought for a moment. Then he grinned. "I think we start by making them paranoid. Make them think law enforcement is breathing down their necks."

"Ooh, I'm in." August's eyes sparkled. "So like, set up

more surveillance, but do it where they can see it so they get twitchy?"

"No." Ricardo shook his head. "Then they'll just find a new hidey hole. I think we take a more direct approach." He eyed his partner. "Do you own any suits that aren't perfectly tailored designer brand?"

August's enthusiasm fell and he huffed indignantly. "You *know* that I do *not*."

"Mmhmm. Well, I think you might need to take a trip to the Men's Wearhouse and buy something off the rack."

The little strangled noise August made almost knocked a laugh out of Ricardo. Touching his hand to his chest, he hoarsely asked, "I need...to do...*what?*"

"It's only for this op," Ricardo said as reassuringly as he could. "Because an FBI agent wouldn't be wearing something quite as high-end as you prefer."

That shifted August's offended expression to one that was still deeply insulted, but was also admittedly curious. "An FBI agent, you say?"

Ricardo grinned as he leaned forward and rested his elbows on his knees. "All right, so first things first..."

IN THE SHORT TIME RICARDO HAD BEEN WORKING WITH August, he had learned that there were some distinct advantages to being partnered with a literal billionaire. While money couldn't magically bring Hollywood-style toys into existence, it did give August access to some real-life toys that made his job *so* much easier. All right, so some of that stuff was stolen, like August's unlimited access to the most advanced facial recognition software that was supposed to be reserved for law enforcement and

Homeland Security. Some of it, though, was purchased outright.

That included the incredibly high-end photo printer that never declared itself out of ink because one of several colors was empty, and that also managed to clearly and flawlessly print almost anything Ricardo asked it to. All in the privacy of August's home, too; there were just some things a man shouldn't risk producing at Kinko's.

Things like, say, fake FBI credentials that would hold up to even the most precise scrutiny.

August also had a 3D printer that could have produced the badge to go along with the credentials, but as it turned out, he already had an FBI badge. Ricardo wasn't sure where he'd gotten it or why he had it, and he didn't ask. One less thing *he* might have to lie about under oath someday.

By the time August had returned from the Men's Wearhouse, holding a garment bag and eyeing it like it contained week-old roadkill, Ricardo had a perfect ID and badge in the usual black wallet, ready to identify one Special Agent Merle J. Thomas, III.

"*Merle?*" August gaped at Ricardo. "Am I a special agent or an ex-boyfriend in a country song?"

"It'll go with your new suit."

That had prompted a disgusted snarl, but August took the ID and the suit, grumbled again about burying Ricardo in the backyard, and changed clothes.

Another advantage of a rich partner? Having that much capital made it infinitely easier to bribe cops.

A few hours, two ten-thousand dollar bribes, and a traffic stop under false pretenses later, Officers Fitzgerald and MacDonald delivered a confused, annoyed, and combative Matt to the designated address. As directed, they brought him in through the loading dock of an abandoned industrial building, handcuffed him to a chair in an old office, and left.

"You're going to hear from my lawyer!" Matt screamed at their backs, his voice tinny on the live feed August and Ricardo were watching from another room. "You can't do this to me!"

"Go." Ricardo nudged August. "He can get out of restraints like that."

Bless him, August didn't make a smartass comment about how Ricardo knew about Matt's abilities when it came to escaping restraints. That would waste precious seconds while a trained Green Beret unbound himself, and no one wanted to risk him gaining the upper hand.

August left the room, and Ricardo chewed his thumbnail. He didn't like being even *this* far away. August could take care of himself, and he was well-armed, but Matt was not someone to underestimate. At least August had in an earpiece so they could still communicate.

About twenty seconds after August had left Ricardo's side, right as Matt was starting to make headway with his cuffs, he strolled into the office and into Ricardo's view.

Matt froze. "What the—You. I know you. What the hell is going on?"

"Oh, you recognize me, Mr. Ashford?" August pulled out the fake badge. "Shame we didn't have time for proper introductions last time. My name is Special Agent Merle J. Thomas, III, and right now I can be your best friend or your worst enemy, depending on how much you like having your balls in a vise."

Instantly, Matt was still. Really still. The kind of still Ricardo had only seen him get when bombs were falling and bullets were flying. That was when he was the most dangerous—when he was scared shitless and wouldn't think twice about literally ripping a person to pieces and asking questions later.

Ricardo swallowed. This was even more dangerous than when August had gone in to charm information out of Pedro Silva, the Cavalcante family's goon-in-charge, and Ricardo was suddenly rethinking the entire plan.

Get out of there, August. Get out!

But August calmly pocketed his badge. "I've got some questions for you." He hooked his foot around the leg of another chair, pulled it close with a piercing shriek, and took a seat, seemingly uncaring about the dust and dirt that had no doubt accumulated since the building was abandoned. Damn. Good thing he was wearing that cheap suit instead of one his designers. He wouldn't have broken character, but he would have had a *fit* afterward.

"What were you doing in my house?" Matt demanded. "You were—wait, you were with the gas company. What the fuck were you doing? *Bugging* my house?"

"Ha!" August slouched back, leaning one elbow over the back of the chair and looking casual, even bored. "There were plenty of bugs in that shithole without any help from me."

Matt glared at him. "What the—"

"I'm asking the questions today, Mr. Ashford."

Matt's jaw worked, but that wasn't all that worked.

"His cuffs," Ricardo said. "He's going to get them undone."

August shifted in his seat, then craned his neck. "Are you uncomfortable, hon? Is it the cuffs? Here, let me undo those for you."

"Undo—August!" Ricardo squeaked. "Don't uncuff him!"

But August ignored him and went around behind the

chair. Ricardo couldn't see what he was doing, though he could hear some rustling, jingling, and clicking. He was halfway out of his chair and ready to bolt for the door, even if that meant letting Matt see his face, when he heard Matt shout, "What the fuck?"

Ricardo sat back down. August stood back, arms folded across the badly-fitted jacket and a smug grin across his face. In the chair, Matt struggled even more, but he wasn't making any headway with August's reconfiguration, which included a second set of cuffs and some zip ties.

"There." August dropped back into his own chair. "Now there's no getting yourself loose, so you can focus on me instead of trying to find a way out."

Matt stilled again, looking hilariously perplexed and dangerously pissed at the same time. "What the fuck do you want? And since when do feds do their interrogations in shitholes like this?"

August looked around, then shrugged. "Budget cuts?"

Ricardo had to put a hand over his mouth to keep from laughing audibly, which would probably make August break character.

Matt was unamused. "Aren't you supposed to read me my rights?"

"Your rights?" August stroked his chin. "Okay. Okay. I haven't done this in a while, but…" He cleared his throat. "You have the right to remain silent, but I wouldn't recommend it because I have a collapsible baton in my pocket. You have the right to walk out of here alive as long as you don't piss me the fuck off, and—"

"What?" Matt was scared now. "You're not FBI, are you? Because this isn't how—"

"Oh, I'm FBI." August crossed his legs and folded his

hands on top of his knee. "Are you familiar with the concept of black ops, Staff Sergeant?"

"Um." Matt swallowed. "Yeah."

"Okay, well. That's my assignment. A black op that has your name all over it." August narrowed his eyes. "Can you think of any reason why the FBI might be running some kind of operation like that? And why it would have anything to do with you?"

Matt didn't answer. Ricardo was legitimately surprised he couldn't hear his old spotter's teeth grinding as they often did when he was angry and/or cornered.

"It's quite simple, Mr. Ashford," August went on. "Or would you prefer I called you Staff Sergeant, since that's a bit more, shall we say, relevant to the situation?"

Shifting nervously, Matt cleared his throat. "Relevant...how?"

"Well, you see..." August inclined his head and looked Matt right in the eyes. "There have been reports of war crimes occurring in both Iraq and Afghanistan, as well as other places American troops have been deployed. In particular, American special ops."

Matt was fair-skinned on a good day, and he was nearly translucent now.

August went on, "Interpol is putting pressure on the United States to investigate some troops who..." He quirked his lips as if he were trying to select just the right phrase. "Troops who went rogue and violated international treaties. Would you happen to know anything about that?"

The cuffs behind Matt clicked and jingled, but he wasn't going anywhere. His hands stopped. Then his shoulders slumped. "What do you want?"

"Well, the powers that be want to know about some of the things you did while you were deployed." August narrowed his eyes a little. "But while we were surveilling you, it became quite clear you were involved in something shady on *this* side of the pond too."

Matt chewed the inside of his cheek. Ricardo was admittedly enjoying this more than he should've been. Both watching August slip easily into a new role (even if he was less than thrilled about the costume) and watching Matt squirm as his numerous sins came home to roost.

August sat back, looking right into Matt's eyes. "As much as I want to cooperate with Interpol, your current activities are definitely more interesting to me. So I'm willing to cut a deal."

The spotter straightened so fast, the cuffs jingled and the chair squeaked. "What kind of deal?"

"The kind where you give me what I want and maybe you don't wind up on trial in The Hague."

"Okay." Matt gulped. "I'm listening."

"This new organization you're involved in, it's—Oh, don't try to shake your head and play innocent." August waved dismissively. "We already know what you're doing. I'm not asking about those details, Staff Sergeant, because I know them."

Was Matt shaking? Holy shit. He was. Ricardo grinned as he watched them on the screen. He'd seen Matt take a dressing-down from a higher-up—the kind where his career was threatened within an inch of its life—and barely flinch. Right now, it was a genuine miracle he hadn't pissed himself, and Ricardo was probably enjoying it *way* more than he should have been.

"I don't want you," August said bluntly.

Matt cocked his head. "You... You don't?"

"No." August lowered his voice. "I want the people you're working for. You give them to me, and maybe I magically don't know your whereabouts and can't give them to Interpol."

"Maybe? How is that a deal?"

"Because the alternative is I speed-dial them right now and deliver you to them on a—" August tilted his head. "Well, not a silver platter, but a rusty folding chair. Whatever."

"So either way, I'm fucked?"

"No, *one* way, you're fucked." August smiled sweetly. "The other way, you have a snowball's chance in hell of not being fucked, and I still have some leverage in case you don't do what I tell you to. I mean, what's the point of letting you go if you just run screaming to your buddies and tell them to disappear?"

"Letting—letting me go?" Matt definitely sounded interested. "You're going to let me go?"

"If you tell me what I want to know, and you wear a wire so I can get the intel I need on the people you're telling me about?" August nodded sharply. "Then yes." He gestured at the door. "You'll walk out of here, completely free and with every piece you walked in with." His voice and features hardened as he slowly drew a serrated knife from inside his jacket. "But if you fuck with me, then all of that becomes negotiable." He held Matt's gaze as he ran his fingertip along the side of the knife's blade. "Including the part about the pieces you walked in with."

Matt drew back as much as the chair allowed.

"Do we have a deal, Mr. Ashford?" August narrowed his eyes. "Or should I say... Sandman?"

And there it was—the killing blow. As Ricardo held back a triumphant laugh, the horror visibly sank into Matt's expression. No one outside of their Green Beret team used that name. He didn't share it with anyone because he didn't want to tell the story.

If August—if Special Agent Merle J. Thomas, III—knew that name, then he wasn't blowing smoke. He knew who Matt was. He knew the things he'd done.

"All right." Matt moistened his lips. "What do you want to know?"

CHAPTER 8

August smiled. "Now we're getting somewhere."

We'd get there faster with a switchblade and a nail gun, goddamn it.

But Ricardo was right—if they wanted to thoroughly fuck up a human trafficking organization as careful as this one seemed, they were going to have to play it cool.

"And the answer to your question is, I want to know everything you know so that I can figure out what you *don't* know. I'm a fisherman, Mr. Ashford, and you're going to be playing the role of bait, but I don't know what part of the pond to fling you into quite yet. So let's start at the source of your...product." He let his lips curl with a fraction of the disgust he felt for this piece of shit. "How do you find the girls?"

"It's, ah... There are all sorts of feeder sites," Matt said after a second. "Places to narrow things down before we —*they*, before *they*—figure out who the best prospects are. It starts simple, like Craigslist and shit, asking for cute girls who want to make decent money as a model for a store's opening or something like that. Then the bosses start cutting the list down more."

Matt was singing like a canary, and August listened and nodded along and did his best not to give into the urge to pick up his chair and bash this fucker across the face with it. It was good that Ricardo was recording all of this, because there was no way he'd be able to write something coherent with how badly his hands wanted to shake.

Scum of the motherfucking earth. And August knew scum—he'd gone to boarding school with a bunch of billionaire brats, after all.

"You sort them by, what?" he asked in a bored tone. "Physical characteristics? Family characteristics? Eagerness and ability to travel? Things like that?"

"Yeah." Matt nodded. "I don't really know much about this part," he cautioned. "I'm not one of the handlers. I just make sure all the necessary parts are moving in the right direction on this side of the pond, if you get me."

August smiled again. "I do, indeed, *get* you, Mr. Ashford. Go on."

Matt swallowed hard. "Uh...yeah, so... Sometimes a client will have a special request for a particular type of girl. Otherwise, you can find a buyer for almost anything as long as she's cute enough."

Wow. Not even trying to humanize his prey.

"Keep it together," Ricardo said over the com, and August knew it was probably because he was clenching his jaw so tight he was on the verge of cracking a tooth. "Keep him talking. The more information we get now, while he's off balance, the better. The longer Matt has to think things through, the more lies he'll figure out how to feed us."

"Cute," he said with a nod. "I see. I assume you want someone poor, as well?"

Matt sighed and shrugged. "Not like you can take a kid who's got family with enough money to go looking for them. They won't *find* them, but it makes all kinds of bad waves."

"Got it. Cute and poor." His smile probably looked demented at this point, but August didn't care to rein it in. "Go on. Once you've identified the best prospects to sell to the highest bidder, what happens next?"

"Most of the next part, I don't really know," Matt said cautiously. "It's all contacting people overseas and shit like that. I told you, I just work on things over here in the States, I don't even—"

Aaand there goes my patience.

"Mr. Ashford," August interrupted, shaking his head. "Stop. Please. You're slipping, and we've hardly been at this for five minutes. What did I tell you about leaving with all the parts you came in with?" He picked up the knife again and turned it in his hand, admiring the way the light played along the wavy surface of the serrated edge. "Our relationship is only going to thrive in an environment of total honesty. I think you're under the mistaken impression that I might not *actually* use this on you. Allow me to assure you that I will."

"Whoa, you—Hey now, there's no need to be hasty," Matt said, his eyes widening a little as August stood up from his chair.

"What the hell are you doing?" Ricardo demanded in his ear. "You can't kill him yet, we need him to lead us to the big fish."

Aw, was Ricardo worried August had lost his mind? He glanced at the camera and, at an angle that Matt couldn't see, gave his watcher a saucy wink. Then he walked around behind Matt and pulled his chair back a foot, so that there was room for August to sit down on the edge of the table in front of him. He twirled the knife, admiring the balance of the five-inch blade.

"Here's the thing that you need to really understand, Matt. I know your history. I know it well. I'm not here to dredge up the past, but when you tell me that you're only of use to these people you're working for here in America, when I know full well that you speak fluent Arabic and that Dubai is a popular destination for these girls...well." He shrugged. "You can see how it leads to a lack of faith in you. So. Let's tackle that issue first."

Before Matt could shout, before Ricardo could protest, August flipped the knife over into a reverse grip and drove it point-first into the tiny triangle of space on the seat of the chair just in front of Matt's crotch. He put all his weight into it, and the *ka-chunk* of metal penetrating metal was quite satisfying.

"Jesus fucking Christ!" Matt screamed, rearing back as far as he could with his arms pinned behind him. His legs scrambled against the floor so hard he was on the verge of tipping the chair over, and as tempting as it was to let that happen, if Matt broke a wrist because he landed on it funny, Ricardo would be having words with August. Not-fun words in a not-fun voice.

"Wow! Settle down there, sport, settle down!" August let go of the knife and put his hands on Matt's shoulders, steadying him enough that the chair's front legs finally touched the ground again. "Did I touch a nerve?" He smirked. "Actually, I was very careful *not* to touch a nerve." Matt just stared at him with wide, viscerally frightened eyes.

Yeesh, tough crowd.

"Deep breaths," August continued, patting Matt firmly

on the cheek. "Just inhale and take comfort in the fact that you've still got your testicles. And all in one piece, too!"

"You can't... You wouldn't..."

"Black ops," August reminded Matt gently. "I can do whatever I want to you as long as I make progress on this case."

"That's not true," Ricardo muttered in his ear. "Especially not while you're working in this country."

August ignored him. "Now, I don't want to make you bleed. Not because it wouldn't get results, but because I don't want to have to send someone in here with a bottle of bleach and a pile of rags after we're done. Nobody wants to clean up that sort of mess, you know? That's not being a team player. So I'll just..." He moved back and sat down on the edge of the table again. "...leave that knife right where it is, and as long as you become a model citizen and tell me what I want to know, it won't move. If you start to try and bullshit me again, though?" August reached out and tapped the toe of his shoe against the hilt of the knife, which wiggled a little. "Well, I guess we'll see if I miss your femoral artery when I kick this into your crotch."

"You're a fucking psychopath," Matt said hoarsely, staring straight at August's face. August wasn't quite sure what the other man was seeing there, but he was sweating like it was a hundred degrees in this dank little room instead of a comfortable seventy-two. "You're nuts."

"Sometimes," August agreed. "When it's necessary to get the job done. And I assure you, Mr. Ashford, my supervisors *love* that about me. Now. Prospects. Bidders. Go."

"Um. Okay." Matt closed his eyes for a moment, clearly putting himself back together on the inside. August had to hand it to him; he'd taken nearly having his balls cut off better than most men did. "Once the best prospects have signed contracts or gotten parental consent we have to get the paperwork together. Passports and shit like that is easy enough. We subsidize it for the girls who can't afford it on their own, but we need realistic work visas for the destination we have in mind. That can be...challenging. It changes a lot, and working with people in the destination country is risky."

"Sure, of course." The more people who knew about an operation like this, the more danger that it would get sniffed out and shut down. Outside operatives were less obedient than the people you kept in pocket in the States, and more likely to turn or abandon things if they caught even the faintest hint of danger. "So I assume you're working with someone in Department of State?"

"A consultant, actually. David Schreiber." Matt's voice was perfectly flat now, speaking solely with the intent to convey information as efficiently as possible. "He works for the State Department in DC. He's been working for the people who put all of this together a lot longer than me, though." Matt smiled thinly. "They have evidence of him sleeping with an underage girl. He's terrified of going to prison."

"It's smart to be terrified of going to federal prison," August said. "This is an excellent beginning Matt; you're doing a lot better. So he, what, fakes the work visas?"

"Something like that. He's got a few people looped in on his side, and I do not know them by name," Matt was careful to articulate. "Once those are ready to go, though, we get the girls to the Madame and let them live it up for a weekend in a decent hotel before shipping out. Gotta keep the product happy. That's where I usually do my hands-on work."

"As a babysitter?" August asked.

Matt did his best to shrug. "Bodyguard, babysitter, whatever. I keep them from doing stupid things for a few days before the Madame escorts them onto the plane. They always send a couple of passengers along incognito to back her up if she needs it, too. Not me," he articulated again. "I don't do international travel on public flights."

"Of course not." Because he was a wanted man in *several* countries due to his war crimes conviction, and facial recognition software was getting better and better all the time. August would know. "Tell me more about the Madame, then. Who is she?"

Matt did his micro-shrug again. "Hard to say. She looks different every time, and her paperwork is always perfect. Some trips she's blonde, some she's a brunette. Sometimes she's Moroccan, sometimes she's English. I think it's always the same woman, though." He smirked briefly. "She's stacked."

"And she's trafficking American girls into foreign countries to become sexual slaves. What a gem," August said dryly.

"It is what it is." Matt met his eyes again. "Seriously, we're not even the biggest operation on the East Coast. You want to take down human traffickers? You should be focused on the pipeline through the old Eastern Bloc, not a little local setup like this one."

If August were actually a federal agent, Matt would have a point. But there was no reason to let him know he was right.

"What makes you think we aren't, sugar cube?" August asked brightly. "The arm of the law is very long, after all. The fact that you're here doesn't mean we're being neglectful. Trust me. Now." He tapped his foot on the knife again, just for the pleasure of seeing Matt wince. "Let's talk timelines and contacts. I want to know everything about your next shipment, —and this is where detail really matters, pumpkin, so don't hold back. When is your next group of girls due to ship out, and from where?"

Over the next two hours, August coaxed details out of Matt—the number of girls in the shipment (four, the youngest of them just fifteen), and when they expected to leave (nine days out as of today—so they'd be getting together at the hotel in seven). He just didn't know *which* hotel, and this city, unfortunately, had many.

"Good job," August congratulated Matt when he finally ran out of new information. "That's some really excellent intel gathering. Now." He smiled and hopped down from the table. "You sit here like a good boy, and I'll be back in a few minutes to discuss next steps."

"Come on, man," Matt groaned. "Can't you give me a break? I've got to piss like a race horse."

"Nope."

"Then at least take the knife away?" He shifted uncomfortable. "My balls are about to retract into my body."

"That's a great trick," August said. "Do you think you can get them to do that before I geld you?"

"Just *move* the *fucking knife!*" Matt shouted. The sweat was back, darkening the pits of his shirt and rolling down his neck. "I'm not fucking going anywhere, just move it already!"

Hmm. This smacked of delaying tactics. August moved around behind Matt's chair, where—"Gosh, you're very industrious!" he said, eyeing the blood running down Matt's wrists. He'd already worked through both sets of cuffs, and had gone after the zip-ties pretty hard from the look of it.

"You are really, really good at this. Houdini-level good. You should have a show. I guess you subscribe to the school of 'if at first you don't succeed,' huh?" If Matt could push hard off the table and twist his arms just right, he might get enough leverage to actually have a hope of escaping...but he couldn't even raise his legs with the knife stuck at that angle between them.

"If I were you," August said, coming around and looking Matt in the eyes again, "I'd stop trying. All you're doing is damaging yourself, and the more you damage yourself, the more lies you have to tell about how it happened. You better get your boss to believe you're into kink, is all I'm saying. Also?" He grabbed a fresh roll of duct tape from his chair, went behind the chair and wrapped half of it around Matt's wrists. "You'd be starting from scratch, and we've got eyes on you, apricot, so don't be more of an idiot than you have to at this point. Mkay? Mkay." He got up and left the room before the urge to slap Matt so hard across the back of the head he got a concussion got the better of him.

Ricardo was shaking his head when August joined him. "What?" August asked, loosening his tie—*fuck* this polyester bullshit, *seriously*.

"You don't think that was a little too theatrical?" Ricardo replied. "You're supposed to be a federal agent; they're not known for their creativity when it comes to questioning suspects."

"Having never been questioned by a federal agent before, I can't rebut that, but Merle J. Thomas III is an inherently theatrical guy. He first met Matt while he was in disguise, after all." August sighed. "It would almost make for a great romcom, if not for the human trafficking angle. And the fact that Matt is *such* a dick. I mean, I like Eve, don't get me wrong, mad respect, but she is shit at picking men. This guy is—"

"August. Focus." Ricardo was frowning, but August sensed it wasn't at him. "We don't have the names of the girls."

"Because this misogynistic piece of shit didn't bother to remember them."

"Without those names we can't warn them."

"We can't warn them yet anyway," August said. "Not until we've got the big players wrapped up. Otherwise they'll be ignored at best or become witnesses who need to be silenced at worst."

"Yeah." Ricardo's far-away look resolved. "First things first, we need to track down David Schreiber and see what he knows."

"We can use Matt for some of that," August said. "Get him to wear a wire before a meeting. I'll find out when the next one is." He eyed Ricardo for a moment. "You're weirded out by something. What?"

Ricardo huffed a sigh. "We have to make sure we don't take Matt for granted. He has reason to cooperate with who he thinks you are—legitimate, self-serving reasons—but he's vicious, and he doesn't like being ordered around."

"Shit soldier, then."

"Yes," Ricardo agreed.

"Aw, Ricky. Don't worry." August leaned in and kissed him lightly on the lips. "We'll make sure Big, Bad Matt doesn't fuck things up. There's two of us—four if you count Eve and Elodie—and one of him. We can cover him."

"We'd better." Ricardo nodded his head toward the door. "Now, go scare the shit out of him some more before we let him go."

"My pleasure!" Really, if he wasn't going to be on

contract for a while, at least he still got to partake in the sheer pleasure of making assholes consider death the better option.

Matt deserved every second of pain, as far as August was concerned.

CHAPTER 9

Before long, Matt was duly terrified and wired enough to be released into the wild. For Ricardo, that process was incredibly entertaining, too; after years of putting up with Matt talking and acting as if he were a god among mortals, it was beyond gratifying to watch him taken down a few pegs. Trust August to be the perfect man to do it, too. Ricardo would have to blow him for that later tonight.

Grinning to himself, Ricardo watched on the monitor as August removed the last of Matt's various bindings.

"All right." August stepped back and extended his hand. "You're free to go, Mr. Ashford. But do remember what I said about removing, disabling, or otherwise tampering with that wire." He smiled brightly.

Matt eyed him, and Ricardo didn't think it was the shitty camera or blanched fluorescent lights making him look that green. Grudgingly, Matt shook August's hand. Then he gestured at the door. "So, uh, are those cops waiting outside to take me home, or what?"

"Waiting out—" August laughed. "You're a big boy with a working cell phone. I'm sure you can find a ride home."

Matt blinked. "Are you... What the fuck? You aren't even going to—"

"If I drive you anywhere," August said, his tone shifting to a menacing growl, "it'll be to catch a plane to The Hague." He nodded sharply toward the door. "Uber might give you a few more options."

The fear that crossed Matt's expression drove a laugh out of Ricardo, and he clapped a hand over his mouth to muffle it even though he doubted his voice would carry.

Matt had apparently decided not to test August's—sorry, Special Agent Merle J. Thomas, III's—patience or good will any further, and he took out his cell phone as he headed for the door. August had also wired the phone, so any calls would be clearly recorded for posterity. They probably didn't need to pay much attention to that right now, so Ricardo reached for the feed to mute it for the moment.

A split second before his finger would've hit the button, though, a voicemail message picked up:

This is Eve. I'm not available right now, so you know what to do.

Ricardo froze, hand hovering over the keyboard. Shock quickly gave way to rage, and then Matt started talking:

"For fuck's sake, Evie," he growled. "Stop fucking around and call me. I need a ride. But... ugh. Fine. You're obviously too busy for me. Again. Just call me. I need a place to crash tonight."

Then he ended the call, and he didn't dial out again. He was probably booking a ride share.

Ricardo clenched his hand into a fist and fought the urge to slam it into the keyboard. They needed this equipment, and he didn't need a broken hand, but he couldn't run out there and bash Matt's face in either. Not yet.

But he was going to kill him. Forget bro code or anything like that—Eve could date whoever she wanted—but if this asshole was going to treat her badly and put her in danger, then he was going to see a side of Ricardo he didn't think existed.

"You know, for a sniper," Matt had teased one day as they'd broken down their weapons in the desert, *"You've got an awfully squishy heart."*

"It's not a squishy heart," Ricardo had said through his teeth. *"We're here to neutralize threats, not make people suffer."*

Matt had laughed at him, and he'd challenged, *"There's nobody out there who you think deserves to suffer?"*

"No one I've ever been told to kill."

Just you wait, Sandman, Ricardo thought in the present, his teeth grinding with barely contained rage. *Because you're about to find out the hard way that I do believe some people should suffer.*

The door opened behind him, and August started to speak on his way in, but Ricardo whirled on him. "When this is over," he snarled, "*I'm* putting a bullet in that fucker's brain. *Me.*" He tapped his own chest. "No one else."

August skidded to a halt, eyes wide, lips still apart for whatever it was he'd intended to say. Slowly raising his palms, he nodded. "All right. All right. You called dibs. I respect that." He glanced at the various electronics Ricardo had been monitoring. "Any particular reason? Because you were chill twenty minutes ago, and now you want—"

"The first person he fucking called for a lift was Eve."

"Are you—" August stared at him. "Eve. He called Eve to—That asshole! He doesn't even give a shit about putting her in Special Agent Psycho Switchblade's crosshairs? What the hell?"

Ricardo nodded slowly. "Yeah. That's why I'm—"

"Oh, don't you worry." August huffed indignantly. "I can't promise he won't be bleeding when the time comes, but the kill shot? Baby, that's *all* yours. And I'll even pay to put the shell casing in a fancy-ass shadow box, because fuck that guy."

That actually drew a smile out of Ricardo, and as his hackles came down, he touched August's waist. "A shadow box, huh?"

August grinned, letting himself be drawn in. "You have to admit—it would be a hell of a conversation starter."

Chuckling, Ricardo brushed a kiss across his lips. "It would be. But for now, we need to—"

A ringing phone turned both their heads.

"Oh, is he calling someone else?" August craned his neck.

"Sounds like it." Ricardo released August—admittedly with some reluctance—and turned to get a better look at the feed. There was a number on the screen, which could come in handy later, but it didn't tell them much yet.

"Come on, you piece of shit," Matt was muttering over the sound of the ringing phone. "Pick up. Pick the fuck up. Where are—"

"Yeah?" came a disinterested answer.

"Thought you weren't gonna pick up." Matt laughed, and he was clearly trying to sound calm and cool, but Ricardo knew him well enough to recognize the undercurrent of nerves.

"I almost didn't. What do you want?"

Matt cleared his throat. "I need a sit-down. ASAP. With the big man."

August and Ricardo exchanged looks.

"The big man doesn't come to you." The response was calm. Bored, even. "You jump when he says jump, not the other way around."

"I get that. But this is important."

"Of course it is." The man on the other end sighed as if this conversation were the biggest imposition he'd ever faced. "Tell you what—I'll set something up with a lieutenant. If he thinks the big man is interested, he'll—"

"There's no time for that," Matt hissed. "It can't wait."

"Then I would suggest you meet the lieutenant at the place and time I give you. We'll be in touch."

The call ended.

Ricardo stared at the now silent screen.

"What do you think he's doing?" August asked. "Do you think he's going to run screaming to the boss that the feds are on to him?"

Ricardo thought about it for a long moment, then shook his head. "No. He's going to try to save his own skin." He turned to August, who was watching him curiously. "He knows we're listening, and he knows we're going to hear this and think he's trying to deliver the big boss to us so he can get a deal."

"So he's a backstabbing little bitch, is what you're saying?"

Shrugging, Ricardo nodded. "It's on-brand for him."

"Ugh." August wrinkled his nose. "Tell me again why you didn't shoot him while he was your spotter?"

"Because if I'd done that, I'd still be in Leavenworth, and I wouldn't have fucked you last night."

That got August's attention. "Oh. Well. When you put it like that, it makes perfect sense." Rubbing his chin, he scowled at the computer. "So he's going to be rallying as many people as he can find in order to deliver them to us on a silver platter and score witness protection or something. While he's doing that legwork for us, what should *we* be doing?"

Ricardo considered it. "I think we need to find the girls."

August turned to him. "How do we do that?"

"You got the name of his contact at the State Department, didn't you?"

"Yeah. David Schreiber."

Ricardo nodded curtly. "Well. I think we know who we need to speak to next."

"We? So we're going to do this one together?"

"Might be more effective that way, yes."

August's face lit up and he bounced a little as he clapped his hands ."Ooh! It'll be like date night!" He flailed a hand at their electronic gear. "Let's get all this shit back to the house. I need to pick out the right shoes!"

Ricardo just rolled his eyes and started shutting down the equipment.

TRACKING SOMEONE DOWN WAS NOT AS QUICK OR EASY as Hollywood liked to portray. Well, that wasn't true. If the person was stupid, careless, and/or cocky, then finding them was generally not a difficult task, and there were a lot more stupid, careless, and/or cocky criminals than most people realized.

The problem was when the mark was smart, careful, and/or cognizant of their own mortality. They were the ones who had scant footprints on the internet, varied their routes when driving, and were generally a pain in the ass to anyone who wanted to find them.

It was in this respect that people like August and Ricardo had a distinct advantage over law enforcement. Not only did they have (highly illegal) access to much of the same surveillance the cops and feds used, they also didn't have to abide by inconvenient things like "rights" or "the Constitution." That wasn't to say law enforcement gave two fucks about those things either, but August and Ricardo didn't even try to pretend they did.

And it was through those highly illegal and wildly unconstitutional channels that, over the course of just under twenty-four hours, they tracked down David Schreiber. Plus Matt had obediently submitted information to Special Agent Thomas, including some criminally damning evidence against Schreiber. Then there were a few more hours of driving to Manassas, the Washington suburb where Schreiber rented the kind of shitty, cramped apartment where well-paid government employees lived when they'd been taken to the cleaners by an ex. According to Matt, the man's ex-wife had taken the kids along with most of his net worth about five years ago, and Schreiber had been living the canned-beans-on-paper-plates lifestyle ever since.

Given what Matt had said about Schreiber, Ricardo had to wonder if the guy was paying her for the same reason Ricardo had been paying Eve all this time—because coughing up that much alimony was a hell of a lot cheaper and less painful than letting her find out about some of his secrets. Secrets such as, say, the one Matt's bosses were using to keep Schreiber at their beck and call.

While Matt continued trying to get an audience with his boss, no doubt so he could throw the whole hierarchy under the bus in exchange for leniency, August and Ricardo zeroed in on the slimeball at the State Department. According to the tracker on his car, he'd left work at five o'clock sharp, and the traffic reports predicted he'd be home in another twenty to thirty minutes at most. It was go time.

Ricardo drove around the block, memorizing every access point to the apartment's parking lot. Then he parked down the street beneath the shade of an oak tree and shut off the car.

August glared at him from the passenger seat. "I can't believe I let you talk me into this."

"What?" Ricardo reached into the backseat to get the necktie he had refused to put on until it was absolutely necessary. "I thought you liked covert ops."

"I do. I love them. But isn't this a little..." He looked down at his white button-up shirt, black tie, and plain black pants. "Do we have to?"

"We have about twenty minutes before Schreiber gets home." Ricardo started tying his tie. "If you've got another idea, we need clothes, identities and back stories ready to go by the time he shows up." He snapped his fingers. "Come on. Out with them."

"I... But I mean..." August closed his eyes and forced a breath out through his nose. "Do we have to wear the nametags, though?"

"Do you want to sell the persona or not?"

August made one of those whiny, defeated sounds that Ricardo probably shouldn't have found quite so entertaining. Then he opened the glove box, took out the two pins, and handed one to Ricardo before fastening the other above his breast pocket.

Gesturing sharply at it, he looked right at Ricardo. "We're going to hell for this. You know that, right?"

"Pretty sure we were going there anyway."

August groaned and rolled his eyes.

Ricardo chuckled as he put on his own pin, which was a black lacquer rectangle that read *Elder Esteban Hernández* in neat white letters. Below that, *The Church of Jesus Christ of Latter-Day Saints*.

Yeah, they probably were going to hell.

With a resigned sigh, August checked his phone. "All right. He should be here in less than twenty, so we'd better get started." He shot Ricardo a look. "What happens if someone actually wants to talk to us?" He picked up their *Book of Mormon* and waved it around. "I didn't exactly have time to read this on the drive over!"

Ricardo snickered. "They won't want to talk to us. Don't worry."

August narrowed his eyes. Then he pointed sharply at Ricardo. "If one person invites us in or keeps us talking instead of just slamming the door in our faces, you are blowing me tonight."

"I probably will anyway." Ricardo shrugged. "Now let's go."

"But wait—they're usually like twenty. Tops." August flailed a hand at Ricardo. "How are they going to buy that you're a missionary?"

"Because I was a late-in-life convert, and I want to share the Word. You, on the other hand, could pass for twenty. Now could we please get moving?"

A compliment like that would usually result in some blushing and preening. August was apparently in no mood for flattery, though. Instead, he let fly a string of commentary that would make his alter ego—Elder Beckett Bradshaw—faint, but he got out of the car, plastered on a manic smile, and followed Ricardo to the apartment building.

It sounded counterintuitive to so brazenly enter a

building like this, but it was actually much less conspicuous than trying to be stealthy. Walking in with nametags on their chests, knocking on people's doors, and introducing themselves to people didn't exactly scream *"We're here to threaten a man's life if he doesn't give us what we came for."* Ricardo was kind of surprised more criminals didn't do this, but... stupid, careless, and/or cocky.

Admittedly, he was rather proud of this particular scheme.

He did, however, misjudge one teeny, tiny detail—just *how* good August could slide into this persona and sell it.

"Well, hello there!" he said with a bright smile to the young woman who answered the door. "My name is Elder Beckett, and this is my companion, Elder Esteban, and we're with the Church of Jesus Christ of Latter-Day Saints. We were wondering if you had a few minutes to talk with us about God!"

She stared at them, eyes flicking back and forth between them as if she had no idea what to make of them. This was where Ricardo had banked on her and all of Schreiber's other neighbors telling them to fuck off before slamming the door in their faces.

She was not supposed to return the smile as she shrugged, stepped aside, and said, "Sure. Can I get you something to drink?"

August kept his smile firmly in place, but Ricardo could almost feel him screaming internally, which in turn almost made him laugh.

Calm down, August, he wanted to say. *This won't take long.* After all, a couple of hitmen trying to pitch a religion they knew nothing about to a complete stranger was bound to end in short order.

In theory.

After forty-five of the longest minutes of Ricardo's life, their hostess, Allison, showed them to the door. "I'll email you all of those links as soon as I'm done studying!"

"Um." August swallowed, and he looked and sounded dazed. "I'll, uh... I'm looking forward to reading it." Clutching his Book of Mormon to his chest like a shield, he said, "You've given me a lot to think about."

She grinned triumphantly, wished them both well, and closed the door.

In silence, August and Ricardo continued down the breezeway toward the next apartment. After several steps, August smacked Ricardo with the book. "Asshole."

Ricardo let go of the laugh he'd been stifling this entire time. "What?"

"I can't believe you." August huffed theatrically. "It was bad enough you thought of this whole hare-brained thing in the first place. But pretending you didn't speak English so *I* had to do *all* the talking? What the fuck, man?"

"I thought you handled it well!" Ricardo shrugged, still snickering. "How was I supposed to know one of his neighbors was a graduate student in comparative religious studies? And besides, you were selling the whole 'oh my God, you're talking me out of my own beliefs'—I wasn't going to interrupt."

August shot him a dirty look. "Fuck blowing me." He jabbed a finger at Ricardo. "You are *bottoming* tonight, good sir."

Right then, a middle-aged couple came around the corner, arms loaded with groceries, and from the wide-eyed stares, they had absolutely heard everything. Their eyes flicked to the nametags, and the confusion deepened.

August instantly bounced back to his cheerful self, and

he held up the book. "Hello! Do you have a few minutes to chat with us about God?"

Eyes widened even more, and the couple hurried away.

"It'll just be a few minutes!" August called after them. "Don't you want to hear about—okay, they're gone." He glared at Ricardo. "Now can we cut the crap and go deal with our mark before he decides to go hook up with someone on Tinder or something?"

"We have to keep up the act." Ricardo plucked the book from August's hands. "If we skip apartments, it'll look suspicious."

"Uh-huh. And what if he leaves?"

"Then we'll be waiting when he comes back after dark, won't we?"

August eyed him suspiciously. Finally, he sighed, and he jabbed the middle of Ricardo's chest. "I mean it—*bottoming*."

The next two neighbors were predictably uninterested in discussing religion with a couple of strangers, and the doorbell on the third door went unanswered.

After that was David Schreiber's unit.

At the door, August rolled his shoulders and set his jaw. Then he poked the doorbell.

No answer.

August rang it again.

Still no answer.

"So help me God," August said under his breath, "if this motherfucker doesn't answer, I'm going to end up on YouTube as a Mormon missionary who snapped."

Ricardo stifled a snort. Sort of.

"I hate you right now," August muttered.

"Admit it. You're enjoying this."

"I am *not*." He jabbed the doorbell a third time. "I had

to spend almost an hour pretending I was—well, hello there!" Like a switch had flipped, he was back to manically bright. "My partner and I would love to chat with you about God for—"

The middle-aged white man on the other side rolled his eyes. "Yeah, I don't think so. Have a nice—"

"Oh, I'm not asking." August's voice was still cheerful, but took on a menacing edge. "We're going to sit down and talk about a few things, and one of those things is how soon you'll be meeting God if you piss me off. So, would you mind if we come in?" He smiled again, and even Ricardo had to admit he was kind of terrifying right now. Hot, but also terrifying.

The man—Schreiber, Ricardo recognized from facial rec—stared at both of them, having clearly also registered that August might be slightly unhinged. "Who the fuck are you?"

"Isn't it obvious?" August tapped a nail on his lacquer nametag. "We're two guys who know a few things about your future and whether or not you'll be around to see it."

Schreiber blanched. He looked at Ricardo, silently asking what the hell was going on.

"You should probably do what he says," Ricardo said casually. "I could tell him not to kill you, but does he look like he listens to me?"

Schreiber's eyes got even wider.

"Let us in." August's voice was still scarily bright and cheerful. "And don't try anything stupid."

The man stared at them for a moment, and Ricardo wondered if he would, in fact, try something stupid.

Don't do it, Ricardo wanted to plead. *If he beats the shit out of you out here, then we might have to deal with the police, and that's just inconvenient.*

Finally, Schreiber stood aside and gestured for them to come in. They did, and he closed the door. "What's this all—"

"We're going to ask the questions." August had dropped the missionary persona and was 100% pissed-off hitman now. He pulled his collapsible baton out of his trouser pocket and snapped it open. "Maybe we should sit down in the living room and get comfortable."

Schreiber slowly raised his hands. "Look, I don't know what this is all about, but I don't want any trouble. Just tell me what you want."

August was clearly about to tell him that he was getting trouble whether he liked it or not, but Ricardo touched his forearm and spoke first: "Let's all sit down and talk, all right? Then maybe we can do this without costing you your damage deposit."

Schreiber gulped. Hands still raised, he nodded. "Okay. Okay. Living room is..." He gestured with his chin toward the couch and chairs gathered around a medium size flat screen TV.

As the trio moved from the entryway into the living room, August muttered, "You take the fun out of everything, I swear."

"I'll make it up to you," Ricardo promised.

Schreiber sat in an armchair. August sat on the couch, one knee crossed over the other and his hands folded on top as he held the baton in a loose grip. Ricardo stayed standing, in part so he could loom over their mark, and also in case August decided to lunge at Schreiber and rip his spine out through his nipple. Having August this heated hadn't been part of the plan, mostly because Ricardo couldn't have predicted that the doctoral candidate neighbor would put their cover to the test like that, and he wasn't sure exactly how volatile August was right now. On the other hand, having him this close to losing his shit was clearly making Schreiber reconsider any thoughts of trying to fuck with them.

"All right." Schreiber flattened his palms on his thighs. "So, what's this about?"

"It's about some passports and visas that you're handling," Ricardo said.

The man's brow furrowed. "You'll have to be more specific. I process dozens of—"

"Think about it, assclown," August growled. "Which passports do you think a couple of lunatics like us might be interested in? Huh?" He narrowed his eyes. "Or do you have so many shady-ass clients that we really do need to be more specific?" He smacked the baton on his palm.

Schreiber eyed the baton, and he gulped.

"Maybe this will jog your memory." Ricardo pulled up an image on his phone, then turned it so Schreiber could see it, and the man turned even whiter.

"Where did you get that?" he rasped.

"It doesn't matter where I got it." Ricardo lowered the phone. "What matters is whether or not I'm going to pass it on to law enforcement." Inclining his head, he added, "Is that what you want? For the cops and your bosses to find out what you did with—"

"No! No!" Schreiber put up his hands in surrender. "Please. I don't know where you got that, but... Look, I know which passports you want. I'll get you the information. Just... Just please don't show that to anyone."

"You've got fifteen minutes." Ricardo started a stopwatch on the screen and showed it to him. "Show me what I want to see, or that picture goes—"

"I can't do it that fast!" Schreiber spoke frantically and

moved to the edge of his seat. "But I can get you what you want. Just... It's..." He paused to take and release a deep breath, and he cut his eyes warily toward August before looking up at Ricardo. "It'll take me more time than that, but I'll get you what you want."

"Fine." Ricardo stopped the timer and pocketed the phone. "Get to work."

"Okay. My..." Schreiber gestured toward the kitchen. "My laptop is in there. Can I go get it?"

"Hurry up."

The man scrambled to his feet and stumbled on the way to the kitchen. From here, Ricardo could see him as he picked up his laptop case and unzipped it. As long as Schreiber didn't try anything stupid—and Ricardo suspected he wouldn't—they'd wait for him in here.

Under his breath, August said, "I still think we should send that picture to law enforcement."

"Oh, we will." Ricardo glanced at August. "I'm using it as leverage now, but as soon as we're done with him..." He nodded.

For the first time since they'd arrived, August smiled a genuine smile, and he relaxed a little. They'd both been surprised when Matt had obediently supplied August with the evidence of Schreiber's transgressions with the teenager, and August had hit the roof, going off on one of his colorful tirades about how he was going to make someone regret being born. Ricardo was more inclined to turn the scumbag over to law enforcement.

"That way the whole world will know what he did," he'd explained in the car. "Instead of someone just finding his body and wondering who could do such a thing to an innocent man."

August hadn't seemed convinced. Now, apparently, he was.

Unaware of them making long term plans for his well-deserved future, Schreiber returned to the living room with his laptop.

"Okay." He looked up at Ricardo. "Tell me what you want to know."

CHAPTER 10

It took a while to get everything they wanted out of Schreiber, not because he wasn't being helpful, but because once he got going, he was willing to be *too* helpful. He definitely wanted to keep the illicit picture that Matt had provided out of the greater sphere, and he was willing to transfer over copies of every document he'd obtained in relation to these girls in exchange for it. He even made hard copies.

When August told him to copy over the passport information and work visas for the other girls he'd done this to, Schreiber had just sighed and said, "I don't have a thumb drive big enough to support all of that data."

"Then get ready to take advantage of the cloud, motherfucker." August knew it was too late for most of them. As soon as they hit ground in a foreign country, they'd been as good as lost, sold into a short and brutal life of sexual slavery that no one, not even this asshole sitting in front of him pushing his glasses up his nose with a resigned look, deserved.

Sex had never been part of August's kidnappings and

subsequent captivity, not any of the times, but he remembered how the men in the first one had talked about his sister. Elodie had been fifteen, a child forced to act like an adult as she tried to shield her little brothers from what was going on. August remembered the way they'd looked at her, the way one of the men had touched her when he'd tugged her off the ground and pulled her in close, ignoring her outcry and evading her attempt to stomp on his foot.

He hadn't gotten far with her—one of the other kidnappers had called him off, like bringing a dog to heel—but August had never forgotten the panicked look on her face, or the way she'd sat down between August and Laurence when she'd come back, surrounding herself with the only two people she could trust in a hostile environment. She'd tucked him in close against her side and buried her face in his hair, while their brother hugged them both as hard as he could.

August had been too young to understand the peril then, too innocent. By the time he understood the potential consequences of something like a kidnapping, Laurence was dead and August had been disfigured. By the third kidnapping, he'd developed a system for dealing with the emotions that came with being torn away from a safe place and thrust into a lion's den. It involved lots of indiscriminate violence and a pathological disregard for his own safety, but it worked for him.

What had Elodie used as her coping mechanism?

He could ask her. She was at his house right now with Eve, putting together a database of everything they knew and everything they needed to know. He'd already forwarded the data to her, and she'd responded with, "Got it." No questions asked. Elodie had allowed him to draw her into a web of pure filth that had to be bringing up some bad memories for her, all because he'd asked. Because she came whenever he called; because she was determined not to lose him, and perhaps willing to let him hurt her in order to ensure that.

Jesus, he sucked.

Ricardo, in a show of the kind of compassion he didn't often put on display, didn't say anything for the first half hour of their two-hour drive back home. August emailed the names of the girls to Eve, then perused the printouts on them in silence, reading about them and memorizing their photographs. He finally leaned back against the headrest and sighed. "I hate people."

"Me too."

August smiled despite himself. "But not you. Most of the time, anyway."

"Most of the time?" Ricardo huffed a dry laugh. "More than I can say about you."

"Oh, fuck off." August smacked his arm. "You're a complete shit."

"You're not wrong." Ricardo glanced over at him, and he turned serious. "We're going to save these girls, you know. And make it so no one in this crew can pull the same tricks."

"I know." August had perfect faith in their ability to fuck up the world of a human trafficking ring like this. "I feel a little hypocritical," he confessed.

"Why?"

He gestured between them. "Look at us. We kill people for money. End lives with dispatch and alacrity, all for the cost of a late-model Lamborghini. Doesn't that make us a lot like these people?"

"I'd argue no," Ricardo said. "Seeing as how every hit we take is vetted and thoroughly researched to ensure a minimum of damage to everyone surrounding the target, and certainly doesn't involve selling their families off to the highest bidder." Which was something a few of others in the hitman community had tried to add on as part of their "services," before Ricardo had gotten ahold of them and eliminated them with extreme prejudice.

"Still, we're profiting off death and misery."

"We're doing a job. One that we have the option to refuse at any time." He glanced at August. "Ever since I left the Army, I've only killed people who I thought deserved it. I might have been wrong once or twice, but the small chance that I am doesn't keep me from sleeping at night."

"Hmm." August thought about that for a minute. "Me neither."

"Good." Ricardo smiled slightly. "You should feel way more guilt about being a billionaire in this day and age than about being a hitman."

"Ouch! Low blow."

"Truth hurts."

"Oh, please. You're filthy rich too—you just don't understand what to do with money other than squat on it like a dragon," August snapped, then took a deep breath and moved on. "We know how to handle the girls now, generally speaking. What we should really be doing is finding out everything we can about the Madame."

"We have an avenue for her," Ricardo said. "You got Schreiber to hand over information of people she's trafficked in the past. If we can match those girls' stays to specific hotel visits, then we can pick out the Madame and see what we can find. Credit cards, phone calls, how she orders her breakfast in the morning—everything that might be useful."

"That's a good idea." August thought about it for a

moment. "You know who would be *really* good at that? Heidi."

"Yeah," Ricardo said slowly, "but if we call her in, I'll owe her a favor. I fucking hate owing her favors."

August laughed. "Really? That's why you don't want to talk to her?"

"She's mercenary," Ricardo insisted. "No. Not unless we can't do it on our own. Or you could ask *your* new liaison to help out."

"Absolutely not."

"See? You feel the same as I do."

"But for a completely different reason," August said. "Because my new liaison is a bitch." God, how he'd argued for Heidi after his last Rate Your Hit liaison was murdered, but it had been dubbed a potential conflict of interest for him to have yet another thing in common with Ricardo. "Greg is an asshole. I'm not letting him anywhere near an outside project; he'll probably try to insert some sort of ridiculous fee structure into it." Greg Larimer had come into hitman management via a suite of nefarious Wall Street shenanigans, and it showed.

"You could fire him, you know."

August sighed. "I'm already on thin ice after what happened with Victor and the thing with the goats. One more strike and they might punitively lower my rating. It's not fair!"

"The thing with Victor wasn't your fault," Ricardo said judiciously. "The thing with the goats, though..."

"The client asked for me to make a statement! It was a *great* statement!"

"Less great when you consider they ate her million-plus-dollar antique Persian rug after you let them into the house."

"Who knew goats can eat rugs? It's a mistake anyone could make." August relaxed into their familiar banter, able to forget about everything except making Ricardo roll his eyes so hard he almost crashed the car. It was its own form of therapy, being with someone who understood him well enough to join in with August's coping mechanisms, and being a sassy, irreverent little shit was the best defense August had ever found for his own mental health.

That and his custom flamethrower, which he only ever brought out for *really* special jobs.

Ricardo parked his awful little car right next to August's brand new Aston Martin, tight enough that August would have to squeeze out on his side to keep from bumping the door into his pristine crimson paint job.

Or...

Before Ricardo could do more than smirk and take the keys out of the ignition, August had twisted out of his seat and straddled Ricardo. His back was pressed too tight against the bottom of the steering wheel and his left knee was jammed into the gear shift, but it was worth it to see the look on Ricardo's face. Irritation at being pinned morphed into appreciation of exactly *how* he was being pinned, and he slid his arms around August's waist and tugged him in and down a little bit more, until...just...*there.*

"Someone's in a mood," Ricardo said, but August could hear the tease in his voice.

"Well, you did make me some promises," August replied, shifting his hips with a grin.

Ricardo shook his head. "We're not fucking in this car."

"Not in *this* car, no," August agreed. "Because it's not

worthy of us. You bought it used and it's never been detailed—who knows how many other people have had sex in this car?" He looked around skeptically. "I mean, probably not many because it's a POS, but still. There are so many other excellent cars here we could fuck in."

"My ex is practically within shouting distance and you want to get naked in the garage? The unlocked garage?"

"We don't have to be completely naked," August said, warming to the idea. "Just naked enough for me to bend you over a seat. Or in the Escalade! Ooh, or over a particularly nice hood maybe. You'd like it." He ground down against Ricardo's cock, enjoying the thrill that went up his own spine at the contact but liking the way Ricardo had to shut his eyes for a second even more. "I'd make sure you liked it. I only do things you like; you know that." That was a bit of a stretch overall, but in the bedroom it was completely true.

Ricardo swore hoarsely in his mother tongue.

"I'd open you up nice and slow," he went on, murmuring in Ricardo's ear as he snaked a hand between them. "Just how you told me to. I'd be so good for you, I would, I'd fuck you just the way you want."

Ricardo swallowed hard. "August..."

The door connecting to the main house opened, and Eve stepped into the garage. "What are you two waiting for, an engraved—oh!" She did an immediate about-face. "Sorry, I'll—inside, later, okay." The door shut again, and so did Ricardo's eyes, but not with pleasure this time.

August sighed. "Mmm, nope, mood gone."

"I *told* you that would happen."

To be fair, he had. August opened Ricardo's door and contorted himself enough to slide out. He glanced down, and... "I'm going to need a minute before I can go in and face your ex *and* my sister."

Ricardo wiped a hand down his face. "Same."

August sighed again, then brightened. "Raincheck on bottoming, then?"

Ricardo glanced at him, then laughed. "Jesus Christ, you're incorrigible."

"Is that a yes?"

"Obviously it's a yes. Now stop bringing it up, or we'll never get inside."

August mimed zipping his lips. Five minutes later, they were in the main house, where Eve and Elodie had transformed the formal dining room August never used into an office supply store. There were whiteboards, a projector, paper and computers and pens and printouts. August was a little surprised his sister hadn't indulged by putting up pieces of string linking pictures together, like something out of a movie.

Eve, still in her casual clothes from the morning, was studiously not meeting either of their eyes, but Elodie just waved from where she sat in one of the chairs, typing away. "It's good to see you both," she said, standing up and coming over to greet them.

For all that she had nearly a decade on August and did most of her business in America, her mannerisms still tended toward French. She had clearly come from the office, but had kicked off her heels, set her jacket aside, and rolled up the sleeves of her blouse. Her light blonde hair was pulled back in a loose chignon, and she had a glass of red wine by her computer. She went to August first, bussing him on both cheeks before pulling him down far enough that she could kiss his forehead.

"I forget how short you are when you're not in your shoes," August said, and laughed when Elodie lightly whacked him on the shoulder with the back of one hand.

"I'm slightly above average in height, thank you." She turned to Ricardo and greeted him with the double kiss, which he returned with perfect equanimity. "You look well," she congratulated him. "So much better than last time. Paschal will be very pleased."

"What was wrong last time?" Eve asked, her voice suddenly sharpened to a point.

Elodie, to her credit, didn't fluster at all. "Oh, these two, they're so clumsy sometimes," she said fondly, as though being shot in the gut was the equivalent of a little tumble off a curb. "I'm just pleased you've managed to put up with this one for so long," she continued, nodding at August.

"Hey! I'm very lovable!" he said.

"Sometimes," his sister agreed, patting him on the cheek before turning back to her computer. "Your facial recognition program could use an upgrade, by the way." She gave a little frown before she sipped up the last of her wine. "We don't have a positive identification of the woman you sent pictures of yet. Too many variables."

Ricardo shrugged. "We can afford to wait on her, since we can get her at the hotel."

"Mmm." Elodie stared at her computer for a moment. "She's very good at changing her appearance, but the shape of her chin is quite distinctive. It could be worse, but we might have to rely on your Matt to know where to dig for more information about her."

August agreed, but at the same time... "I hate relying on that fucker for anything," he confessed. "Even with the fear of God in him, I don't trust him not to try and wriggle out of this."

"He can squirm as much as he likes," Ricardo said. "We have enough to go on now that if he fucks things up, at worst we can rescue the girls who were meant to be sold this time around and seriously scramble the organization on a base level. Has he got a meeting with the lieutenant he was talking about yet?" They'd handed the surveillance equipment over to Eve before going to scare the pants off of Schreiber.

"Not yet, but he *has* left three messages for me, in addition to calling a hooker to come help him 'blow off some steam.'" She sounded disgusted. "He better have taken the wire off for that, because I refuse to listen in. It's bad enough I have to replay my own sex with him in my head."

"Ugh, yes." August was pretty open-minded when it came to sex and relationships, he thought, but there was never a good time to listen to a ex have sex. Unless you were the ex having the sex, and your former lover was watching from across the club and seething about it, and you could look at them smugly while your newest boytoy fucked you against the railing along the edge of the mezzanine and—

Yeah, no, *that* had never happened.

He cleared his throat. "I'm going to get some wine," he said to the surprise of no one. "Elodie, would you care for another?"

"Not for me, darling, I have to head home soon." She picked up her empty crystal glass. "I'll just drop this in the kitchen. I'll be back tomorrow, though. I'm rather enjoying the opportunity to take personal days for something that isn't company-related."

"Do you not understand the concept of personal days?" August asked, walking with her into the kitchen. Eve was already speaking to Ricardo in a low voice behind them, and August was more than happy to let him field any questions Eve might be throwing his way right now. "You can do anything you want with them, but spending them working on company projects is *work*."

"Oh, you sweet pet," Elodie said with a shake of her head. "Don't you know that when you inherit your company, every day off is a day that your father asks you why you aren't working to keep the company, his life's blood, his precious baby, solvent in an unstable age?"

"Aw." He leaned in and hugged her around the shoulders. "I'm sorry he's giving you hell."

"He's Papa. It's what he does." She set the glass in the sink, then pulled down a clean one for August and poured it half-full. "You do seem well," she said more quietly. "Like you're happy."

"I am." August had always made it his business to be satisfied by his life, but happiness had been a much more elusive beast before Ricardo shot his way into the picture. "I really am. Very unexpected, I know."

"No, not so unexpected." She smiled at him, looking tired but pleased. "You were a happy little boy. Always playing and laughing and enjoying life. I'm glad that you can still be happy, no matter how you do it."

"Even when the way I do it is all...shooty?" He'd asked her this question a long time ago—demanded her support, more like—and she'd told him yes, of course.

"Yes, of course."

Damn, I love you.

"You know what you need?" August ignored his glass of wine and pulled her in for another hug. "You need a real vacation. Something for you and Paschal and nobody else, someplace where Dad can't harp on you and Mom can't insist you give her grandchildren for the twelve-thousandth time—" Which, if his parents really knew his sister at all, they would know was never going to happen. "—and where Paschal can't be on call. Doesn't that sound nice?"

"Sounds like a place that doesn't exist," Elodie said

wryly, but she hugged him back hard. "We'll get a chance to relax for a while soon, I hope. In the meantime, this really is quite nice for me."

August kissed the top of her head. "I know, you're such a freak."

She punched him in the ribs hard enough to make him wince. "Watch how you speak to your big sister! I might be smaller than you, but I'm twice as mean."

"I know that! When did I ever say you weren't a mean and vengeful bit—ow! Stop hitting me! I *will* tell Mom!"

"You're such a spoiled brat!"

Ricardo stuck his head around the corner of the kitchen. They stopped playing as soon as they saw how serious he looked. "Matt's meeting with the lieutenant," he said, and August forgot all about his wine as he and Elodie hurried back out to the dining room to listen in.

CHAPTER 11

Eve took the armchair. August sat on the couch next to her with Elodie to his other side, while Ricardo—far too restless—stood. The laptop that had been monitoring the call was on the coffee table with Matt's voice coming through loud and clear, along with the man who was apparently a lieutenant.

Most of the conversation was boring and irrelevant. Small talk, really. Theoretically, August and Ricardo could have had Elodie or Eve listen until there was something interesting, but they weren't trained to pick up on the little things people let slip. Things like names and coded phrases. As boring as this was, they all needed to listen.

After Matt and the lieutenant had gone on at length about last night's game, Ricardo seriously wondered if they were speaking in code. Carefully worded discussions about benign, everyday matters were the best way to transmit covert information, and without some sort of cipher, everyone in this room was dead in the water. There was no way to know if "fumbled two yards from the end zone" really meant an overpaid athlete had screwed up on the field or if someone delivering hot merchandise had been busted by police just before reaching the drop house. Which meant it was entirely possible this was a waste of time.

Though with Ricardo's knowledge of Matt's obsession with sports, and with Eve's "Jesus fuck, I don't want to hear one more word about this" expression, odds were that this truly was a discussion about what people in this country called "football" for some reason.

Then Matt's tone shifted. "Look, I need to see the big guy. ASAP."

"He's a busy man. What makes you think he's got time for you?"

"Because this involves issues with the State Department that he needs to know about."

"What issues?" The lieutenant sounded bored.

"Issues I need to take up with the big guy," Matt snapped. "I can't fuck around here, all right? Just meeting you to try to set up a meeting with him is a waste of goddamned time."

"Uh-huh. And that's how shit works. You want to talk to the man, you go through the right channels. Now. What is this about?"

Matt made a frustrated sound. "It's need to know, all right? It's need to know, and it's *bad*. Bad like if it goes to shit and the big guy finds out he wasn't notified because you didn't think it was important, you're going to be as dead as I am. You feel me?"

There was no response. None that could be heard, anyhow.

"Can you set me up a meeting with him or not?" Matt demanded.

Long silence. Long, uncomfortable silence. Then something pinged like a text message had come through, and the lieutenant grunted. "All right. It's in the works. Keep your phone on, and Calabrese will be in touch with a time and place."

August's teeth snapped shut so hard it was audible in the same moment Ricardo's heart dropped. They exchanged wide-eyed looks, and August whispered, "Did he just say—"

"Yep."

"As in—"

"Uh-huh."

They stared at each other. Ricardo sensed Eve watching them, probably wondering what connection they'd made, but she stayed quiet as Matt and the lieutenant kept talking.

The rest of the conversation wasn't particularly interesting, but that brief exchange had Ricardo's blood running cold. The fact that there was a "big guy" and that there were "lieutenants" had made Ricardo wonder, but there were plenty of small-time crooks who used that rank structure. A ranked hierarchy like that was technically a form of organized crime, but it wasn't what lawmen or laymen meant when they used the phrase. It was organized like a mom and pop business as opposed to a powerful and multi-tiered corporation. One was crime that was organized. The other was *organized crime*.

Ricardo had really, really hoped this was the former option, and if it was the latter, it was a one-trick pony—a gang who existed solely to be involved with one aspect of crime. In this case, human trafficking. Those existed, especially in the narcotics or gun-running trades, and they were a whole lot easier to take down than the alternative.

But luck was rarely on Ricardo's side, and if the lieutenant meant the Calabrese that Ricardo thought he meant —and he most likely did—then luck definitely wasn't on their side this time. Because in the circles where he and August moved, there was only one Calabrese, and that was Cristiano Calabrese.

Cristiano Calabrese, the consigliere of Sebastiano Basile.

Sebastiano Basile, the boss of the extraordinarily large pain in everyone's ass known as the Vaccaro crime family.

Instead of that one-trick human trafficking pony, Ricardo and his partner were going up against the superstore-that-didn't-need-to-be-named of the underworld: a huge and obscenely wealthy organization that had its hands in multiple industries, numerous powerful politicians in its back pockets, and little regard for human rights.

Taking them down was a bit more David and Goliath than Ricardo liked to think. Especially since the whole reason David and Goliath was noteworthy was that David *won*. It didn't make the news when Goliath won because, hello, "giant stomping the little guy into the dirt" was kind of the expected outcome.

Ricardo really did not like being David.

Especially not when Goliath was the motherfucking *mafia*.

On the other end of the microphone, there were sounds of Matt walking away and getting into his car. Nothing left to hear, at least for the moment.

"Oh, shit," August breathed, wiping a hand over his face. "This is bad."

"Yeah. It is." Ricardo rubbed the back of his neck. This was *really* bad. It had been already, but the conversation between Matt and the lieutenant took them from "well, this sucks" to "oh *shiiiit*, we are in way over our heads."

August looked up at Ricardo. "We can't do this on our own. Not when we're going up against the damned Mob."

"No, we can't." Ricardo chewed his thumbnail. "I think we might need to call in reinforcements."

August's eyebrows climbed as his spine straightened. "Do I even want to know who you have in mind?"

Sighing, Ricardo shook his head. "No, because you'll be about as happy as I am."

"Oh yeah?" August narrowed his eyes. "So who is—Oh, you have got to be shitting me. Tell me you're not thinking who I'm thinking."

Ricardo eyed him.

August glared back. "Ricardo, I swear on all that's holy, if you tell me we're bringing Pedro fucking Silva into this..."

Ricardo just grimaced.

"Oh my *God!*" August flew to his feet. "Are you insane?"

"Do you have any better ideas?"

"Yes, I absolutely—" August halted, eyes losing focus. "I mean... We could..."

"Any time you're ready," Ricardo taunted.

August flipped him off. "I... Okay, I don't have a better idea. Yet. But Pedro Silva hates us both, especially you, and I do not want to get tangled up with the damn Cavalcante family."

"Neither do I. But given the way they dispatched Bruno Cavalcante for his involvement with human trafficking, I don't think we'll have a hard time persuading them to get on our side. Pedro doesn't have to like us, but the family got rid of one of their own over trafficking, so..."

August scowled, and Ricardo knew he had him cornered. The two of them had met because they'd both refused to assassinate the judge presiding over Bruno's case. The judge had ultimately been killed by someone else, and Ricardo had learned later that a bought-and-paid-for judge had granted Bruno bail. That had given the family the opportunity to bail him out and take care of him themselves before he'd had a chance to stain their good name—well, "good" name—with the stench of human trafficking. Ricardo didn't know who'd taken him out, but word on the street was that Bruno had been killed slowly and painfully to make sure no Cavalcante even *thought* about getting into that particular side hustle.

"Okay. Okay, fine." August folded his arms. "So...which of us reaches out to him?"

"Given how things went last time, I think you know the answer."

August scowled. "Ugh. You owe me so—"

"Um, question?" Eve raised her hand like a kid in school, and Ricardo's heart plummeted into his stomach. He'd been so focused, he'd forgotten she was even here. *Shit*. She glanced back and forth between them. "I hate to tap the brakes here, but could you boys back up just a *wee* bit and fill me in on a few things? Like the part where members of organized crime even know who you are, never mind hate you, never mind hate you because 'last time'?" She practically squeaked as she asked, "What the hell is going on, Ricardo?"

"Uh..."

Elodie made a face like she hoped the ground would open up and swallow her, and then she quickly excused herself under the pretense of needing to call her husband about something.

"You know." August side-stepped Ricardo and held up his phone. "I'm going to go give Pedro a call while you—"

"Oh, no you don't." Ricardo grabbed for August's arm, but his partner was faster and danced away from him. "August, don't you dare—"

"Gotta call Pedro!" August yelled over his shoulder as he ran for the kitchen, waving his phone over his head.

"You asshole," Ricardo muttered.

"Ricardo?"

He turned to see his ex-wife watching him, that one eyebrow raised the way it had been the first time—and every time thereafter—she'd accused him of cheating on her.

Voice low and cold, she growled, "What's going on?"

He closed his eyes and exhaled. Then he moved to take August's spot on the couch. Eve wasn't stupid, and anyway, given the shitshow this whole debacle was turning into, she deserved to know what she was up against. She deserved the opportunity to bail out before things went nuclear. Because he had a feeling that was the direction this was headed—wars between crime families were *always* messy.

Resting his elbows on his knees, he met her gaze. "This is not going to be easy for you to hear. And you'll probably hate me afterward. I..." He shook his head. "I can't really blame you."

Her eyes were huge, her mind probably reeling with all manner of possibilities.

"The short version," he said, "is that August and I are..." Christ. How was he even supposed to explain this? He'd always dodged the subject out of necessity, and the only people who needed to know what he was already knew. This was, by design, not a closet he came out of with any regularity.

"What?" Eve demanded. "Are you guys hitmen or something?"

His head snapped up.

She stiffened. "You're... That was a joke. Ricardo, you're not." She glanced toward the kitchen, where

August's voice was audible even if the words were muffled. Facing Ricardo again, she whispered, "You're not, are you?"

Ricardo swallowed. "I am. We are."

Her lips parted, and she stared at him as if she didn't understand the words he was saying.

He took a deep breath. "It's what I was in the military, Eve. When I came back... I'm—"

"That's different!" she hissed. "You were killing people in a warzone!"

"Is it, though? Because the people I kill now are criminals. Drug lords. Weapons dealers. Murderers." He paused. "Human traffickers."

She closed her eyes and leaned forward, raking both hands through her gray-flecked red hair. "Oh my *God*."

He grimaced, and he sat quietly while she absorbed what he'd told her. Guilt wasn't a frequent emotion of his, but he didn't like hurting the people close to him, whether by lying to them *or* telling the truth. In his line of work, the best solution was to not get close to people. August was an exception because they shared one secret and respected the rest.

"Jesus Christ." Eve sat up, staring skyward, and her voice was full of exhaustion and exasperation. "Is *every* man I fuck a goddamned criminal?"

Ricardo masked a laugh with a cough. From the way she glared at him, it didn't work. He sighed and reached for her hand. "I know you don't like it. I never expected you to. That's why I didn't tell you."

She looked at him, narrowing her eyes a little. "How long have you been doing this?"

"Uh..."

"Was—" She yanked her hand away. "You weren't

cheating, were you? You were... Oh my God, Ricardo. You were *murdering* people? For money?"

"I was—"

"Jesus fuck." She threw up her hands and stood. "Okay. I need... I need to process this." She started out of the living room, heading for the dining room, which had a door going out to the backyard.

"Eve, wait!" He hurried after her.

"No." She spun and jabbed a finger at him. "You need to give me this, Ricardo. You can't just expect me to absorb all—"

"I'm not. But please..." He sighed. "I know I'm asking a lot, but please, don't go to the cops."

She set her jaw. "I'm not going to the cops. Because as much as I hate this, I don't know anyone else who can take down Matt and all the shit he's involved with. Which apparently involves organized crime." She planted a hand on her hip and rubbed her forehead with the other. "Which somehow involves you. Oh my God."

Still muttering to herself, she continued out of sight. A second later, the door slammed, rattling the entire house.

He sighed and pressed his shoulder against the wall. He believed her that she wouldn't go to the cops. In part because she needed him for this, and in part because she was proud to a fault. Admitting to anyone that she'd been married to a hitman and had lived with a human trafficker would be too much for her. Though he supposed she could submit an anonymous tip after all this was over. That would be...not good.

"Ricardo?" August's voice was cautious. "Everything all right?"

Ricardo turned around to see his boyfriend in the living room, cell phone still in hand. "She's...processing."

August's eyebrows climbed. "How did she take it? I mean, she didn't claw your eyes out, so that's a good sign, right?"

"Something like that. What did Pedro say?"

"Well, it wasn't him, but the random unnamed-in-the-credits goon I talked to said someone will call us tomorrow with a time and place to meet Silva."

Ricardo grunted. It wasn't ideal, but such was arranging a meeting with someone that powerful.

"Are you just letting her cool off for a while?"

Ricardo nodded. He leaned against the wall and sighed. "I hoped I'd never have to tell her. And now it's even worse because she probably feels like she can't get away from me. Not until this shit with Matt is over."

"All the more reason to get it over with, then," August said. "So you two can either sort your shit out or vow never to speak to each other again."

Ricardo studied August, whose face was full of sincerity. He knew August had a bit of a possessive streak, but he seemed oddly comfortable with Eve, and with Ricardo and Eve needing to iron things out between them. No judgment. No insecurity. He always seemed to intuit when Ricardo needed space to handle something on his own. Even when that meant space with the only person who'd ever been as close to him as August was.

It made Ricardo more grateful than ever to have August.

Without a word, he reached for August and reeled him in close. August tensed, but he let himself be wrapped up in a tight embrace, and after a second, he returned it.

When Ricardo let go, August eyed him. "What was that for?"

Ricardo shook his head. "Don't worry about it."

"But it—"

"We should figure out our game plan. Once he's knows it's us, he's not going to be interested."

August pursed his lips. This wasn't over and Ricardo knew it, but for the moment, August wisely said, "He will be once he knows his biggest rival is involved in human trafficking." He gave a haughty sniff. "And I think he *owes* me after the way things went down after he hooked me up with his 'fixer'."

"Do you?" Ricardo quirked a brow. "Do you think he sees it that way?"

"He should. Fucker almost got me killed."

"Mmhmm. Maybe we shouldn't go into this by telling a high-ranking mobster that he owes you a favor right after you show up with me. You know, the guy you told him you wanted to kill last time? In order to get him on your side?"

August's eyes widened. "Oh. Shit. Good point. Glad you brought that up, or he might've shot us both."

"It's disturbing how casual you are about that." Eve's voice spun Ricardo around. She was watching them from the dining room, arms folded and a bemused look on her face. "It's actually disturbing how casual you two are about any of this, but given your line of work..."

"You *told* her?" August exclaimed, staring in horror at Ricardo. "About me? And...that..." He threw up his hands. "But that was our secret!"

"She asked." Ricardo shrugged. "I've lied to her enough. She deserved the truth."

"But..."

"Relax, August." Eve shook her head as she gave a resigned sigh. "Now that I've thought about it a little, it's almost a relief, knowing he was working as a hitman instead of cheating on me."

"A hitman?" August put his hand to his chest and exhaled

with melodramatic relief. "Oh, *that's* what—oh, thank God. Here I thought you'd told her about the *other* thing."

Eve's eyebrows shot up. "What other thing?"

Ricardo glared at August.

"What?" The idiot offered up an innocent look that wasn't convincing in the slightest. "I mean, listen, if you want your ex-wife to know you like to dress up like a squirrel in the bedroom, I'm not—"

"Oh, for fuck's sake." Ricardo rolled his eyes. "Shut up."

"Oh, that?" Eve waved a hand. "Please. After the Elvis costume, nothing surprises me anymore."

Ricardo stared at her, slack-jawed. "*Really?*"

"Elvis?" August perked up. "Are we talking young and sexy Elvis? Or rhinestones and—"

"Ugh, fuck you both," Ricardo groaned.

"A threesome?" Eve asked. "Oh, honey. I don't think you could handle both of us at the same time."

Ricardo shot her his most plaintive look as August was overcome with hysterical laughter.

She narrowed her eyes and smirked as if to say, *Admit it —you deserved that.*

A second later, Ricardo was mercifully rescued from the relentless crap from his current and former partners, and that rescue instantly sobered all three of them: August's ringing cell phone.

Humor gone, August eyed the screen. "That's probably Silva." He put it to his ear and adopted his entitled rich asshole voice. "This is Augustus. Uh-huh. Right. Yes, I'm aware of—okay. Oh really? That soon?" A long pause. "Got it. I'll see him there." He ended the call, and when he looked at Ricardo, he was completely serious. "Silva wants to meet us in an hour. We have to go."

Ricardo's heart jumped into his throat. Silva was moving fast, which likely meant he didn't trust them. He wasn't giving them time to put into motion any kind of plan that might actually work. "All right. Let's go."

"I'll get my gun." August glanced at Eve, then back at Ricardo. "Your usual?"

Ricardo recognized the out—August was going to get his gun for him *and* give him a minute to make sure Eve's feathers were truly unruffled. "Yes. Thank you."

August beat feet out of the room, leaving Ricardo alone with his ex-wife.

"So, a meeting." She swallowed hard, her own humor a distant memory. "And this guy is...what?"

"A boss. A rival of the man Matt is apparently working for."

"Whoa. And, um..." She chewed her lip, shifting her weight with obvious discomfort. "This guy knows you. And August. And he doesn't like either of you."

"That's right."

"So is this safe?" She studied him. "Are you guys walking into a deathtrap?"

There was no way to tell her the truth without sending her into a panic. Whether he liked it or not, a deathtrap *was* a distinct possibility, and that was even before Silva realized who was with August. Silva could shoot Ricardo, and then continue his meeting with August without blinking, simply because he'd never let go of his grudge against Ricardo for disrespecting him.

But he couldn't tell her that.

"It's safe," he said. "The man's a criminal, but he's a businessman. And once we tell him we're there to stop a rival of his, especially a rival engaging in a business that crosses a red line for Silva and his own boss, he'll listen to us."

"Are you sure?"

Holding her gaze, he hated how badly he wanted to both be honest with her *and* lie to her. He'd lied to her enough, and he'd lost her as a result. But tonight, the truth would only terrify her.

"I'll be fine." He paused. "I'll text you when we leave the meeting. So you know it went all right."

Some tightness in her neck and shoulders relaxed. "Okay. I can live with that." Then she stepped closer and hugged him, catching him off guard like he'd caught August off guard a few minutes earlier.

"Be careful, Ricardo," she whispered. "Promise me."

"I will." He returned her embrace. "I promise."

"Good." Drawing back, she looked right in his eyes. "Because I just found out you're not actually a cheating bastard, so don't get yourself killed before I've had time to decide if I like you or not."

He just laughed.

But he hoped like hell she got that chance to decide.

CHAPTER 12

So. Pedro Silva and the Cavalcante crime family.

Hooooo boy. Things were about to get... Well, complicated would be the least violent way of putting it.

It had taken a while for August to get a handle on the politics of organized crime when he was first getting his feet wet as a hitman. Someone like him, while in a squint-to-see-it similar line of work to the mafia, was considered an outsider, not the sort of person a family would rely on unless they were desperate or meddling. Hiring Ricardo, which August presumed Pedro had done before things turned sour between them, would have been very expensive but worth it to someone who wanted to ensure that their target was handled swiftly and with no links back to the people who'd done the hiring. Everything of lesser importance was kept in house, and that house was kept in *order*. Seriously, you didn't fuck with the guy running things and you didn't go behind their back, because if you got caught...

Well, Bruno Cavalcante had been caught stepping out of line, and he'd paid with his life.

Honestly, August had done a great job of steering clear

of the East Coast mafia organizations for the most part. Given his predilections—jobs that paid extremely well that targeted extremely rich assholes—he wasn't the perfect fit for working with the mob.

Ricardo, on the other hand, not only had a reputation that preceded him, but he oozed vicious-minded, bloody-handed competence. It was no wonder Silva had hired him for a job.

The wonder was that Ricardo hadn't completed it.

August hadn't asked, and he wasn't planning to. A part of him was desperate to know what had been bad enough to make Ricardo balk, but he trusted his partner. Besides, right now really wasn't the time to reminisce about anything from "back in the day" when Mrs. Back In The Day was literally staying in one of their guest suites.

Mind in the game. You've got to convince Silva not to shoot on sight, after all.

Which meant that the best place to start was the most obvious one—the "don't shoot the rich douchebag because it's more trouble than you want to call down on yourself" gambit.

Hell, it had worked for August last time. It would probably work again.

He straightened the lapels of his Kiton K-50 bespoke suit and grinned. Commissioning this garish monstrosity had nearly cost him the privilege of ordering *any* suits from Antonio's stores, but it was worth it. The fit was superb, the fabric was top of the line, the stitching was exceptional…and it was the color of a swimming pool.

This suit was a shade of aquamarine that seared the eyes, and August might be trim, but anything in this color big enough to fit him was more than big enough to make everyone around him wince. He'd done his best to tone it back with the plain white shirt and semi-casual loafers, but there was no excuse for an outfit like this except pure, unadulterated hubris.

Perfect for Augustus.

He slid on a chunky Garmin watch—as if Augustus Mason had ever bothered with GPS in his life—and slicked back his hair, then turned in the mirror a few times to make sure the line of the jacket hid his gun well enough. Not even a hint. Almost perfect; he just needed something to tip things over into truly ludicrous territory... Ah.

The chain was solid platinum—a thick, chunky Byzantine style that stopped just beneath his collarbones. Apart from redoing the clasp—because August would be damned if he died because some opportunistic fuckhead managed to choke him to death with his own jewelry—it was as true to Augustus's style as he could make it: slightly outdated, decidedly ostentatious, and yet somehow it worked for him.

Now, time to go foment war between two rival mafia families. August grinned manically. It had been a long damn day, and sleep was nowhere in sight, but he'd mainlined enough caffeine that he would be bouncing through these next few hours. He could handle himself.

You'd better. Otherwise the wrong someone might get killed.

He headed out of his closet with the confident strut of a man who didn't acknowledge the opinions of others because they were all wrong, wrong, wrong, and downstairs to where Ricardo was waiting for him. He was just holstering another gun—his third, it looked like—in the small of his back when he glanced up at August.

Ricardo's entire body shuddered as his mouth fell open, and he dropped the gun.

Dropped.

The.

Gun.

It hit the couch cushion, then slid to the floor. There was no danger, of course—the safety was on—but it was entirely possible August would die from laughing anyway.

"Your *face!*" He grabbed the rail of the stairs and leaned against it, doing his best to keep his volume down so he didn't draw Eve's attention. "Oh my God, is it that good? I mean, I thought it was—I had it made for just this kind of thing—but it must be *really* good! What else do you think I can make you drop?" He tried to lift one eyebrow suggestively, but he was snickering too hard to really pull it off. "Maybe your pants?"

Ricardo's mouth worked silently for a moment before he finally ground out, "I will not hesitate to cut you."

"Well, you certainly won't shoot me, that much is clear." August suppressed the worst of the giggles and straightened up, looking down at his suit once more. "Do you think I should get another one done in, like, a lemon chiffon? No, too yellow, it doesn't work with my complexion—but what about a salmon color? But metallic? Wouldn't that just be perfect?"

Ricardo regained enough control of himself to grab his gun and smoothly tuck it into his hidden holster, as if he'd never flubbed the dear little thing in the first place. "Perfect for making people want to take potshots at you? Yes, it would be perfect for that. Are you an idiot? Do you realize what a target you're going to make of yourself in this?"

"I'm operating on the assumption that I won't be a target, because we're going to use our words instead of our guns." And if that failed... Well, better that August draw some fire than let Silva focus it all on Ricardo.

Ricardo shook his head. "I don't need you to protect

me."

Trust Ricardo to see right through August's clever scheme. Fucker. "So self-centered," he said with a huff, shooting his cuffs like Augustus always did when he was feeling put-upon. "Not everything is about you. Most things, in fact, are about me. So!" He reached into the pocket where he'd customarily have a pocket square and pulled out a pair of gold-rimmed sunglasses. "Be honest with me. Too much?"

"The odds of you getting punched in the face just went up by a factor of ten."

August nodded and threw the sunglasses onto the couch. "Right, no. You've got to know when to call enough enough." He clapped his hands together. "Let's head out, then! I'm driving. We're taking the Audi tonight, because it's the only vehicle I own that won't clash with my suit." It also had, much like the Escalade, half a million dollars of custom bulletproofing installed just two months ago, a fact that was surely not lost on Ricardo.

But he was nice enough not to mention it.

THE RESTAURANTS PEDRO SILVA MANAGED WERE legitimate businesses ninety-nine percent of the time. August had met him in one of them the last time; it was a nice, low-key Italian eatery that leaned hard on accordion music and ceramic kitsch to set the mood. Staffed by local teenagers, frequented by families, a significant donor to local food banks—it was beyond reproach...which made it perfect for the occasional "business meeting." Last time, it had gone okay.

For tonight's rendezvous, though, Silva had selected a

venue with a decidedly more limited menu and less charming ambiance. Namely, another restaurant that the Cavalcantes were allegedly renovating and getting ready to open any day now. Given the purposes August suspected this facility was actually used for, calling it a laundromat would be somewhat on the nose but definitely more honest.

It was also in an incredibly shady and rundown part of town. Silva, being the family's public face, had made a lot of noise about revitalizing the neighborhood and gentrifying it within an inch of its life.

Whatever you say, Silva. Whatever you say.

The area gave August the creeps. It was almost devoid of life most of the time. Even the homeless avoided this area, and given some of the places where they found shelter, that said something. During the day, people locked their car doors if they had to drive through here. At night, it was even creepier—no one bothered locking their doors because no one in their right mind came down here.

A rich asshole in an expensive car was basically asking for it.

August shuddered, shifting behind the wheel. He had to give the impression of a clueless billionaire with no survival instincts. That had been relatively easy last time; pretend not to notice the bouncer reaching for a weapon, turn his back on someone who was armed, go shopping for a few hours until the guys tailing him got bored—shit like that made his skin crawl, but it sold the act of dumbass douchebag with too much money.

It was going to be a lot harder to suppress those instincts and reactions out here. And it didn't help that, unlike last time when they'd met in the middle of the day, it was one in the morning. He also hadn't had Ricardo riding shotgun toward a man who wanted him dead.

But meh, details, details. He rolled his shoulders under his electric blue jacket. This would be fine. All August—or rather, Augustus—had to do was break the ice and get Silva into that slightly-contemptuous-but-still-humoring-the-rich-guy state, and then he'd drop the bomb about the Vaccaros. Then, if things were looking good, he'd bring Ricardo into the picture. Hopefully they'd have enough common ground at that point to keep things civil.

Fingers crossed...except for his trigger finger.

The restaurant was lit when they got there, the only well-lit building on the entire block. It actually looked like it was open, even though August doubted they'd ever served so much as a breadstick here.

Swallowing his nerves, August pulled into the handicapped spot right in front of it with a flourish, because Augustus really was that kind of asshole, and he took a deep breath. "Okay, just...stay in here until I tell you to come out, all right?"

"Don't give me any reason to worry about you and we'll be fine," Ricardo retorted.

"Aww, Ricky!" August pressed a hand to his chest. "You worry about me? That's so sweet!" Three men had appeared at the restaurant's front doors, two with their hands already on the butts of guns they weren't even bothering to conceal. The third was a foot ahead of them, his face illuminated by the street lamp.

Pedro Silva.

"I'm serious. Don't get shot."

"When have you ever known me to get shot?" August asked. "You're the one with a predilection for taking bullets."

"August..."

"I'll be fine." This wasn't the place for a kiss, but August gave Ricardo the closest thing to a real smile he could muster before plastering Augustus all over his mind. "Later, honey!" He killed the ignition, opened the driver's door and stood up, leaning one elbow on the roof but keeping the car between him and Silva for now.

"Hey! Long time no see, you look..." August paused and did a very visible once-over of Silva's body. "You look like someone went to Build-A-Bear and made themselves a bespoke, middle-class daddy. A short-sleeved, button-down shirt? That's some serious papa energy right there, Pedro."

Silva sighed the sigh of the truly put-upon. "And you look like a goddamn neon sign in a bar window," he snapped. "You called *me*, Mr. Mason. It's late, I'm tired, but you promised to make this bullshit meeting worth my time, so how about you get over here and we take this conversation inside before we wake anybody up?"

"Gosh, someone woke up on the wrong side of the bed," August said sotto voce, but still loud enough for Silva to hear. He closed the door of the Audi and came around the hood, stepped up onto the curb, and—

"*Fuck!*" The toe of his right shoe slipped into a divot in the pavement he couldn't even see in the darkness, and before August knew it he'd stumbled down onto his hands and knees.

"Are you drunk, Mr. Mason?" Silva asked sarcastically. "Can you even remember why you're...here..."

"I'm not drunk, I'm just bemoaning my misappropriated tax dollars, because the city must think that your goddamn sidewalk is not worth fixing," August snapped, glaring at Silva. Then he realized that Silva wasn't looking at him. He was looking *behind* him, where the passenger side door of the Audi had opened just a sliver.

The hell, why did he open it?

But August already knew the answer to that. Ricardo couldn't shoot through the windows now that they were reinforced, couldn't hear him well through all the armoring, and August had just klutzed the fuck up where Ricardo couldn't see him.

We should have worn our comms.

It was too late to correct that mistake, though. August had to try and roll with it.

"Who else is in the car?" Silva barked, waving his two men forward, guns drawn.

"No one important," August said quickly, standing up and straightening his jacket as he tried to brush the whole thing off. "My chauffeur, but I felt like driving myself tonight and he still wanted to get paid. Unions, man. So many rules."

"Yeah? Well, get your chauffeur out where we can see him."

August cocked a hip and sighed. "Seriously? Just let the man sit in the car where he isn't bothering anybody and get me a goddamn drink already, all right?"

Now Silva drew his gun, a little snub-nosed revolver that looked like it had come straight out of a gangster movie. He didn't point it at the car, though. He pointed it at August. "Mr. Mason," he said grimly. "I get the feeling you're lying to me. And I don't. Like. Liars."

"Then you're really not going to like what comes next."

August shut his eyes and swore at the sound of Ricardo's voice.

"You!" Silva was stunned stock still for a full two seconds before anger overwhelmed him and he changed targets, firing wildly at Ricardo. His men followed suit, and August had to jump out of the way to avoid getting caught in the crossfire. Except...

Except there wasn't any crossfire. Not really. There were bullets coming from Ricardo's gun, but they were going so wide that he might as well not be firing at all, except for how they made Silva and his men cringe. Missing close shots like this was a deliberate act, which meant Ricardo was hoping they could still salvage this. If he killed anyone now, it would all be over, and they'd have no hope at all of getting help with the Vaccaros *and* probably make enemies of the entire Cavalcante family.

Time to hit the brakes.

August didn't bother dealing with either of Silva's goons. He didn't have to—they were fixated on the car door Ricardo was using for cover, which was becoming increasingly dented. It would hold, of course—it was going to take more than three little handguns to make that much armoring break down—but if one of them got a lucky shot, or a bullet ricocheted in just the wrong way...

Nope. August needed to stop this cold, which meant staying Augustus was out of the question. He pulled his own gun as he rolled to his feet, slid in behind Silva before the other man even registered he was there, and got one arm around his neck as he pressed his gun's muzzle to Silva's throbbing temple.

"Ah-ah," he said in his own voice now, quiet and dead serious, as Silva began to fight. He gripped deep around the collar of Silva's terrible shirt and twisted it up in his fist, turning the cloth into half a chokehold. "Keep fucking with me and I'll shoot you through the ear. Tell your people to stop."

"Hold your fire," Silva gritted. His men turned and startled simultaneously, like a pair of enormous bunnies who'd missed the fox slipping up on them until it was too late.

"Good. Now, I want you to know that I really did set up

tonight's meeting in good faith," August went on. Silva scoffed. "No, I did. We have a common enemy and, shockingly, it's not Mr. Garcia." That was Ricardo's name as far as Silva knew. "But we can't have a decent conversation when there's gunfire involved, hmm? What are the odds the cops are on their way already?"

"Eh." Silva managed a shrug. "If it had been one shot, we'd be fine. That many, though..." He scowled at Ricardo, who'd straightened up behind the car door with an almost offensive nonchalance, like this was something he did every day. "And none of them even did their job," he said. "Torralba, you piece of shit—"

"I'll give us a five minute window," August decided, and backed toward the front door of the restaurant with Silva in tow. "That's all we need of your time, Pedro, I swear. Less, even. Then we'll be out of your hair, hopefully for good."

August felt Silva's teeth grind where his jaw was pressed to August's forearm. He could see the man assess the situation, taking better stock now that his blood had cooled a bit. He had two men with him, probably more just a few minutes away. If he could fight his way free, he might still be able to get his revenge.

August tightened his grip. "I think you'll find the new me is harder to shake than Augustus," he murmured. "And I'm dead serious about shooting you through the head if you try anything on Ricardo. I won't even flinch."

"*Ricardo*, is it?" Silva asked. "Was any of that song and dance you sold me last time the truth?"

"Enough to make it sound good," August said with a shrug. "Now stop wasting time and come along like a good boy."

Silva's jaw tightened again, but he didn't fight August's grip as they entered the restaurant, and he didn't say a word as Ricardo got out of the car and joined them. "Keep an eye on my car, gents!" August called out before locking the door on Silva's backup. One of them rattled it while the other raised his gun, but Silva shook his head.

"Let us know quick if you see a problem coming," he called out. They backed off, grudgingly, and then it was just Silva, August, and Ricardo in the brightly lit foyer of the restaurant.

"You've got some fucking nerve, don't you?" Silva said, finally shrugging off August's restraining arm. He didn't go for his gun, though, which... Well, it wasn't perfect amity, but August would take it. "Both of you, coming here like this. You think the fact that you've got a reputation is going to keep us off your backs, now that we know who you are?" He glanced at August. "And where to find you? You think—"

"You have bigger problems than us." Ricardo's voice cut through Silva's threats like a knife. "Specifically, the Vaccaros."

"Like *hell* the Vaccaros," Silva spat. "We have a truce. They don't fuck with us, we don't fuck with them, and they've held to it."

"They're involved in an international human trafficking ring," August said. "Girls, young ones, sent overseas. None of them have been seen again."

Silva paused for a moment, then shook his head. "No. I know a setup when I see one, and this stinks of a setup. A bad one."

"We have proof."

"Fuck your proof," he snapped. "You think I'm going to trust anything you give me? I'm just a few seconds away from having you two blown to pieces, and damn the consequences."

August sighed and glanced out into the street. This was getting them nowhere, and the more time they wasted on banter, the closer the cops got. Even in a mostly abandoned area like this, there was always the chance someone had heard the gunshots and (though it was unlikely) actually called the police. Or the police had heard them. He could talk *himself* out of a situation with the police, but Ricardo was another story. Maybe it was time to cut their losses and run.

Ricardo, it seemed, had other ideas. He stepped closer to Silva, who couldn't quite hold his ground.

"You ever ask yourself where Bruno Cavalcante got his ideas?" he asked, quiet and menacing. August grinned, barely holding back an appreciative shiver. "Who made him decide to try his hand at selling people into slavery, even though he knew your family didn't care for it? Do you think Bruno was the only one of your people the Vaccaros have been working on? Or even working *with*?"

"Now *that* you can't prove," Silva said, but he didn't sound certain.

"I can prove plenty." He thrust the thumb drive they'd loaded with copies of their most salient files at Silva, who took it gingerly. "I can prove the Vaccaros are linked to the kind of crimes that make the feds sit up and pay attention. I can prove that there are a lot of business ties between the Vaccaro and Cavalcante families. And I can publicize it all, big time." He nodded at August. "You really want to bet that you can take on the kind of organization that supports people like *him*? He's a fucking billionaire."

"Guilty as charged," August murmured. Was that sirens in the distance? Oh shit. Someone actually *had* called the cops. "Do you want to bet the feds won't start looking into you when we blow this thing open? Because that's not a bet I'd take."

"What the hell do you want from us?" Silva asked at last, looking uncomfortably sweaty.

"I just want you all to do your part," Ricardo said, giving Silva enough space that the man's shoulders finally unhunched. "That is to say, no help for the Vaccaros. No deals. No amnesty. You get your distance from them *now*. Use whatever excuse you have to, but keep us out of it. That way, when the feds start to investigate, you not only save yourselves, you help take out some true scumbags. And any of your people who get caught up in it, well..." He shrugged. "You won't be able to say they weren't warned."

"You want us to sever operational ties with a family two times the size of ours on your say-so." Silva chuckled nervously. "Damn, but you do have some balls."

"You do whatever the fuck you want to, that's up to you." Ricardo's eyes narrowed. "But you know me well enough to know that when I tell you I'm going to wring these fuckers so hard they look like blood-soaked rags by the time I'm done, I'm telling the truth. I will set them on *fire*, and if you try to warn them or help them in any way? I'll fucking set you on fire too. Got it?"

"Fuck you," Silva whispered, but his eyes were wide, and his hands shook. "You're just one guy. One guy can't take on the whole mafia."

"Aw, sweetheart, no," August interjected. "There's two of us now. That you *know* of. So listen to Ricardo, okay?" Yeah, that was definitely sirens getting closer. August looked over at Ricardo. "And Ricky, I think it's time for us to make our exit."

"Yeah." In a show of pure contempt, Ricardo holstered his gun. "Let's go."

CHAPTER 13

Ricardo had a lot of patience for a lot of things—he lived with August, after all—but he did not have the patience to deal with the cops tonight. His adrenaline was spiking, and there'd been a few too many close calls during their brief encounter with Pedro Silva. Too many moments when August could have been gone in a muzzle flash.

Between him and August, though, they'd reacted quickly and kept control of the situation, and there was nothing to do now except get the fuck out of Dodge before the night turned strobing blue.

Fortunately, August didn't protest when Ricardo demanded the keys. As they bolted from the building, putting perhaps a little too much faith in Silva's halfhearted orders for his men to stand down, Ricardo glanced around, and yep, the blue lights were closing in. More from the south than the north, at least as far as he could see. The sirens seemed to be coming from everywhere, but such were the acoustics of brick and asphalt—too many disorienting echoes from too many different directions.

Ricardo slammed the car into reverse. August hadn't

even put on his seat belt yet, and he tumbled forward with a choked, "Shit!"

Ricardo grabbed his shoulder, pushed him back against the seat, and then shifted gears again, and the tires squealed loud enough to drown out the approaching sirens. He seriously expected August to give him crap about tearing up his undoubtedly expensive tires, but August just rolled down his window and leaned out, pistol in hand. He was probably listening and watching, so Ricardo didn't say anything—he just tore down a street at Mach 3.

Once he'd put a couple of blocks between them and the scene of the crime, he slowed down. After a few more, he decelerated from reckless driving to *"I'm going to let you go with a warning,"* and he and August both exhaled. They both kept shooting looks at the rearview and side mirrors, though—it wouldn't be below Silva to tell the cops to come after them.

Ricardo shifted uncomfortably as he drove. In his hurry to get away, he'd hastily tucked his gun into the back of his waistband, something he rarely did. It wasn't a bad spot, just not a great one, and right now it was annoying as hell. The SIG-Sauer P226 was a great gun, but it didn't offer the best lower lumbar support.

"I think we're good," August said after a while.

Ricardo nodded. "Yeah." He glanced in the rearview. "We're good."

He eased off the accelerator. The getaway had been anticlimactic, but that was how getaways should be. Dramatic chases meant something had gone seriously wrong. When gangsters were involved, Ricardo greatly preferred when things didn't go seriously wrong. They very nearly had, but he and August had defused the situation quickly, had the conversation they'd needed to have with

Silva, and booked it out of there like the place was on fire. Not the best-case scenario, but far from the worst-case. Ricardo would take it.

"Jesus fuck." August flopped against the passenger seat and huffed dramatically. "I can't *believe* I tripped like a wimpy character being chased in a horror movie!"

With a quiet snicker, Ricardo said, "Well, that's what you get for that remark about me taking bullets instead of you."

He didn't have to look to know August was giving him that narrow-eyed *how dare you* glare. Partly because August was that predictable, and partly because he could feel it.

He didn't *have* to look, but he *did* look, and oh, yes—

Wait. No.

That wasn't that look.

He glanced at the road. August. The road again. "What?"

August cleared his throat, shifting in his seat with a little less melodrama this time. "I'm not sure if anyone's ever pointed this out to you before, but you're fucking hot when you're making Pedro Silva your bitch."

A laugh burst out of Ricardo. "You're the one who put a gun to his head. I think that means *you* made him *your* bitch."

August was quiet for a moment. "Are you saying that was hot?"

"I'm saying..." Ricardo trailed off, and goddamn, now that he thought about it, there was something almost offensively sexy about August getting the drop on Silva like that. Even the garish suit couldn't detract from how phenomenally hot he'd been the moment he'd ripped off the Augustus persona and jammed a gun against Silva's temple, especially when it was just seconds since Ricardo had been hit with the icy near-panic that he was about to watch August take a bullet, and... *Ooh*, fuck. Okay. Yeah. That *was* hot. Jesus.

He glanced at August again, and he damn near drove onto the curb and into a row of newspaper boxes. The glint of wicked curiosity and trademark feistiness in his man's eyes did nothing to quell the heady mix of fierce protectiveness and weak-kneed hunger August had been stirring up in him tonight.

"Fuck," he whispered, forcing himself to watch the road so he didn't wreck the damn Audi and keep them from getting home. The gun in his waistband was uncomfortable as hell, and so was the hard-on swelling against his zipper, and couldn't August have chosen a vehicle with a damned backseat? Did tonight's car have to be a two-seater?

August laughed softly. "What's wrong, Ricky? You seem...flustered all of a sudden."

"I'm fine." Ricardo licked his lips. "But we need to get home before—shit!" August's hand slid over his thigh, and Ricardo jumped, hitting the gas pedal harder than he intended. In his moment of distraction, the car fish-tailed, and August laughed triumphantly; he always knew when he'd gotten under Ricard's skin. The fucker.

"So, you never answered my question." The grin in August's voice made Ricardo roll his eyes, but it wasn't doing a damned thing to *down boy* Ricardo's dick. Still grinning, August asked, "Was it hot when I made Silva my bitch?"

Gritting his teeth, Ricardo plucked August's hand off his thigh before he crashed the car. "We'll talk about this when we get home."

August snorted. "You know, that would usually make me think I'm in trouble or something, but I have a feeling we're going to be 'talking about it' while your dick's down my throat, so—"

"Damn you." The words came out as a moan. What the hell was wrong with him? It had to be the adrenaline from their encounter with Silva. It needed an outlet, and what better outlet than the other man who'd made it out unscathed? They'd survived, they were safe, and they'd gotten their message to Silva, so they were one step closer to stopping the Vaccaros and their human trafficking operation. Why not take a few minutes—because God knew that was all either of them would need—to release that pent up stress?

August chuckled like the evil bastard he was. "Maybe we should go park somewhere and—what the fuck?" He flailed as Ricardo turned so hard he almost put the Audi up on two wheels. "What are you doing? Where are we going?"

Ricardo didn't answer. He just aimed the car at the parking garage of a mall that had closed hours ago.

"I was kidding," August said. "About parking? That was a joke."

"Uh-huh." Ricardo pulled into the dark, deserted garage, ignoring the posted speed limit. "I'm not."

"Oh. Fuck. Are you... Are you serious?"

Ricardo threw the car around a corner and damn near drifted into a parking space near the electric car charging stations. With the car still idling, he met August's enormous eyes across the console. "Do you think I'm not serious?"

August stammered a little, then, "You know there are cameras in here, right?"

Ricardo's eyebrow flicked up. "You trying to talk me out of this?"

"Fuck, no." August undid his seat belt, lunged across

the console, and, just before their lips met, he growled, "Just wanted you to know how hot it is."

And then they were kissing. Greedily. Hungrily. Messily. Somehow, Ricardo managed to set the parking brake and shut off the engine. Without the need to keep his foot on the brake anymore, he focused completely on August, turning toward him and seizing a handful of his hair as they kissed deep and hard.

But that damn SIG at his back.

Still making out with August, he reached for the gun. Damn it. With the way he was twisted, and the way they were leaning...

August lifted his head. "What?"

"Nothing." Ricardo seized the opportunity, arched his back slightly, and freed the gun. "This was in the way." He held it up like a rock he'd taken out of his shoe.

August's eyes widened. "Wait, you take guns off when you fuck?" He huffed a breath and shook his head, drawing away. "Well, that's a turn-off."

"I still have three others on me." Ricardo put the SIG on the dash, grabbed the front of August's shirt, and pulled him back. "Get over here."

"Ooh, well as along as you're still armed..." August nipped Ricardo's lower lip. "What else you packing?"

"Only one thing you need to be worried about."

August slid a hand over Ricardo's uncomfortably hard cock. "But I want to know what else you have. You don't usually accessorize." He kissed under Ricardo's jaw. "Indulge me, baby."

Ricardo bit his lip, closing his eyes and pressing back against the seat as August kissed his neck and teased his cock. "You think... You think I can remember anything about guns when you're... *Fuck*, August."

The breath of hot laughter across his skin shouldn't have made him shiver that hard. Had he really been this wound up after the encounter with Silva? Apparently so, because he was more turned on than he'd been in a long, long time. He couldn't think about anything except the man driving him wild, and he didn't *want* to think about anything else.

He grabbed August's hair, pulled his head back, and kissed him, and August rewarded him with one of those soft, helpless whimpers that always made Ricardo dizzy. Something about the sound was like a reminder that August was a lot of talk and bluster, but when a certain switch flipped in him, he was pliant and sometimes even submissive.

Ricardo wanted him. He needed him bent over something and taking Ricardo's dick and begging for more.

Except…

"This car is too fucking small," Ricardo murmured against August's lips.

"I thought you liked tight."

"Mmm, I do. But there's tight, and there's not being able to move." He nudged August back and nodded toward the passenger door. "Out."

August blinked. "What?"

Ricardo opened his own door. "*Out.*"

August got the message, and as Ricardo came around the front of the car, August stepped out. Ricardo didn't let him get his feet under him before he shoved August up against the rough concrete wall between a painted arrow and a sign he didn't care to read.

"You're going to get my suit dirty," August panted.

"And?" Ricardo kissed him again before he could object, and August just clawed at Ricardo's shoulders and eagerly returned that kiss. Yeah, the suit was going to get dirty. Hell, it was probably going to be torn by the time Ricardo was done with him. But August didn't seem overly concerned with that anymore, especially not as he started fumbling with Ricardo's belt and zipper.

As soon as the zipper gave and Ricardo's cock was no longer being restrained, he shivered, sighing into August's kiss. One stroke of August's warm hand, though, and Ricardo had to break the kiss with a gasp.

"Fuck..."

"Mmm, good idea." August grinned. "But unless you brought some lube..."

Ricardo closed his eyes and groaned. "Goddammit."

"We really need to start including it in our go bags." August brushed his lips across the side of Ricardo's neck as he found a slow, steady rhythm stroking him. "Because every time you go all badass, I want you to throw me down and fuck me."

Ricardo's hips jerked, and he was genuinely surprised he didn't come. "Yeah. Good idea. Because after watching you threaten Silva, *I* want to throw you down and fuck you."

August whimpered, tightening his grip on Ricardo. "Maybe we should just go back to—"

"You really want to stop?" Ricardo panted.

"Hmm, good point."

"That's what I thought." Ricardo kissed him again, and though his hands didn't want to cooperate, he managed to undo August's zipper too. In a matter of seconds, they were both stroking each other, gasping for air between kisses as they rutted together and muffled each other's needy groans. Ricardo had never been more frustrated in his life that he didn't have some lube handy—

being balls deep in August sounded fucking amazing right about then.

He had to make do, though, and he had an idea.

He turned August around and pinned him against the wall with his body. Reaching around, he started stroking him again, and he thrust against August's ass. As hideous as the suit was, the material was soft and smooth, and his head spun as he buried his face in his man's neck. "Fuck, August…"

"Oh God," August breathed, flattening his hands on the dirty wall. "You really are going to ruin this suit, you know that?"

"That a challenge?" Ricardo gritted out. "Or do you want me to stop?"

"Don't you—don't you *dare* stop." August shuddered, and pre-cum started making Ricardo's strokes slipperier. "Oh, fuck… Promise… Promise me something."

Ricardo squeezed his eyes shut, trying not to lose it yet. "Hmm?"

"After you trash my suit… Take me home and *fuck me*."

Groaning, Ricardo thrust harder, the promise of being inside August driving him on as much as the friction against his dick and the slickness in his hand.

August moaned. "Promise?"

"Uh-huh." Ricardo shuddered, and in the same moment he let go, he mumbled, "P-promise."

And then he was coming, and August shuddered between him and the wall, crying out something that echoed off the parking garage's labyrinthine walls as cum erupted over Ricardo's hand.

With one last shiver from both of them, they stilled. Ricardo wiped his hand on his pant leg—he was going to wash these pants when he got home, so whatever—and

August turned around and draped his arms over Ricardo's shoulders. As the dust settled and the smoke cleared, Ricardo held August close, both of them still trembling and panting. His thoughts began to clear, too, and he couldn't help holding August closer as the entire evening rolled around in his mind.

Tonight had been a nearly simultaneous glimpse of two sides of August that never failed to hit Ricardo in the feels—the vulnerable, mortal man who could be snatched away from him in a heartbeat, and the fearless badass who'd threaten a high-ranking gangster in the name of protecting Ricardo, Eve, and scores of victims whose names he didn't even know. This man was human, and he was a superhero, and he was Ricardo's kryptonite. No wonder Ricardo was so far gone for him.

Sighing, he pressed a kiss to August's temple.

August murmured something, then lifted his head to meet Ricardo's eyes. And there it was—the third side of August that had Ricardo wrapped around his finger: in that moment after an orgasm when he was shaky, sweaty, and disheveled.

It was satisfying, knowing he'd left August this wrecked, but it was more than that. Everything about August stirred up feelings in Ricardo that shouldn't have gone together. Like he wanted to fuck him until neither of them could stand, and he wanted to wrap him up and protect him from everything, and sometimes he wanted to strangle him, and there was no one else he wanted beside him going into the fray.

Beyond being his lover, August was what Matt should have been in their combat days—the man who'd have his back, who'd bleed to save him, and who'd draw blood from anyone who tried to hurt him, and Ricardo would do the same for him. He trusted August implicitly and without reservation, exactly the way he should've trusted his spotter back then. They'd each proven they'd walk through fire to drag the other out of danger, and in between the explosions and gunfire, August was everything Ricardo and Eve had never figured out how to be for each other. He drove Ricardo insane sometimes, but other times, he was the only thing anchoring Ricardo's sanity. The right amount of sass and pushback balancing out the empathy, the understanding, the respect, and the...

Why did he even try to deny it anymore? Because standing here with August, both of them shaking and debauched against the dirty wall of a parking garage after a harrowing encounter with a gangster that Ricardo couldn't imagine surviving with anyone else, it was so painfully obvious.

Heart thumping, he ran a trembling hand through August's sweaty hair. "August..." He swallowed. "I love you."

August blinked, his lips parting. Ricardo fully expected a smartass response, because that was how August responded to everything. If August had a love language, it was brazenly unbridled snark.

But this time, his expression softened, and his voice was barely a whisper as he said, "Really?"

"Yes. Really." Then Ricardo kissed him, because he wasn't good at moments, and he couldn't handle the silence or—worse—whatever August might expect him to say next.

August wrapped his arms around Ricardo's neck, and this was the kind of silence Ricardo could handle—a long, deep kiss laced with an entirely different kind of hunger. They both held on, still leaning against that concrete wall for support. It occurred to him that it didn't matter how bad he was at moments, because August understood him. He *got* Ricardo. He knew Ricardo struggled to articulate the things partners always wanted him to say, and when those words did come, August took them and didn't push for more. He didn't give Ricardo grief for the timing, for the setting, for the fact that it had taken him so long. It was like he knew how and why that would shove Ricardo right back into his shell, and he rolled with it just like he rolled with everything else that was part of being with Ricardo.

A renewed surge of protectiveness had him holding August even tighter as they kissed against the wall. In the beginning, after he'd stopped wanting to kill August himself, Ricardo had been ready to go to the ends of the earth to save him from danger.

Now? There wasn't a thing in this world he wouldn't burn to the ground to keep him safe.

August drew back and gazed up at Ricardo. Voice soft and ragged, he said, "We should get out of here."

He was right, but Ricardo wasn't quite ready for this to be over. "Why's that?"

"Isn't it obvious?" August tsked, rolling his eyes. "I want to start picking out wedding invitations!"

Ricardo raised an eyebrow.

The corner of August's mouth twitched.

Then they both laughed, and they sank into another embrace, this time burying their faces against each other's necks.

Stroking Ricardo's hair, August whispered, "I love you too, by the way."

Ricardo smiled and pressed a soft kiss to August's neck.

As romantic moments went, it wasn't one they could exactly tell people about. Elodie might think it was funny as long as they left out exactly what they did to August's suit.

Eve would probably find the whole thing hilarious and adorable as long as they glossed over the guns and gangsters. Everyone else...

Well, this would be something just for him and August.

And Ricardo decided he was okay with that.

CHAPTER 14

August blinked his way awake, quiet and careful not to move, and gradually became aware of three things. First and most important, Ricardo was still in bed beside him, so close he could feel the blanket move with every one of his breaths. It was a rare thing for August to wake up before Ricardo, even after late-night jobs and marathon fucks, so he was determined not to ruin it by rousing him if he could help it.

Secondly, if the distant noise he heard was any indicator, Eve was already at work in the command center that had taken over his dining room. Good for her—it showed initiative, and better yet, it showed tact, since she hadn't come up to wake them and instead just got to work. August appreciated that, especially since he wasn't sure he could look at her right now without thinking smug thoughts about how Ricardo was his now. Yes, it was childish, but he was only human.

Thirdly, if the sun was strong enough to wake August even with the UV shielding on his bulletproof windows, then it had to be pretty late in the morning. They didn't really have time to waste lying around in bed together, but...

Eve can handle things by herself for a little longer.

August scooted an inch closer to Ricardo, enough so that their shoulders brushed together. Ricardo made an adorably disgruntled face, then sleepily reached out and hauled August in close, until his head was on Ricardo's shoulder and their bodies were pressed together. "F'kin ticklish bullshit," he muttered.

August chuckled. "I know, sorry. Go back to sleep." He didn't really think Ricardo was going to, but to his surprise the other man gave in, settling back into a state of quietude in under a minute.

August looked at him, cataloguing every inch of skin that he could see: the tiny scars along his shoulder and chest, the callouses on his palm, the astonishingly long fan of his dark eyelashes against his cheek. His jaw was rough with stubble, a few strands of gray showing here and there. His face was weathered, skin walking the line between sun-kissed and sun-damaged, and his morning breath was none too sweet. August was stupidly enamored with it all. Ricardo wasn't the best looking man August had ever spent the night with, but he was the only one August planned on waking up next to from here on out.

God, it was *ridiculous* to feel this way about another person, so soft and vulnerable. It was maddening and cloying and cute, and it made August want to put a pillow over his head and scream for a while, just to try and exorcise the tenderness inside of him before someone could jerk it all out of him with a meat hook. Of course he had to fall in love with Ricardo Torralba. Of course. He didn't do anything dumb by halves, and yet...

Maybe it wasn't so dumb. At least he wasn't alone. The

weight of all these soft, heavy emotions wasn't just his to bear, because Ricardo felt the same way. And he'd said it *first!* That had been unexpected. August knew Ricardo appreciated him—who wouldn't appreciate him? He was hot and rich and had excellent aim!—but knowing that Ricardo loved him made August's stupid heart ache with happiness.

He'd teased Elodie mercilessly when she'd been swept off her feet by her now-husband. Admittedly, August had been a shitty teenager back then, but he'd still laughed at her sappy expression whenever she talked about Paschal. He owed her the biggest damn bouquet of apology flowers now, because damn. He knew he was being sappy, and he *still* couldn't stop.

He'd get control of himself in the shower. August carefully pulled away from Ricardo, wincing at how his thighs stuck together—he should have cleaned up before going to sleep, but his last orgasm had been the straw that knocked the camel unconscious, or however that saying went. He let himself have one last, long, embarrassingly appreciative stare at Ricardo, then walked into the bathroom and turned the shower on. He adjusted the heat and pressure to "scalding" and "bruising" respectively, then got in and let the water pummel him for a while, washing his mind and body clear.

Loving Ricardo out loud didn't have to change anything. Hell, August had loved him before their confessions last night. Putting it out there in the world didn't mean it was going to get taken away. He wasn't tempting fate. He *wasn't*.

August washed aggressively, brushed his teeth and did his skin care routine, and finally emerged from the bathroom in a cloud of geranium-leaf-scented steam.

Ricardo appeared reluctantly awake where he lay on the bed, and he yawned before he said, "You look like a lobster."

August laughed. *Way to cut the tension.* "The hotter the water, the easier it is to cleanse my delicate pores," he replied. "You should try it sometime."

"Mmm, no." Ricardo yawned again, then squawked as August threw his damp towel on top of Ricardo's head before strutting toward his closet.

It still felt good. It still felt *easy*, even with the words out there now. August relaxed as he surveyed his clothes. Hmm...what did you wear when you were in a great mood even though your partner had abso-fucking-lutely ruined the worst-best suit you owned?

Probably Armani. Maybe—

Snap.

August screeched at the sudden pain in his ass from where the wound-up towel had snapped him, and he flung one of his cedar shoe-stretchers straight at his assailant's head. Ricardo ducked it, then snapped him on the right thigh.

That was it. He had to die now. August threw another shoe-spreader, then charged, knocking Ricardo back onto the floor.

Fifteen minutes later August had rug burn in places he didn't want to contemplate. On the plus side—morning blowjob! So at least there was that.

As they walked past the dining room on the way to the epic kitchen, Eve glanced at both of them and laughed. "Ten a.m.!" she crowed. "You're getting lazy in your old age, Ricardo."

August smirked at her. "Oh, there's nothing lazy about

this guy. Especially not the way he gets a really good grip around your waist with his hands and then—"

"Never mind, that's enough, we're good."

"If you say so." August made coffee, then let Ricardo have the stove to himself to cook up the huevos rotos August knew he was probably craving, and joined Eve in front of the computer. "Have a good night?" he asked pleasantly as he sipped his coffee.

"Very good," she said, not quite looking him in the eye. "There were no alerts from Matt, so I slept the whole way through. I can't remember the last time I didn't wake up at least twice before morning."

"That bed has a very good mattress."

Eve smiled at him. "You have a very safe house too, August. It's nice to be somewhere that makes me feel safe. I don't think I realized how unsettled I was in my own home until all of this came up, but now?" She sighed. "I think I'll be selling in the near future."

Oh. "That sucks. I'm so sorry."

She shrugged. "It's all right. I've lived through two major failed relationships in that house; it's probably steeped in bad karma at this point."

August had no idea what to say to that, so he opted for changing the subject entirely. "Anything interesting from our spotter this morning?"

"Nothing so far." Eve frowned. "He's been very lowkey, actually. I don't know if it's because he knows someone is listening or if he's really this boring, but he's mostly been watching sports. Jesus Christ, how did I live with this much football in the background?"

"We all make sacrifices for the ones we love." August made an exaggerated expression of suffering. "Speaking of football...*soccer*. Oh my God, the soccer."

"It's *real football*, you ingrate," Ricardo called out over the sizzling of the stove. "And it's amazing."

"It's populated with pussies who fall down every time someone bumps them," August called back. "No, so much wimpier than pussies—dicks! It's a game for dicks!"

"I'll drink to that." Eve clinked her coffee mug gently against August's. Ricardo lapsed into grumbling, irritated Spanish, and she laughed.

"He's insulting your despicable American taste," she informed August.

August sniffed indignantly. "I'm half French."

She smirked. "Annnd now he's moved on to your regrettable *French* taste."

August opened his mouth to fire back—probably something about Ricardo's regrettable camouflage wardrobe, which was so hideous it had to be relegated to its own room upstairs—when the computer's volume automatically rose, projecting the conversation the bug was recording.

"—the fuck you get off trying to tell me what to do, you piece of shit?" That was a new voice, and from the sound of things it was a very, very disappointed one. "I hired you because you said you were gonna make my life easier, not add to my problems. What the fuck is this all about?"

"Mr. Calabrese," Matt said placatingly, and oh—that wasn't a good tone. August was glad this guy wasn't *his* boss, because if a hardass like Matt was trying to jolly him up like this, it had to be bad news. "I'm not trying to make anything harder, I promise. I just wanted to pass on that a few issues have come up with the work visas, is all. It might be better for us to put off—"

"Issues. *Issues*. The fuck is an *issue*, Ashford? Issues are things you talk about with your shrink. I don't have time for issues. I only make time for problems." His voice dropped an entire register, going from menacing to downright Satanic. "Are you bringing me a *problem*, Ashford?"

"Nothing unsolvable," Matt said, the slightest tremor audible in his voice. "Just an issue with a little too much oversight. Schreiber's getting some unexpected pushback on the visas, so it might be best for us to move the delivery to another few weeks out, that's all."

Another moment of what sounded like dead air. "Tell me you're not this stupid."

"Sir, I—"

"No, truly, I wish you were here right now so I could look you in the face and decide for myself whether you're as stupid as you seem to be, you dumb piece of shit. Listen to me. We don't renegotiate timelines with product like this, do you understand? *Freshness* is of paramount importance to our clients, and the longer we take to deliver, the less trust is going to be there between the buyer and the seller. Do you hear what I'm saying?"

There was a moment of silence, and then—"Yeah. I hear you."

"And do you understand that when we say we can deliver something of this magnitude, something that comes with the kind of payout we're expecting, there's no way to make it right other than to do the goddamn delivery? We can't add a couple of extra kilos of product to the next shipment to smooth things over if we don't get this right. Nobody wants a random piece of one of these items put in a suitcase and flown overseas with a box of fucking apology chocolates shoved into the middle of it. Do you follow me?"

"Yes sir, I follow you."

August followed too, although he really wished he didn't. He'd seen and heard a lot of utterly disreputable, disgusting people, but Christiano Calabrese was right up there in the top ten.

"For fuck's sake." The disgusting man sounded disgusted himself. "I don't have time for this right now. I'm telling you, Ashford, I fucking don't. This has been the day from hell, and it ain't even noon yet. Shit is falling out of the fucking sky right into my lap. I would *pay* to switch places with you for a day and let you worry about the goddamn Cavalcantes suddenly getting a termite's mound up their collective asses while I fussed around with a bit of government paperwork. I would fucking *pay*, Ashford, do you understand me?"

"Yes sir."

Calabrese sighed heavily. "Listen to me. I have a meeting with Mr. Basile in an hour. Do you want to be a problem I bring to this meeting, or do you want me to give him the good news that hey, turns out our product can get to where it's going even earlier than we expected? Do you want to be the person who puts a smile on his face, or the person who makes him clutch his mama's rosary and start saying preemptive Hail Marys?"

"You want me to move the delivery ahead of schedule?"

A sarcastic-sounding clap came over the line. "Look at this, the jarhead can be taught! Yes, I want you to fucking move up the delivery. We're gonna need the money, if these Cavalcante sons of bitches have decided they want to get high-handed all of a sudden. So do it, Ashford. Make it happen. Or something unfortunate just might happen to you. You understand me?"

"I... Yes. I'll get it done."

"Good. Don't forget to coordinate everything with the Madame. If this shit goes south, I'm holding you personally responsible. Don't fuck it up." He ended the call, and after a vociferous barrage of swear words, Matt finally hung up too.

August looked at Ricardo, who was now leaning in the doorway, absently wiping his hands on a dishrag.

"Well. I mean," August said. "It looks like our play with Pedro worked out, so yay for us?"

"What the hell did you do to this Pedro guy?" Eve demanded. "Because it sounds like Matt's boss is on a warpath because of it." She looked at Ricardo too, a warning in her eyes. "You know what Matt gets like when he's under the gun."

"Yeah." Ricardo didn't look pleased by that knowledge, either. "Get ready to be Merle J. Thomas III, because Matt's definitely going to make his new problem our problem as well."

"We can handle that," August said confidently. Neither Ricardo nor Eve looked very enthusiastic. "Can't we?"

"As long as Matt thinks *he* can still handle things, it'll be fine," Eve said—murmured, actually, and more to herself than to them. "As long as he believes he can control it."

August wondered, not for the first time, just how afraid Eve had gotten of her ex-boyfriend to take the step of contacting Ricardo. She seemed like a badass through and through, but Matt frightened her. How far had he taken his threats? How close had he come to hurting her?

He might have asked, but just then his phone rang. It was his "special agent" phone, and since only two people had that number and one of them was standing right here, it had to be Matt. "That was fast." He reached for the phone on the table.

"Don't let him work you up," Ricardo said before he could answer the call. "Matt always liked to spread shit around once he got caught with his hands dirty. He'll try it with you too."

"Aw, Ricky." August blew him a kiss. "I love that you care so much about my emotional well-being, but I'll be fine. Promise." He grabbed the phone and answered on the fourth ring. "Special Agent Thomas."

"I need a meeting."

"Ah, Mr. Ashford! I was wondering if you'd be calling." August decided to double-down on honesty. "Especially after that takedown by upper management. Brutal, just brutal. I hope you didn't clench up too hard."

"I *need* a *meeting*."

"Why do you need a meeting?" August asked. "You've been asked to move up the timeline. So do that—tell people that you're leaving early, keep me apprised of the new timetable, and prepare to get out of the way once we get your compatriots in one place."

"It's not that easy!" Matt snarled. "I can't get these people to the hotel if the paperwork isn't in order, and I can't *get* the fucking paperwork in order on my own! Not this fast!" He was shouting now, all of his composure completely gone. "You want this done? You want to get these people? Then it's time for you to help *me* out instead of the other way around, motherfucker, do you understand me? Otherwise we're both screwed."

"Take a few deep breaths," August advised. Both Ricardo and Eve put their heads in their hands. "Recite a calming mantra, do some—"

"*I will shoot you through the head, you asshole son of a bitch!*"

"Goodness, Mr. Ashford." August let his tone become darker, more serious. "That's quite the threat to make to an FBI agent. For someone who ostensibly wants to keep himself out of federal prison, you're not very good at taking a long view, are you?"

"I..." Matt stopped speaking for a minute. When he came back, he sounded completely calm. It was almost eerie, how steady his voice had become. "We're in a position of mutually assured destruction at this point," he said. "I can hurt you just as badly as you can hurt me. You think being an FBI agent will protect you from someone like Calabrese? Think again."

"There's those threats again." August tutted. "Why don't you just tell me what you want, Mr. Ashford?"

"I need a meeting with you. *Today*. I need you to make these work visas happen. *Today*. I need to move up the flight to Dubai. *Today*. I can only handle one of these things on my own. If you want to do what you say you want to do, then you'll help me with the other two."

"All you had to do was ask nicely, Mr. Ashford." August let Matt stew for a moment, then continued, "Of course I can do all that. We don't want your boss to pull you from this little project of yours before we get what we need to deconstruct it, after all. Let's meet on the bottom level of the parking garage on Fifth Street in the warehouse district at noon, how does that sound? I'll bring hard copies of the updated visas with me." August had fond memories of that parking garage—it was the first place Ricardo had killed someone specifically for him.

Hopefully he wouldn't need to repeat the feat this time around.

"You can get this done that quickly?"

"You'd be amazed at the latitude I'm being given with this case, Mr. Ashford. There's almost no limit to what I can get done in order to get this wrapped up in a bow," August replied. "Don't be a stranger, and don't get into any more trouble, okay?" He ended the call with a smile, then looked at Ricardo and Eve. They were both frowning. "What?"

"We can't get those visas changed in an hour and a half," she said.

"Of course not." August waved her concern away. "But I've got a great printer that can mimic almost any government document, and we've got a mole—Mr. Schreiber, in this case—who we can get to tell Matt that we really *have* updated the visas. It's not like we're planning on letting these girls fly anywhere anyway, so it doesn't matter if we've got the real thing as long as it *looks* like the real thing."

"The parking garage?" Ricardo demanded. "Really?"

"Hey, I like that place!"

"You realize Matt could try to kill you there and no one would find your body for days."

"Ricky. Baby." August crossed over to him and put his arms around Ricardo's neck. "Nobody is dying in that parking garage today, least of all me." He kissed the tip of his lover's nose. "Because you'll be watching my back. Right?"

Ricardo sighed, all the tension going out of him like a cat finding just the right spot in a sunbeam. "Of course."

"There we go." August kissed him again, more decisively this time, until a theatrical throat-clear from Eve made him finally pull away.

"We're still working on a tight timetable," she pointed out, her cheeks slightly pink. "You should get ready."

"So I should." August sighed. "Back into federal agent chic. I may never wear another decent suit again, at this rate. It's not a death joke!" he added quickly when Ricardo glared at him. "How could it be a death joke when I'm not going to die? Anyway...my printer and my polyester await! I'll be back in, like, fifteen minutes." August grinned at him.

"You could tell Eve about the fun we had with Bubba in the meantime, if you want?"

He turned and headed upstairs, hearing Eve say, in a voice drier than a Harmattan wind, "Wait, who's Bubba?"

THE FIRST SIGN THAT SOMETHING HAD GONE WRONG was the fact that there was no one waiting for August on the bottom level of the parking garage, even though he was ten minutes late. Or rather, Matt was *waiting*, according to Ricardo; he just wasn't waiting where *August* could see him.

"He's got a perch half a block to the west," Ricardo said over the com. "Second floor, empty apartment. Son of a fucking bitch."

August hummed in acknowledgement, and touched his earpiece to make it look good for Matt.

Just like a fed, can't talk without telegraphing it.

"Not that I think he's really going to shoot me," August said, "but you *are* totally going to avenge me if he does, right?"

"Shut up and call him."

"Touchy, touchy," August griped, pulling out his "Matt" phone. "It's like that blowjob this morning didn't even relax you. How many times do I have to make you come before you finally take that stick out of your ass?"

"Guys," Eve said in a reluctant tone of voice. "If we could please focus right now?"

"I'm very focused," August said, then called Matt. "Mr. Ashford," he said as soon as the call was picked up, "I'm not feeling the love. You're the one who asked for this meeting, not me, and now you won't even meet with me face to face?"

"I don't trust you that far, Special Agent Thomas," Matt said coldly.

"Goodness, you know how to hurt a man, don't you?" August pressed a hand to his chest as he slowly turned in a circle, as though he were searching for Matt's location. "You realize I didn't come here alone, right? If you're looking at me and thinking about making a bad decision, think again."

"No bad decisions. Just leave the documents on the ground and drive away. Then I'll give you a new time and place for the girls."

August shook his head. "That's not how this works. You don't dictate the terms, Mr. Ash—"

A bullet sent concrete spattering just a few feet away from him, particles spraying into the air. August took a second to be grateful that he hadn't jumped, because there was every chance that Ricardo would have overreacted if he thought August was hurt.

Whatever you do, August, don't trip again.

But that didn't mean he was going to let Matt off the hook now. "Oh, Mr. Ashford. You do love practical demonstrations, don't you." He sighed, then lowered his phone and nodded.

If he hadn't been listening for it, August wouldn't have heard the sound of shattering glass half a block away over the noise of the city. As it was, he *did* have that pleasure, followed by the pleasure of Ricardo saying, "He's rethinking his life choices," even as Matt started shouting into the phone.

"What the fuck was *that*? What the fuck are you—"

"I told you already I didn't come alone," August said. "I'm

not sure why you didn't take me at my word, but I hope you do now." He let his tone go from stern to conciliatory. "Look, this doesn't have to be more than a bump in the road, Mr. Ashford. I want to work with you. I'm prepared to protect you. I'll get you out of this part of the country, away from all the bad people who are going to be out for your blood once this mess is over, as long as you don't play me for a fool. Now get your ass down here within the next five minutes, or I'll let my backup start calling the shots." He smiled without meaning to. "And you should know that he takes those shots very, very seriously."

There was a long pause filled only with heavy breathing before, "I'm coming." The call ended.

August paced in a slow circle. One of his cheap shoes had a scratch on it—already, and *How?* He hadn't even *jumped*. How did these pieces of trash get marked up so fast?

"Think he'll show up?" he asked Ricardo quietly

"He knows he'd better."

"That doesn't mean he will."

"He's too paranoid not to."

"You sound very certain," August commented.

Ricardo huffed. "I know more than I want to know about Matt's paranoia. I had to handle more than my share of it. Trust me, he'll be here."

"I trust you," August said quietly. Ricardo sighed, but before he could speak, Matt was walking up the ramp of the parking garage, no gun in sight but still brushing bits of glass out of his hair. One of them had left a cut on his face, and a thin trail of blood ran the length of his right cheek.

He stopped about five feet away from August and held out a hand. "The work visas."

"Show me your mic."

Matt's face crumpled with anger. "Give me the—"

"Another condition of our working together is that you remain an open book to us, Mr. Ashford, and that means wearing our listening gear at all times," August interjected. "If you take it off to shower or shit, you put it right back on afterward. Where is it?"

Matt dropped his hand. "In my car. I'm going to have a lot of facetime with my crew coming up. If they find out that I'm wired—"

"Don't let them." August was inexorable. "Keep their hands off of you, and keep my equipment on you. The more conversations we collect, the easier it will be to put your crew in prison and save your ass, do you understand?"

Matt ground his teeth but eventually said, "Yes."

"Good." August withdrew an envelope from inside his jacket and handed it over. "Modified work visas. Enjoy. I'll expect details on when and where the girls will be staying by this evening. Now, I think we're done here, so—"

"Where's your sniper?"

August blinked. "I beg your pardon?"

"Where's your sniper?" Matt repeated. "I scoped out all the best perches for two blocks in every direction, and I should have been free and clear where I was. Where the hell did you set up your sniper?"

"Mm, put a pin in that, and we'll come back to it if I feel like you do something deserving of a reward," August said with a smile. "For now, consider the question a fun mental exercise."

There was that blank look again. August had to resist the urge to wipe his face—being stared at so intently made his skin crawl.

"Bye for now, Mr. Ashford."

Matt turned and walked away without looking back.

August blew out a breath as soon as he was out of sight, then turned around and—

"Jesus Christ!" Ricardo was *right behind him*. "Aren't you supposed to be perched somewhere being menacing?"

He shrugged. "I came down once he got into close quarters range, just in case. I menace just as well from close up."

August wanted to be annoyed, but instead he just felt protected. It was *weird*. "I had it handled. You're supposed to be a secret, remember?"

"He wouldn't have seen me cut his throat."

Awwww. His boyfriend said the nicest things. August resisted the urge to grab Ricardo and defile yet another parking lot with him. "C'mon, let's get home. We can give Eve a break from monitoring."

"Whatever you want."

Love had definitely made Ricardo squishy. But that was all right. As long as the only one who got to experience it was August, he was good with it.

More than good.

CHAPTER 15

Walking out of the parking garage, Ricardo's senses were all on high alert. He hadn't been that close to Sandman in way too long, and he wasn't going to draw an easy breath until he was absolutely sure they'd left his old spotter in the dust. He could say a lot of things about Matt, but the guy wasn't (usually) stupid, and Ricardo didn't buy that he'd walked away from Special Agent Thomas without looking back. Or circling back. Or...something.

August seemed in tune to Ricardo's wariness, and he wisely followed suit. That, or he was just wisely on edge himself. He did, after all, have solid survival instincts.

At each curve and corner on the way down to street level, they both slowed, listened, looked around. People had this idea that hitmen were apex predators of the criminal world, but the assassins who stayed alive were those who understood there were times when it was prudent to behave as prey.

Times such as when they were navigating a building full of blind spots out into a street in view of numerous sniper perches when there was someone with spec ops training lurking in the shadows.

For all Ricardo knew, Matt had bolted for his car and high-tailed it to some hidey hole or another. But he doubted it. He'd spent too much time with Matt when the man was amped up, cornered, and downright terrified. Much like a wild animal, Matt was at his most dangerous when he had his back to a wall, and Ricardo had seen for himself how quickly Matt could decide everyone around him—including his fellow Green Berets—were threats to his freedom or safety. Given the way both the Vaccaro family and "Special Agent Thomas" had Matt's balls in a bear trap, Matt was bound to be in "lash out at anyone, including the hand the tries to feed me" mode.

To Ricardo's surprise, though, the only signs of life they encountered were a dumpster-diving stray cat and a young couple having an argument beside a minivan.

Dropping into the driver's seat in a lot two blocks away, he indulged in a sigh of relief. They weren't out of the woods yet, and God knew this whole op was far from over, but he felt a lot less exposed and vulnerable now. And a lot more like Matt really had left.

"For the record," August groused as he buckled his seat belt, "I hate that guy."

"Most people do," Ricardo muttered.

As Ricardo pulled out of the parking space, August twisted around to look in the backseat. "Where's your gun?"

"It's safe. We'll come back for it."

August turned to him. "You really think it's safe up... Wherever it is?"

"No," Ricardo admitted. "But Matt knows you brought a sniper with you. If he sees someone walking with a gun like that—or even something that could be a disassembled gun in a case—he'll zero in on them." He tapped his thumbs on the wheel. "I made sure it's as well-hidden as it can be, and I'll come back tonight after dark and pick it up."

"Oh." August sounded nervous. "You're really worried about him, aren't you?"

"I know him," was all Ricardo could say.

They drove in uncomfortable silence for a while. Ricardo once again appreciated that for all August could be an insufferable pain in the ass, he knew when to flip the switch and be serious. On the other hand, he didn't like that August sensed that this was one of those times. The usual snark and bullshit would be annoying as hell right about now but not nearly as unnerving as the *oh shit* silence. When August shut off the snark and bullshit, it was like when all the birds stopped singing and the wildlife started running for higher ground. A silent forest meant bad shit was afoot, and anyone with a shred of self-preservation got the hell out of Dodge.

As subtly as he could, Ricardo accelerated, pushing the car a couple of miles over the speed limit. It wouldn't accomplish much, but it made him feel a little better without alarming August.

What *didn't* make him feel better was when the car behind him also accelerated.

The driver was still hanging back rather than being on Ricardo's bumper, but he matched Ricardo's speed.

Without signaling, Ricardo took an abrupt left turn. August's hand smacked the armrest and he made a small yelp of surprise as he was thrown off-balance, but instead of demanding to know where Ricardo was going, he said, "We're being followed?"

"We're being followed."

He was sure now—the other car nearly lost its ass when

it course-corrected, but it was behind them now. The driver didn't bother hanging back anymore, either, and he was nearly tailgating them.

August muttered a few curses as he shifted in his seat. He didn't whip around to conspicuously look at their tail, and he didn't panic, but the tension in his body was unmistakable. He rested his pistol on his thigh. When he spoke, he gestured with his free hand—the aggravated flail of a passenger annoyed by the erratic driving—but his voice was calm and level. "How long?"

Ricardo returned the gesture, giving their follower the impression they were having an animated disagreement even while they spoke quietly and evenly. "Couple of miles."

"You think it's Matt?" August's gestures were almost comically juxtaposed with his unusually mellow voice. "Or is this a Vaccaro?"

Ricardo's frustrated wave wasn't entirely an act—he really was frustrated because he didn't have an answer. Still, he kept his tone level: "Could be either. Could be Cavalcante for all I know."

"Oh God," August groaned. "As hot as it is to watch you make Pedro Silva cower, I am *so* not in the mood."

The joke brought Ricardo's blood pressure down a couple of notches. Not because he thought August was dismissing the danger they were in, but because he could sense August pulling on his game face. Whatever they were about to face down, Ricardo wasn't facing it down alone, and it looked like there was only one person in the car behind him. They had a two-on-one advantage. His partner had a clear head. They could do this.

He looked around—this unstriped back road was almost entirely deserted except for them. Then he glanced at August. "I'm going to stop, and we're going to face him."

"You think that's a good idea?"

"No. But the alternative is giving him a chance to gain the upper hand. If we do something he's not expecting, then he won't be the one in control."

"What do you have in mind?"

"Exactly what I said." Ricardo glanced at his partner again. "I'm going to stop. And we're going to face him. Guns out. Catch him by surprise."

August lit up. "Ooh, I'm already playing an FBI agent, and now I get to play felony stop cop?"

Ricardo chuckled. "Something like that." He shifted a little as he pulled his pistol from his shoulder holster and rested it on his thigh. "You ready?"

"Pfft. I'm not bottoming right now, baby. You don't have to prep me."

Indulging in an eyeroll, Ricardo silently chastised himself for not enjoying that blessed—if unnerving—period of August's silence.

Then he slammed on the brakes.

Instantly, tires were squealing, and not just his. The car behind him veered to the left to avoid colliding with them.

Before the other driver could recover, August and Ricardo were out of their car, weapons trained on him.

"Hands where we can see them," August barked in his special agent voice. "Then get out of the car. *Slowly*."

Ricardo was taken just a little aback by the goose bumps from August using that voice. That was something he'd have to remember for later. Right now, though, he focused on the other driver, who had presented two shaking white palms to the windshield.

August came around to the driver's side, and at his

order, the driver opened the door. Then August growled, "Get out."

Hands still upraised, the driver stepped out.

And turned to Ricardo.

And blinked.

"Hurricane?"

Ricardo swallowed. This was not ideal, not in the least, but there was nothing to be done about it now. "You want to tell us why you were following us, Sandman?"

Matt stared at him. Then at August. Then back at Ricardo. "How the fuck... You're working with..."

"You're working with human traffickers and the Mob," Ricardo growled. "You don't get to judge me for working with the—"

"I'm not judging *you*." Matt sneered and cut his eyes toward August. "You're working with this asshole? Seriously?"

August shrugged. "I kind of thought the same thing until I ended up working with you. But you've really put things in perspective." He smiled brightly. "So thanks for that."

The look of shock and horror on Matt's face, coupled with the smugness on August's—Ricardo had to fight a laugh. He masked the amusement with a cough and stepped closer, weapon still fixed on his old spotter's face. "Why are you following us?"

Matt narrowed his eyes. "Because I wanted to know who the fuck this guy"—he jabbed a thumb at August—"is working with." His jaw worked as cold contempt rolled off him. "You, though? Seriously? I can't believe the FBI even let you in." With a bitter laugh, he shook his head. "Guess I should've taken that job when it was offered. If I'd known the standards were so low..."

Ricardo sighed. "Are you finished? Because I've been finished listening to you run off your idiot mouth since the last time we were deployed together."

"Oh, *damn*." August guffawed, nudging Matt with his pistol. "He told you, didn't he?"

Matt glared at him, which only amused August further.

Matt was livid, and now that Ricardo was in the asshole's presence, he was too. There was a lot of history here—personal and professional—and there were a lot of reasons why Ricardo wanted to pound Matt's face into the pavement until he was guaranteed a closed casket funeral. He'd wanted to do that for a long time, but now that he knew Matt had been such an asshole to Eve, and now that he knew what kind of unforgiveable crimes Matt was involved in, Ricardo's rage for him burned hotter than ever.

I should have shot you when we were downrange.

God, there'd been so many opportunities in combat. So many chances to make it look like an accident or enemy fire. But Ricardo didn't kill indiscriminately, and thanks to his crisis of conscience, Matt had lived long enough to become a civilian, abuse Ricardo's ex-wife, and destroy the lives of countless girls and young women.

Shooting him here and now didn't feel like murder the way it would have back when they were deployed, but he also couldn't justify it because, goddammit, they *needed* Matt. He was the lifeline for the very girls he'd put in danger, and until they were safe, so was he.

You have no idea how lucky you are right now, you puto gilipolles.

Ricardo lowered his gun, but he didn't holster it. "All right. So you followed us. Now you know who he's working with. Is there anything else?"

Matt's jaw worked again. "No." He looked Ricardo up and down. "I think I know everything I need to."

"Good," August said coldly. "Then get your ass out of here and get me the information I asked for before I decide to nix our deal and make sure you go to prison for your involvement in human trafficking." He jabbed Matt's shoulder with his pistol. "Because the longer you're standing here with your thumb up your ass, the longer I have to wait for locations on those girls. You feel me, dumbass?"

Matt actually looked startled, and Ricardo swore that if he hadn't already been in love with August, he'd have fallen for him right then and there. How could he not love someone who could rattle Sandman's cage like that?

"All right." Matt showed his palms. "All right. I'm..." He nodded toward his car. "Can I go?"

"Yes. Go." August took a step back. "I need that information. *Now*."

"I'm going. I'm going." Matt inched toward the open door of his car. When he was apparently satisfied neither man was going to shoot him, he got in. August and Ricardo both leveled their weapons at him, and they kept them on him as he executed a slow three-point turn to head back the way he came.

Before he drove off, though, he lowered his window. "Oh, hey, Hurricane?"

Ricardo ground his teeth. August would be asking about that nickname soon, he just knew it. "What?"

With a smug grin even by his standards, Matt said, "Just thought you'd like to know, Eve covered up the butterfly."

Then he winked, squealed the tires, and took off.

Ricardo's temper flared so fast and hot, he very nearly shot out Matt's rear window just for spite. Instead, he let fly a roar of, "Hòstia!" before shoving his gun into its holster and stomping toward the car.

August got in, and they continued toward home.

And to his credit, he didn't ask about Hurricane or the butterfly.

"So Matt knows?" Eve put a hand to her mouth. "Oh God. I'm surprised you two didn't kill each other."

"They thought about it," August declared over the edge of his coffee cup as he leaned against the kitchen counter. "I mean, I'm no psychic, but..." He nodded sharply. "They thought about it."

Eve turned to Ricardo for confirmation. He just shrugged before taking a pull from his beer bottle. Literally the only thing keeping Matt alive right now was those girls bound for Dubai.

Once those girls were safe... Well.

"So what happens now?" Eve folded her arms loosely and leaned against the island. "Is he actually going to cooperate and get you the information he needs?"

August snorted. "If he wasn't going to before, he is now." He tilted his cup toward Ricardo. "One look at him, and he definitely rethought a few of his life choices."

Eve gave a quiet, dry laugh. "I guess I'm not surprised. As much as I'm sure he'd love to sabotage this as a fuck-you, he's still as afraid of Ricardo as he ever was."

Ricardo flicked up an eyebrow. "He's afraid of me?"

She huffed with amusement. "Oh come on. Don't act like you don't know." She paused. "Wait. You did know, didn't you?" When he didn't respond, she blinked a few times, her jaw falling open. "As much time as you two spent joined at the hip, and as observant as you are about everyone, you never picked up on that?"

Ricardo thought about it, then shrugged again. "I always thought he was too arrogant to be afraid of anything."

"Pfft." Eve shook her head. "There is a very short list of things that man is afraid of, and you are definitely on it."

"Explains why you came to me when he started—"

"No, it doesn't," she snapped, and pointed a long nail at him. "I came to you because you're the only one who understands how dangerous he is when someone crosses him."

"Which *you* knew when we met, but you still dated him after—"

"You really want to get into that now? Huh?" She glared at him. "It's not like I can undo it. If you'd rather I get someone else to—"

"Okay, okay." August casually slid between them, patting the air with both hands. "Look, I'm not about to get in the middle of an argument between ex-spouses, but I *am* going to ask you to put a pin in it until the fire's out, okay? We've got a shitstorm coming, and you and I"—he looked pointedly at Ricardo—"have got to be able to focus. Got it?"

Eve made a disgusted noise and muttered, "Fine," before stalking out of the kitchen.

Ricardo slumped back against the counter. He wanted to argue—with him, with her, with anyone who'd put up a fight—but August was right. Once they knew where those girls were, the clock would be ticking, and they'd need to be ready to make their move. That meant more than just strapping on a few weapons, tossing go bags in the car, and formulating a plan. He had to have his head in the game. Those girls were counting on him.

And it wasn't like him to be this volatile or to pick a fight with his ex-wife. Truth be told, if August hadn't stepped in,

Eve and Ricardo would probably be deep into a shouting match that would last until they'd both run out of steam. It took a lot to set off either of them, and August must have seen the telltale smoldering of both their fuses.

He looked at Ricardo. "You good?"

"Yeah." Ricardo took another long pull from his beer before setting it aside. "You're right. We... We don't need..." He closed his eyes and tilted his head back, letting it rest against a cabinet. "What the fuck is wrong with me tonight?"

"Well, if I had to guess," August said, sounding uncharacteristically cautious, "your former spotter stepped on a few nerves, and you're looking for an outlet."

Ricardo opened his eyes.

August was watching him, forehead creased, and he took a cautious step closer. Sliding his hands up Ricardo's chest, he softly said, "I mean, I'm sure just seeing him brought back some unpleasant memories, but the way you clearly wanted to rip out his heart and feed it to him?" He grimaced. "I'm not surprised you're pissed at him. If we didn't need him for this op, I'd have pistol-whipped him just for being a dick to you."

At that, Ricardo couldn't help chuckling, and he wrapped his arms around August. "You just want another chance to drag someone into a meth lab and 'interrogate' him."

August's eyes were so big and innocent, a Disney character would've been jealous. "You say that like you didn't enjoy the hell out of it. And look how much we bonded! It was almost like our first date!"

Shaking his head, Ricardo laughed. "Our first date? Really?"

"Well, yeah." August shrugged, draping his arms

around Ricardo's neck. "What better way to kick off our epic romance than removing a few swastikas from a shrieking white supremacist? Mark my words, baby—when they make a romcom movie about us someday, that'll be the scene where everyone knows we're meant to be."

Ricardo stared at him, wondering if there would ever come a time when he wasn't surprised by what came out of this man's mouth. "A romcom movie, huh?" He pulled August a little closer. "So who's playing us?"

"A couple of foxes, obviously."

"Foxes? Like who?"

"Like Robin Hood."

Ricardo blinked. "Wait, you mean like cartoon foxes?"

August's face lit up. "Exactly! I mean, come on, Robin Hood was basically my gay awakening five years before I realized I was gay."

Well. Speaking of Disney characters. "A cartoon fox. Was your gay awakening."

"Uh, yeah? Have you *seen* that movie?" August touched his chest and shook his head, sighing wistfully. "So, yes, I will absolutely be a cartoon fox in our movie. You? Hmm, well, maybe a wolf?"

"A wolf? Really?"

"Well, like..." August shrugged. "A sexy wolf."

Ricardo stared at his partner. He really, really wanted to be seething over his ex-spotter and the snide comments the douchebag had made—especially the dig at Eve—but... Goddammit. Despite once being the target of Ricardo's murderous thoughts himself, August was surprisingly adept at not only defusing him, but shifting gears from violent homicide to playful laughter.

Chuckling, he cupped August's face. "Just one problem with your movie idea." He brushed their lips together. "I don't think they'd let us cut off a Neo Nazi tattoo in a kids' movie."

"Kids' movie? Please." August leaned into him. "Who said anything about a kids' movie?"

Ricardo had to give his partner credit. Between the ridiculous conversation in the kitchen and the quickie in the bedroom that nearly resulted in some broken furniture, August had definitely left him feeling closer to normal. As Ricardo wandered downstairs, hips feeling vaguely disjointed, his mind was clearer and his mood had leveled out. Oh, he still wanted to beat the holy hell out of Matt, but the exchange in the street didn't feel so recent or raw.

The exchange with Eve, however...

Stomach tight with nerves, he went looking for her, and he found her in what was becoming her favorite place—the covered patio beside the pool. She was leaning back in a chair in an old faded T-shirt and a pair of shorts. They were short, too, possibly short enough he'd be able to see the tattoo she'd had on her inner thigh. But he didn't look. Partly because he didn't want her to think he was perving on her, and partly because he didn't want to take Matt's bait. If she had, in fact, covered the tattoo or had it removed, that was her business. If she hadn't, and Matt had just wanted to rub it in his face that he had intimate knowledge of Eve, well, it was still her business and Matt was still an asshole. He didn't own Eve. Never had, never would, never wanted to. He just hated the idea of her being with him because he knew how horribly Matt treated women, and the jackass apparently hadn't made an exception for Eve.

She looked up from the paperback she'd been reading.

"Hey." Her tone was flat in that, *Did you come to apologize because we both know you're wrong?* way it had been at times during their marriage.

He didn't let himself get defensive. Not this time. "Do you mind if I sit?"

Her eyes flicked toward the seats on either side of her at the small round table, and she shrugged.

He pulled out one of the chairs and sat. "Listen. I'm sorry. About earlier." Shaking his head, he sighed. "That wasn't fair, taking a swipe at you for being with Matt."

Eve exhaled and put the book on the table. "I mean, you're not wrong. I was stupid to get together with him."

"Still. What's done is done. And I'm going to get him out of your life." He hesitated, then touched her arm. "I mean it. I'm sorry."

She nodded slowly. "Okay."

Slowly, the knot in Ricardo's stomach unwound. It hadn't been a huge blowup, but they were still finding their footing with each other after all this time. Plus, there was all the shit Matt was involved in, and that was clearly stressing Eve out as much as it was August and Ricardo. Better to settle the small issues as they came up than let them fester into something worse at exactly the wrong moment.

Eve rolled her shoulders and met his gaze. "So, what happens next? With Matt?"

"If he knows what's good for him, he'll tell us where the girls are."

"Do you think he will?" She paused, then laughed softly. "Oh God. Of course he will. If he thinks the feds *and* you are on his ass..."

Ricardo allowed himself a quiet chuckle. "Let's hope." Sobering, he rubbed the back of his neck. "Because there isn't much time."

Her humor vanished too. "What if he doesn't get the information in time?"

Pursing his lips, Ricardo shook his head. "Well, then as far as he knows, he'll have the FBI coming for him."

"That actually sounds less scary than a Mafia family."

Ricardo shrugged. "General population in a federal prison isn't a good place for a man who's been involved in what he has. He'll think twice."

"Ooh, right. Good point. So he'll probably—"

"Hey, I don't mean to interrupt." August's voice turned them both around, and he leaned out of the sliding glass door, gesturing with his cell phone. "We've got a location, and a *very* brief window."

"Well, that answers that." Eve stood as quickly as Ricardo did, and they followed August inside.

Ricardo shut the door behind them. "So where are they?"

August faced him and Eve. "The girls are at the Coleman Hotel downtown, and they're staying in the Royal Suites. They're basically living it up and being treated like princesses to keep the whole charade going."

"So they don't suspect they're being trafficked," Ricardo said.

"Exactly." August nodded sharply. "Where the window gets tight is that the girls are going to be moved first thing tomorrow morning. To a hotel closer to the airport."

"Oh, shit," Ricardo breathed.

"Yeah. They're due to fly out tomorrow night." August folded his arms and shifted a little as if he were warding off a chill. "Once they leave the Coleman, there will be too many people around. Their escorts. Vaccaro muscle. Generally not people we want to hassle with."

"They don't have escorts and muscle with them now?" Eve asked.

"They do," August said. "But it's a smaller presence. Enough to make the girls feel like VIPs without tipping them off that something's amiss. And given that they're going to be moved tomorrow, it's a safe bet that there will be more muscle showing up soon."

"Which means we need to make our move sooner than later," Ricardo said.

August nodded. "Matt thinks our window is between now and about eleven o'clock tonight. So four hours tops."

Eve cocked a brow. "Can we trust him, though?"

"Oh, I don't trust him any farther than I can yeet him," August said, disgust dripping off every word. "But I do trust that he's going to do whatever it takes to save his own ass, and right now, that means cooperating with Special Agent Thomas. As far as he knows, if he gives us bad intel and sends us into a death trap, he's looking at a federal prison sentence so harsh, the government will hire a necromancer just to make sure he serves the whole thing. And that's not even taking into account the charges he thinks he's facing in The Hague. He is, shall we say..." August grinned wickedly. "Motivated."

Her eyes widened, and she looked at Ricardo.

Sighing, Ricardo nodded. "I don't like taking Matt's word for anything either, but August is right. And even if we didn't have Matt by the ball hairs, erring on the side of caution now would mean possibly letting those girls leave the country." He shook his head. "I don't want to take that chance."

"Those girls are *not* leaving the country," August growled. "And if we move fast, I think we can do this without traumatizing them more than we have to."

"What do you have in mind?" Eve asked.

"Well." August pressed his palms onto the kitchen island and pushed out a long breath. "I do have an idea..."

"Would you stop staring at me like that?" Ricardo groused from the driver seat of August's seriously swanky and bulletproof-to-hell-and-back Cadillac Escalade.

"What?" August shrugged. "I'm allowed to gloat that Mr. I'm-Never-Going-To-Need-A-Suit-This-Fancy is wearing the suit I made him get."

Ricardo rolled his eyes. "Shut up."

August just snickered, but neither of them said anything more. Ricardo suspected there were some nerves underneath the gloating; as arrogant and self-assured as August was, tonight's op was close to home for him. Even over the road noise, Ricardo could hear August rubbing his shoe against the floormat as if he might be able to push away the physical and emotional remnants of the kidnapping that had cost him three toes, a brother, and the ability to sleep soundly.

Without a word, Ricardo put his hand on August's thigh. August slid his hand over the top. They were still silent, but the shoe-rubbing was a little less pronounced now, and Ricardo only tugged his hand away when he needed to adjust a vent or something. Then he put it back.

Up ahead, the Coleman came into view, its distinctive French Renaissance architecture standing out from the shining glass and dull concrete buildings around it. The hotel was allegedly a knockoff of New York's Plaza Hotel, and it had the same reputation as being the place where movie stars and dignitaries stayed when they were in town.

The list of people who'd stayed in the famous Royal Suites just below the penthouse read like a guest list for the Oscars or the United Nations.

Tonight, two of those suites were occupied by four girls with dreams of becoming models and pop stars, and Christ, Ricardo was feeling the pressure to get them out safely and without scarring them for life.

As Ricardo slowed in front of the hotel, August exhaled heavily.

"We've got this." Ricardo wasn't sure who he was trying to assure.

"I hope so," August whispered.

They exchanged uneasy glances.

A valet stepped out, clearly expecting them to ask him to park the car, but they waved him off and continued into the parking garage. It was underground, which Ricardo didn't like, but it had three exits, so he could live with it. And if nothing else, the car was insured, so if something happened to it... oh well.

With the car parked close to one of the exits, they got out, and Ricardo buttoned his suit jacket. Though he'd never admit it out loud under torture, this suit was actually quite comfortable. August's tailor was a miracle worker, and the material of both the shirt and the trousers was surprisingly soft. Well, maybe not surprisingly, given how little tolerance August had for anything but the finest in textiles.

Either way, August was not to know how much Ricardo liked this suit.

From the trunk, August produced a pair of garment bags. He shoved another bag into Ricardo's hands, then smiled with almost manic glee. "Ready to sell dresses to some young ladies?"

Ricardo had to suppress a groan. He hadn't been sure

which persona August was going to adopt for this, but he could feel August slipping into it already. Fuck.

August slammed the trunk and swung the garment bags over his shoulder. "Let's go!" As he walked, he fell into the animated gait of his most boisterous and flamboyant persona, which also happened to be one of his most annoying. Ricardo reminded himself that killing him would be counterproductive.

Get the girls out. Then kill him.

At the entrance to the lobby, a pair of security guards watched them. One squinted a little, watching August, and Ricardo's gut clenched. They recognized him, didn't they? They'd seen Augustus Mason's photo on the news or something, and they—

"Do you need a hand with that, sir?" the security guard asked.

"Oh, no, I'm good." August smiled brightly as he strolled past them. "Thanks, boys!"

Ricardo kept his surprise under the surface. And really, he shouldn't have been surprised. While August's face *was* somewhat well-known, given his high-profile existence as Augustus Mason, he was also a master at hiding in plain sight. He was a magician when it came to styling his hair and applying subtle but effective makeup. At worst, if he had to use his FBI badge to get them out of a jam, someone might notice a passing resemblance between Special Agent Thomas and the billionaire philanthropist. If the cops were actually as observant as they were trained to be, they might sneer at the idea of a man—especially a man in *law enforcement*—wearing makeup.

But they wouldn't connect the dots. As skeptical as Ricardo had been in the beginning, he had to admit that the very fact that August could still exist as Augustus Mason was proof enough of his ability to keep his job as a hired gun a secret.

The hallway took them into the hotel lobby, which was, unsurprisingly, ritzy as all hell. Enormous crystal chandeliers sparkled overhead, bathing the tall drape-framed windows, rich paintings, grand piano, and plush furniture in warm light. The floor was gleaming marble, because of course it was, and every fixture was either sleek hardwood or spotless metal.

August made a quietly disgusted noise. "It looks like they were going for Versailles but decided to get drunk instead."

Ricardo bit back a laugh. He wasn't wrong.

The humor only lasted for a second, though, because up ahead… Matt.

As soon as he saw them, the temperature in the lobby plummeted. Matt's jaw tightened, and he started toward them. They came together by some empty couches near a couple of water coolers stuffed with cucumbers and God knew what else. "Right on time," he said through his teeth.

"Of course we are," August said cheerfully. "Now how about you take us upstairs so we can put those young ladies into some nice dresses?" He jiggled the garment bag on his shoulder as if Matt might have forgotten the plan.

Matt didn't look thrilled, but he gestured for them to follow him to the bank of elevators. Inside one, with August between him and Ricardo, Matt swiped a card, entered a code, and punched the button for the Royal Suites floor. No wonder the Vaccaros were keeping the girls here; the luxury floors were incredibly secure.

As the elevator groaned into motion, Matt quietly said, "You've got about an hour and a half before the real designers get here. So whatever you're going to do, do it fast."

August and Ricardo nodded. Ricardo didn't like the tight window, but Matt had been able to get them in ahead of the people who were really scheduled to fit the girls for some dresses. If those designers showed up early, this could get messy.

"Is everything where we need it?" August asked.

"Yes," Matt said tersely.

"Good." August stared up at the numbers above the door, his flamboyant persona and fake smile still firmly in place. "By the way, I hope we're clear on something, Mr. Ashford."

Matt glanced past him at Ricardo, then looked at August. "What's that?"

"No matter what past bullshit you have with my partner..." August turned that bright, phony smile on Matt. "If you cross me tonight, so help me, whatever your worst nightmare is right now, you'll be *begging* for it by the time I'm done with you. Got it?"

Matt's eyes widened. He looked at Ricardo as if to ask, *Is he for real?*

Ricardo just shrugged. Because, yeah, August was for real, and if Matt interfered with August rescuing some trafficked girls, Ricardo wasn't sure there was much he could do to stop August from eviscerating Matt. Not that he'd try.

The elevator let them off at the Royal Suites floor. There were security guards in the hall. Too many for Ricardo's liking. If Matt hadn't held up his end of the deal...

Well. He'd deal with that if he came to it.

Matt tapped on a door. A moment later, a middle-aged woman opened it. Her eyes went right to August and

Ricardo, and she grinned. "Ooh!" She looked over her shoulder. "Girls! The designers are here!"

She stepped aside and gestured for them to come in.

Ricardo's heart sank as soon as he saw the girls. They were all seventeen or so, but they looked so much younger. They looked so innocent, smiling excitedly as they hurried up to see what kinds of dresses the new arrivals were going to put them in.

Fuck. What if Eve had never come to him about Matt? And how many more of these girls were already gone?

He swallowed against the acid rising in his throat. They had to focus. Here. Now. Tonight. *These* girls. Once they'd helped them escape, then he and August could think of something to help all the others.

August didn't miss a beat. He launched into his sales pitch, opening up the garment bags to show off the sample dresses (which they'd raided from Elodie's closet and would probably be replacing before too long) while Matt and the Madame watched.

Ricardo's phone vibrated. Discreetly, he checked the message.

In position, Eve had written. He didn't like that she was even here, but they'd needed as many hands on deck as they could get. As long as he could keep her and Matt from crossing paths, maybe they could do this without bloodshed.

He thumbed back, *Same. Be at the window shortly*.

Right on cue, the Madame's cell phone rang. "Excuse me a moment." She took the call, and her voice quickly became flustered. "What? But I don't have time to—I have people in here with the girls right now. I can't—" She huffed angrily and lowered the phone. "Matt, keep an eye on them." Then she stormed out of the room.

August watched her go. The instant the door closed

behind her, he dropped his flamboyant persona and turned to the girls. "All right, I need you all to listen very carefully."

All four stiffened, as if startled by his sudden shift.

"My name is Special Agent Thomas with the FBI." August held up his fake-but-convincing credentials. "There's no time to explain all the details, but we're getting you out of here and back to your families."

While August gave the girls a quick rundown of the plan, Matt and Ricardo went to one of the windows and opened it.

"You better hope this works," Matt hissed. "Or we're all dead."

"Says the man who got involved with this shit in the first place," Ricardo growled. He carefully removed the screen from the window, then leaned out and looked up. As expected, a window in the penthouse was open too.

Elodie leaned out, the Pest Assassin overalls baggy on her small frame. She gave a thumbs up. So did Ricardo. Then he turned to August.

To his surprise, August was in the process of comforting one of the girls, who had apparently not taken the revelation well.

"But everything they told us..." She shook her head, tears streaming down her face. "They were going to... Oh my God, what if they catch us now? What's going to happen? We're... Oh God. Oh God."

"Hey. Hey." August touched the girl's arm and looked right in her eyes, his voice and expression softer than Ricardo had ever seen. "Breathe, okay?"

She breathed, and she whimpered, "I'm scared."

"I know you are. So am I."

Ricardo barely stifled an aggravated noise, and he was

ready to smack August for panicking the girls, but then August went on.

"We're both scared." He nodded toward Ricardo. "That's how you know we're going to be smart about this. We're not ten feet tall and bulletproof, and we know it. If someone rescuing you said they weren't scared, that would mean you've got someone who's too reckless to stay out of the line of fire. Us?" He gestured at himself and Ricardo. "When the bullets start flying, we're gonna duck! We're going to do everything we can to keep all of us—you and ourselves—safe so we can get out of here in one piece. Okay?"

That...actually helped. The girl was still crying, but she started to calm down. So did the others.

And damn if Ricardo didn't fall just a little harder for August.

"This sucks, and we all know it," August said. "But I've been through something like this myself, okay? I was kidnapped as a kid. I know you're scared, because I've been scared like that too. But we're here to help you get back to your families. Okay? Just take a deep breath." He took one himself, which encouraged her to do the same. "Stay as calm as you can. And we'll all get through this. All right? We ready?"

The girl took another breath, but then she nodded meekly. "Okay."

"All right." He gave her arm a squeeze and turned to Ricardo. "Let's go."

CHAPTER 16

S*IT*. T*IE*. L*IFT*. R*EPEAT*.

It was August's mantra right now. The words he lived by. Breathed by. The distance between the penthouse and the suites below it was substantial, and it had taken a while for them to figure out the best way to get the girls up there from down here. It had to be fast, it had to be safe, it had to be something they couldn't fall out of or off of, and it had to be discreet. Unfortunately, every floor except the penthouse up above them only had access to the fire escape via the hallway, so there went their chances of easy.

Instead, discreet evacuation was handled by the quick application of a tubular, tent-like structure Eve and Elodie had set up on the outside of the building. At first glance, it would just look like some covered construction. It was lightweight, and easy to get into place and remove. Inside of it was a sling, complete with a secure harness and a simple pulley system to get the girls up safely.

"Where the hell did you even get all this?" August had asked a few hours ago when Elodie had brought all of this equipment with her.

"Pasqual likes mountain climbing, you know that," she'd replied, smoothing out the harness. "Here, let me show you how to get into this—"

"This is not regular climbing gear, this is—what does he do, *sleep* on the side of a cliff?"

"Exactly."

Shit, the things August didn't know about his brother-in-law. "I'd have thought he'd be more careful with himself. Isn't he a doctor?"

"He's a surgeon," Elodie corrected. "Nine times out of ten that means adrenaline junkie. I'm just glad he's not a narcissist as well. I'm more than happy to fly him to Nepal for some life-threatening fun as long as he keeps refining his technique when it comes to eating my—"

"Lalalalalalala!" August clapped his hands over his ears.

"Hypocrite," his sister sang at him.

Right now, August was grateful for his adrenaline junkie brother-in-law. He was grateful for Eve and Elodie's calm, no-nonsense presences upstairs, getting the girls in safe but fast. He was especially grateful that Ricardo was the one running interference with Matt, because if it had been up to August, he would have tied him to a chair and taped his mouth shut five minutes ago.

"What part of 'dead' don't you morons understand?" Matt snarled for the second time in three minutes. "I can't stop the Madame from coming in, and the second she sees what's going on here, she's going to put everyone else on alert. You're a decent shot, Hurricane, but not even you can handle four on one."

"Shut up and let Thomas handle it," Ricardo snapped back. "He's on the last girl."

August was, and she was taking all of his focus. She was the youngest of them all, just turned sixteen from what her paperwork said, and probably the prettiest when she wasn't crying her eyes out like she was now. "I—want—my—mom," she gasped around the tears. "I—want—my—mommy—"

"We're going to make sure you get to her." August took one of her shaking hands and placed it high up on his chest, letting her feel his slow, deep inhalations. "We're going to get you out of this, but you have to breathe, Gina, okay? You have to calm down a little. Being calm right now will get you back to your mom faster, I promise. Deep breath, come on. With me." He managed to calm her down enough to get in the sling, and soon she was safe in Elodie's arms.

It was a start, but it was only a start.

"Time for us to get out of here," August said to Ricardo. He watched his partner's eyes light up. "Yeah, exactly."

"Exactly what?" Matt demanded. "Assholes, have you forgotten that you've got to do something for *me* before you—"

He didn't even see it coming. If August had been the one with bad blood between him and Ricardo—and he'd been there—he would have been a lot more diligent about keeping his guard up. As it was, Ricardo's sucker punch to the face hit Matt like a pneumatic hammer, knocking him out instantly.

Ricardo even caught him before he could fall like a noisy-ass paperweight to the floor. August...was conflicted about that.

"You said I could hit him," he complained as he headed for the sling.

"You can." Ricardo gestured to where Matt lay crumpled, like a broken Ken doll. "Go for it."

"It's not the same when he's not awake to experience it."

"We don't have time for bitching." Ricardo double-checked August's straps, then helped heave him up the side of the Coleman.

"Oh please," August said down to him, "there's always time for bitching. I'll make the time to bitch at you on my death bed."

Elodie happened to be the one pulling August into the room, and to her credit, she got him all the way inside and the harness off before punching his shoulder.

"Ow, why!"

"Don't joke about that," she snapped as she sent the harness back down for Ricardo. "Didn't we have this talk? How many times do I have to intervene before you stop being an idiot?"

"Fine, but you don't have to be so mean about it!"

There was a throat-clear. August and Elodie both turned to look at Eve, who was standing in front of the wide-eyed teenage girls with an expression on her face that clearly said, *My patience is dangling by a thread and when it snaps, I'm coming for you.* "Let's get Ricardo up, shall we?"

"Yes, of course." She and Elodie got to work, and August put on his "Special Agent Thomas" persona again as he smiled gently at the girls.

"Okay, so the nice thing about the penthouse suite is that it has its own private elevator," he said. "We should be able to take it all the way down to the garage, at which point we'll get into a special car and get you all out of here without any problems."

"Seriously?" This was from Zoey, whose nails were probably long enough to reach all the way to the back of someone's eye socket. Huh, there was a thought... "Those guys have guns! Like, so many guns! I thought it was weird that they were all dressed like John Wick, and now you're telling me they're, like, gangsters, and just—where are the rest of your people? Shouldn't they be arresting everyone right now?"

"That is an excellent question and a valid point," August replied. He did have a few numbers from his own kidnapping days programmed into his phone, but those weren't going to be helpful until they got the girls out of here. Life as a federal desk jockey—it killed your motivation. "But the reality right now is that we're on our own. There's four of us, there's four of you, and I promise, we're going to take care of you as long as you all keep it together for a little bit longer. Okay?"

There was a round of nods, and August gave them one last smile before heading over to the elevator along the nearest wall, right between a mirror the size of a Cadillac and a plinth with a vase full of dried flowers on it. Expensive dried flowers, but still...what the fuck? Who was this decorator, and what had they been smoking? August pushed the button for the elevator.

Nothing. No movement. No light. No indication that it was working at all.

Well, shit.

He had rented this fucking suite. Under a pseudonym, of course, but still—he was paying for it, right now, and that meant the elevator should be in use. It was one of the Coleman's claims to dubious fame, that they gave their top tier clients extra perks. This elevator was a ten-thousand dollar perk, and it. Wasn't. Working.

Something must have clued Ricardo in to the fact that things were, in fact, shit, because a second later he was by August's side. He asked in a low voice, "Elevator?"

"Unresponsive."

"Someone threw a breaker in the basement."

"No." No, because August had done more than his fair

share of researching this world of bullshit after his second kidnapping, and he knew more about the subject than most kidnappers ever would. He also really, really hated the fact that he was going to have to come back to this hotel once this was all over and shoot someone in the head.

Fucking loose ends—Did he have time for this? No!

"The odds are someone on the staff shut off operations," August said, keeping his voice low and calm so the girls wouldn't get more nervous. He was glad he hadn't shared the initial plan with any of them, given how it was working out. "This particular model of elevator has its own alarm system and emergency switch; if it stops working for any reason, an alarm is sounded at the front desk. Whoever cut the power also deactivated that alarm." Which meant they were looking for a manager...

One job at a time.

Ricardo caught on. "They're working with someone on the staff."

"Someone who's been alerted to the fact that things aren't all copacetic up here, so that means the Madame probably found Matt. It won't take much digging for them to figure out we brought the girls up here."

They stared at each other for a moment. August could practically see a plan forming behind Ricardo's eyes. "We can't use any of the elevators," he said a second later. "Not the main ones or the service elevator. Can't take the stairs either, it would be a kill box."

"Oooh, yeah, baby, hit me with more of your military lingo."

Ricardo rolled his eyes. "The girls will have to go down via the fire escape."

August frowned. "That's risky, given the show we

already put on. If we're seen out there, it would be a simple thing to kill all of us."

"The fire escape is just for the girls, Eve, and Elodie," Ricardo clarified. "We're staying here."

"Ah. *Ah,* okay, yeah." They would be the perfect distraction, especially once August called down to complain to their partner in crime. He pulled out his phone. "I'll make an asshole of myself while you inform them of the new plan."

Ricardo sighed. "I'd rather be the asshole."

"Don't worry, Ricky." August put a hand on Ricardo's shoulder and batted his eyelashes. "You'll always be an asshole as far as I'm concern—hello!" He reoriented himself as soon as the front desk picked up. "Yeah, so, I'm in the penthouse suite, and I'm thinking that you owe me a goddamn refund."

"Excuse me, sir?" The young man on the phone sounded confused. "I'm—um, I'm very sorry you're upset, can you tell me more about whatever the problem you're experiencing is?"

"I thought you'd never ask! In fact, you *didn't* ask, I had to call you in order to get this taken care of, and don't think this won't be going in my Yelp review." As August filled the air with chatter, Ricardo headed back over to Eve and Elodie and started talking to them in a low voice. The girls, clinging to each other like barnacles, looked worriedly between them and August.

He gave them a thumbs up as he continued, "Anyhoo! This elevator—this very expensive and supposedly very nice elevator of yours—isn't working. I'll have you know, I chose the Coleman for this elevator. Why? Because I like to have my personal space and I'm willing to pay a premium for it. Now I've got a car coming for me in less than five minutes, and if you think I'm walking my ass down a flight of stairs so I can join the rest of the plebes in your dank-ass *group* elevators, you've got another think coming."

"Um...sir...I...really, I—let me get a manager, and I'm sure they can—"

August could imagine exactly who the manager who took over the call would be, and he didn't want to get distracted with thoughts of killing them when he was supposed to be focused on killing a bunch of child traffickers. "Nope, you picked up, you take some responsibility. You've got four minutes before I call a helicopter to come and pick me up from the roof. Bye!"

"Sir, we don't have a landing pad up there! Sir, you're joking, ri—"

August ended the call and smiled at the girls as he walked over to one of the Pest Assassin bags that Eve and Elodie had brought up with them. He unzipped it and pulled out a bullet-proof vest. Gah, it was going to *ruin* the lines of his jacket, but safety first. Then he pulled out four more. "Okay, ladies, let's gear up and get you out of here."

August had found over years of dealing with hostile negotiations—and plenty of people begging for their lives—that there was a place between the screamy initial terror response and the desperate, teary-eyed, snot-faced bargaining phase. Keeping people in that place of calm shock was an art, and the most important thing when it came to ensuring they could still function was embodying pure confidence. When August put his shields up, not even Ricardo could always tell when he was bluffing and when he wasn't.

None of the girls asked questions about the vests as he helped them into them. None of them questioned the fact that they were going out the window and climbing thirty stories down to the ground. None of them blinked when they saw Ricardo pull a pair of Glocks out of the Pest Assassin bag and hand one over to August. They were in the zone of obedience, and as long as they left *now now now*, they would probably stay there long enough for the ladies to get them out of here.

"Keep the line open," he told his sister, tapping his Bluetooth. "If you run into trouble, let me know. One of us will be down to take care of you."

"Movement in the stairwell," Ricardo called out from where he'd positioned himself beside the ornate doorway to the stairs. Simultaneously, the elevator suddenly began to move, the numbers rising until it got to floor Twenty-Nine, where it paused.

Picking up some friends. This was going to be more than four people. August chivvied the girls and their escorts onto the fire escape as fast as he could. "Keep going, don't stop for anything, especially not us," he instructed them. "If everything goes well, we'll meet at the safehouse."

"Be careful," Eve said, low and serious. In that moment, she reminded August of her ex-husband.

He smiled brightly at her as he gave her a little wave. "Always! Bye now, ladies. See you soon. Don't do anything I wouldn't do."

"That statement is ridiculous," Ricardo commented, toppling one of the couches over so that he could crouch behind it. It was a solid couch, heavy wood and metal springs, not the lightweight cheap décor that most hotels sourced. Huh, who knew August would be grateful to the hotel for one of their decorating choices after all? "There's nothing you wouldn't do."

"I have limits! Not *many* of them, but they do exist." August shoved a bedside table over beside the couch for himself. He set his up so that he had a good view of the elevator door, then grabbed one of the smoke bombs from his bag, as well as an extended magazine for the Glock. "For example, I don't go outside without sunscreen. I'd sooner skip my moisturizing regime altogether than forget sunscreen."

Ricardo snorted. "I didn't realize there were people as fussy as you outside of the *Real Housewives* franchise until I got to know you."

"You love my fussiness," August said, tossing Ricardo one of the gas masks and taking another for himself. It was nice that they could be together for the shooting—the penthouse was huge, but both entrances were relatively close to each other, and it was good for concentrating their smokescreen. "You love that it means the nicest sheets and the best-tasting coffee and the finest food and, oh hey, the most fantastic sex, because I don't accept anything but the best." He put his mask on, made sure Ricardo did the same, then tossed out a few smoke grenades. They began to hiss, obscuring his view of the elevator.

"Sounds like more of a compliment to *me*, doesn't it?"

"Take it however you like it, Ricky." Ah, there was the final ding. The elevator had arrived, which meant the stairwell would be opening any second now as well. August switched his vision over to infra-red, because he didn't stint on hardware any more than he would on anything else—and a second later...

Blamblamblam!

Two men charged out of the elevator, already firing—like *idiots*, were they trying to kill their product? Or had Calabrese already called the operation and told these people to clean up the mess?

Either way, they stumbled when they were less than a

foot into the room, blinded and coughing on smoke. August heard the door bang open, but he focused on the targets ahead of him.

Bang.

Bang.

Two headshots. Two dead mafia goons.

Gosh, that was...brief.

The edge of the table beside him splintered from another bullet, sending woodchips flying into the air. August ducked, then watched as Ricardo very quickly, very cleanly, killed the other two attackers. Each of his shots went right between the eyes.

Fucking showoff.

The smoke began to dissipate. The four stone-cold killers got, well, colder. After a minute of no further incursions and no sign that anyone else was on the way, August pulled off his gas mask and said, "Huh. Is that really it?"

"It seems so." Ricardo took off his mask as well and frowned at the bodies. "It doesn't seem like enough."

"I agree." Where was Matt, after all? Where was the Madame? August hadn't expected them to be up here, certainly not in the first wave, but they ought to be seeing *some* sign of these guys being missed. Yet there was nothing. Complete silence. "Do you think—"

"Guys, we've got trouble!"

That was Eve. August let Ricardo take the lead on talking to her as he ran around repacking their gear.

"What's going on?"

"We got the girls to the SUV, but someone must have recognized them, because we're taking fire from two guys by the main elevators. One of them's Matt," she added angrily.

"Drive out of there—"

"We can't, someone else is blocking us with a car! We

can't get past them! There aren't any civilians down here yet, but I don't know how long that's going to last."

"We're coming." Ricardo stowed his gun and grabbed one of the bags. "Hang in there. We're on our way." He headed for the elevator, but August pulled him back.

"We should split up. You take the stairs."

Ricardo narrowed his eyes for a second, then nodded. "I'll be slower," he warned. "They'll have easy access to you."

"The private elevator is more shielded than coming out right behind them in the other one, I'll be fine," August scoffed. "Besides, better them firing at me than at the girls." He didn't bother mentioning that there was no way his feet could tolerate running down thirty flights of stairs. He'd be crawling by the time he got to the bottom.

"I'll handle the car," Ricardo said after a second, then pulled August into a hard, fast kiss, the kind that left him breathless and wanting. "Be careful."

"I will." That was the best he could offer. Ricardo nodded, then took off down the stairs.

August took a deep breath, then shouldered both the bags and walked over to the elevator, careful to step around the blood stains that were still spreading out across the carpeted floor. He got inside and pressed the button for the parking garage, then waited. The doors closed, and canned saxophone music came on as he headed down.

August shook his head at his reflection. "Ridiculous," he muttered, adjusting one of the bags. There was a camera in this elevator... He wondered if it was still recording, or if the helpful manager had turned it off so no one would see they'd just aided and abetted people trying to kill four innocent teenagers. "Fucking ridiculous."

He wondered how fast Ricardo was taking those stairs,

whether he was still running down them or if he'd resorted to jumping entire floors yet. How his knees were still so functional at his age was a mystery...

Ding. He'd arrived at the parking level. August moved in sync with the left sliding door as it opened, keeping the cover for as long as possible, but—

Bangbang!

Yep, they already knew their guys were dead. Probably missed some sort of check-in. Greeeeeeat. The mirrored panel behind him shattered as August ducked down, then fired back at the guy who was targeting him.

Who was Matt.

Motherfucker.

It would be bad form for either of them to kill the other right now, especially since Matt still thought August was FBI. Still, the temptation to take the shot was intense...but if he missed, Matt would almost definitely retaliate, and a guy who'd trained with Ricardo wasn't someone August wanted to be on the wrong end of a gun with. At least he wasn't still firing at the SUV, although the other guy was using a goddamn P-90 on the poor thing. Armored or not, that left a mark—the windows weren't going to hold much longer.

There wasn't enough room behind the SUV for them to get up the speed to make a dent in the car holding them in place, either, which...that was the Madame driving? That was more hands-on than they'd anticipated she would be.

And where the fuck was Ricardo?

August's question was answered about four seconds later when all of a sudden, his own 1964 Aston Martin DB5—driven by Ricardo, no less—crashed headlong into the car behind the SUV. It sent the car rocking violently to the side, the Madame's head snapping so hard against the side window that it looked like she'd been knocked out.

Elodie—and August was sure his sister was driving, she was worse about letting other people drive than August was—rammed the SUV into reverse and smashed the car further back. Then Ricardo hit it again. Then Elodie, and then—they were free.

And Mr. P-90 had a new target.

He got exactly one shot off at Ricardo in the Aston Martin before August fired at him. It wasn't his bullet that took the guy out, though.

It was Eve's.

Her window was shattered from the inside out—she'd smashed through it somehow, and was leaning out with the intent expression of a person with a goal, gun in hand. *Bang bang bang*, and the target was down.

August had never found a woman so sexy before.

Elodie gunned it out of the parking garage, and August took the opportunity to walk briskly over to Matt, who looked shocked—absolutely dumbfounded. He turned to August, mouth gaping, and August smiled and said, "We'll talk soon, Mr. Ashford! Don't call me, I'll call you," before knocking him down and dazed with an elbow to the temple.

That's more like it.

August ran back for their bags, then to the wrinkled but running Aston Martin. As Ricardo gunned the engine and guided them up the ramp and out into the evening sunset, August snapped, "You killed James Bond's ride, you're dead to me.".

"Do you think Matt saw Eve?"

The rapid subject change made August's brain skip a beat. "What?"

"Do you think he saw Eve? When she took that shot, before they drove away?"

"I..." August wanted to say no, but... he recalled the

dumbfounded look on Matt's face just before he stunned him with an elbow. "I'm... not sure. Do you think he did?"

"I think if he did, we're in a shit-ton of trouble. You left him alive, right?"

"Yeah," August said a little grimly, wishing like hell he hadn't. "I did."

"Then if he recognized Eve, you'd better bet he's going to be out for blood. If he knows—"

August's phone rang. His Agent Thomas phone. And since Ricardo wasn't calling him, and the only other person who had that number was Matt...

"Shit. He knows."

CHAPTER 17

August put the call on speaker. "Mr. Ashford, how's your—"

"Someone needs to tell me what the ever-loving fuck is going on," Matt snarled in a voice that raised the hairs on Ricardo's neck. "What was that whore doing with you?"

August's eyes went to Ricardo and he put up his finger as if to say, *"Shut your mouth and let me talk."*

Ricardo hadn't even realized he'd been about to verbally eviscerate his old spotter until August stopped him. He closed his mouth, clenching his teeth painfully tight and gripping the steering wheel so hard it was a miracle it didn't snap off, and he let August do the talking.

Voice calm, borderline patronizing, August said, "Mr. Ashford, I'm not sure I know what you're talking about."

"The woman! That bitch with the red ponytail! You've got Torralba working with you, so you know exactly who—"

"Red? Ponytail?" August asked stupidly. "What are you talking about? There's no one in our crew who looks like—"

"Don't fuck with me!" Matt barked. "I saw her! I fucking saw her!"

"Mr. Ashford, the only woman in our crew was Natalie, the blonde."

Ricardo cocked his head, but when August said "blonde," he realized he was talking about Elodie.

"There was no one else in the crew," August went on.

"I. Saw. Her." Matt was fuming now, his rage coming through the phone so clearly it was almost visible to the naked eye. "Don't try to gaslight me, you son of a bitch. I know Torralba never got over her, and I know what I saw in—"

"Have you seen a doctor yet for that concussion?"

"Concussion?" Matt sputtered. "Concuss—What? I don't have—"

"Oh, I beg to differ," August said with a condescending laugh. "You were punched hard enough to be knocked unconscious. If you don't have a concussion, might I suggest buying a couple of Powerball tickets?"

Matt made one of those infuriated noises that meant he was close to losing his temper and breaking something. "For fuck's sake! I—"

"Listen," August pressed on. "We're not going to leave you high and dry after your help with the op. Give me your location, and we can either have an ambulance sent to you, or we can come collect you and take you to the nearest emergency room."

Ricardo's jaw fell open. They were going to what now? If they picked up Matt, Matt was going to start shooting at them, assuming Ricardo gave him the chance before he blew his head off just for spite.

August made a *"calm your tits, I've got this"* gesture. "We owe you that much, honestly. A CT scan just to make sure there's no lasting damage. After all, my partner did hit you pretty hard, and now you're potentially hallucinating."

"*I am not hallucinating!*" Matt bellowed. "I saw Eve. I saw her. You're working with Torralba, and now you've got that fucking whore on your payroll, so someone needs to tell me what's going on."

Much more of this, and Ricardo was going to snatch the phone, reach through it, and rip Matt a new one. It wasn't out of possessiveness over Eve. Ricardo just didn't tolerate disrespect toward the people he loved. Well, except for August, but he usually deserved it.

What Ricardo couldn't do right now was read Matt the riot act. Not without fucking up their entire op, and this op wasn't over yet. There were pieces in motion right now, and if anything interfered with them getting to their destinations, the results could be disastrous. Until he had confirmation that all the girls and their families had been safely secreted away into witness protection, he had to tread carefully.

Which meant letting August take point.

Which meant keeping his trap shut no matter how badly he wanted to give Matt anatomical instructions for where he could shove his bullshit.

So he did the next best thing: he pulled over and got out of the battered car.

They were on a side street now, far from the Coleman Hotel. The team's other vehicles were long gone in a completely different direction. No one who saw him or August now would have anything to do with the op, the human trafficking ring, or even law enforcement. Worst case, a cop might happen by and suggest that they move along instead of loitering, though some hyper-rich *"Do you know who I am?"* from August would probably encourage the cop to be the one moving along.

While August stayed in the car and continued trying to

talk Matt down, Ricardo paced outside the car, fists balled at his sides as he seethed with fury. In his mind, he saw himself punching Matt several more times in the room at the Coleman. Even now, his hand hurt from the blow that had knocked Matt cold, but he'd have happily endured some fractures in the name of relieving Matt of most of his adult teeth and maybe an orbital bone.

He didn't know when Matt had turned into this monster of a man, or if he'd always been this way, but Ricardo had had enough. More than ever, he regretted not taking the opportunity to end Matt's reign of terror via some accidental friendly fire. Then Matt wouldn't have lived long enough to murder more innocent local nationals. He would never have dated and abused Eve.

On the other hand, this human trafficking ring would have continued on its merry way without August or Ricardo ever finding out about it by way of trying to fuck up Eve's asshole ex. God, what kind of messed-up, butterfly-effect-meets-trolley-problem, "you could've saved these people but then all these people would've suffered" horseshit was this? And what did it say about Matt that every option on the "does Matt live or die?" flow chart resulted in more people suffering?

Ricardo wiped a hand over his face and swore in almost every language he spoke. He didn't know what future fuckery awaited if Matt was allowed to live long enough. What other crimes he'd lead them to so lives could be saved and evil people could be put away. He also didn't know how many more innocent people would suffer or die as a direct result of Matt continuing to consume oxygen and wreak havoc.

Absently kneading the butt of the pistol on his hip, Ricardo ground his teeth and vowed that Matt was a dead man. Enough was enough. Especially since, if the fury in that phone call was anything to go by, Matt was going to get back at Eve for her involvement in this op, and Ricardo wasn't about to wait and see how that revenge would play out. If the choice was Eve or Matt, then he didn't even need to think about it.

I don't know if you're still Catholic, Sandman, but if you are, might I suggest visiting with a priest sooner than later?

The car door opened, and Ricardo turned.

August stepped out, expression unusually—and unnervingly—serious. "He's threatening to blow the entire op."

"How can he?" Ricardo growled. "He doesn't know where the girls are." At least that much they could be sure of; while there was always a certain amount of danger when assets were in motion, Matt's knowledge of their whereabouts or destination was deliberately limited.

"No." August folded his arms and shifted his weight. "But he's in scorched earth mode. Like he's fucking lost it."

Ricardo arched an eyebrow. "More than he already had?"

August nodded. "I don't know if you really rang his bell, or if he's just that butthurt over realizing Eve is working with us, but he's out for blood, and he doesn't care who gets fucked over." Exhaling, he ran a hand through his hair, letting the fatigue show for the first time. "Honestly, from the way he's ranting, he's going to turn loose anyone he thinks will make our lives hell, and he's going to murder anyone who gets between him and getting his hands on Eve. Literally."

Ricardo's teeth snapped shut. "He lays a hand on her, I'll rip him to pieces."

"Oh, you won't be alone. Assuming there's anything left of him once Eve rips into him, I'll be right there with you."

August scowled. "But Eve isn't bulletproof. And we need to keep that in mind, because I get the feeling he will happily take advantage of it."

A shudder went through Ricardo so violently, it almost made him physically sick. No one knew better than him how brutal Matt was, or how willing he was to draw blood from someone who'd crossed him or even looked at him the wrong way. He'd grudgingly and suspiciously accepted Ricardo's role, but Eve? Now he knew *something* was up, and he probably didn't give a damn what that something was at this point. He just knew he'd been duped, and he didn't take humiliation lightly.

"I gotta know," August said. "How unstable is this guy? I mean, I know he's a lunatic, but how much of this is talk, how much of it is the concussion, and how much of it is 'madman with a gun makes headline news'?"

Ricardo sighed. "The concussion is probably the only thing working to our advantage. It'll slow his reflexes and concentration. But trust me, this isn't the concussion talking."

"Shit."

"Uh-huh."

"Well, you know him better than I do. What do you suggest?"

Ricardo thought about it. "What all did he say?"

August took a deep breath as he leaned against the car. "Mostly that he's going to kill you and... I mean, the shit he said about Eve doesn't bear repeating, but I'd say we'd be wise to keep those two apart."

"He's not getting to her except through me," Ricardo said on a low growl.

"I know." August came closer and put his hands on Ricardo's chest. "That's exactly what I'm afraid of."

The candor startled Ricardo. "What?"

"Look, he was your spotter, so the two of you were close. All that insight you have on him? I guarantee he's got plenty on you, and any idiot knows you are murderously protective of the people you love, even when they're perfectly capable of taking care of themselves. Which means the easiest way for him to get to Eve is to rile you up enough to try to protect her." He slid his hands up and wrapped his arms around Ricardo's neck, looking him right in the eyes. "That's not a weakness, okay? But Matt is going to exploit it like one, and if you don't tread carefully, you're going to basically be his spotter while he snipes Eve."

Ricardo blinked.

"We have to play this smart," August continued. "Which means we need to get Eve as far away from you as possible until we've handled Matt and any of his cronies who might try to take her out."

Ricardo closed his eyes and exhaled. Early on, he'd hated it when August was right because that meant... Well, it meant that August was right, and that usually meant he was insufferable too. But this time the issue was that August had seen right through to Ricardo's willingness to play human shield if it meant keeping Eve safe from that psychopath. Ricardo himself hadn't even realized it, but August did, and... Fuck. What could he say? It wasn't that he thought Eve was a damsel in distress who needed a valiant male protector—she'd remove his testicles with her mind if he ever even entertained the idea —but Matt was dangerous, and helping to keep her safe would be a lot easier if he could see her and provide cover fire.

But August was—damn him—right. Matt knew Ricardo was fiercely protective of the people he loved, and he'd absolutely exploit that to get to Eve.

Looking at August again, Ricardo pushed out a resigned sigh. "So what do we do?"

Arms still resting on Ricardo's shoulders, August held his gaze. "Step one, we convince Eve to get the hell out of Dodge. It would probably be best if even we don't know where she's going."

Ricardo nodded silently.

"Step two..." August's voice hardened. "We make sure Matt isn't anyone's problem anymore. Ever."

Ricardo raised his eyebrows. "What do you suggest?"

"Murder," August said casually.

With an exasperated sigh, Ricardo glared at him. "No shit. More specifically."

"Don't know." August shrugged. "At first I thought we should get him sent to prison and let the general population find out about his crimes, but the thing is, he's a white, decorated war veteran. Quite frankly, I don't want to take chances on the legal system actually doing the right thing and putting him away, never mind where he can get what's coming to him from the other inmates. So. I say we focus on getting Eve someplace... Someplace not here. Then for Mr. Sandman, I say we skip the prison thing, express ship him his just deserts in the form of a well-placed bullet or twelve, and be done with it."

Ricardo couldn't help himself, and he laughed. "I feel like you're looking forward to that second part."

"And you're not?"

"I didn't say that." Ricardo bent and brushed a kiss across August's lips. "All right. Let's get back to the house and start getting Eve out of here."

August grimaced. "How do you think she's going to take that?"

"Well, we might want to do it in a room without anything fragile or expensive in it."

August laughed, but then he sobered. "Wait. Are you joking? I can't tell if you're joking."

Ricardo patted his hip and gently steered him toward the car. "Guess you'll find out, won't you?"

"No, really. Are you serious? Do I need body armor for this?"

"Just get in the car."

"Excuse me?" Eve glared across the living room at Ricardo. "You want me to, what, just go hide somewhere?" She stood straighter, setting her jaw. "I am not one of those little girls, Ricardo. I am not going to be sent into hiding while—"

"Eve." Ricardo put up his hands. "You're not a little girl, but you *are* a target. Matt saw you tonight, and he's pissed."

"So the fuck what?" She folded her arms, her narrowed eyes flicking back and forth between August and Ricardo. "I'm just supposed to go hide until you convince him to stop being an asshole? Do you think you're going to talk him out of trying to kill me, and then tell me it's okay to come back out? What the hell is your endgame here? Because so help me God, Ricardo Torralba, if you think I'm going into witness protection permanently, I will—"

"We're going to kill him," Ricardo snapped.

Eve stopped mid-syllable. Beside him, August stiffened.

Ricardo exhaled. "We just need you out of the line of fire long enough for us to take care of him. Permanently."

She swallowed. "You're..." She glanced at August. "But that's... You're going to *murder* him?"

Ricardo shrugged stiffly. "Well, we can let him keep selling children, hurting people for money, and terrorizing you. Or I can do what I should have done in the Army before he had a chance to make so many people suffer."

Her lips parted. He understood, and he gave her a moment to let it all sink into her brain. Eve had always had an aversion to violence. She didn't like hearing Ricardo and the guys tell war stories, and the thought of cold-blooded murder—even when it was clearly in the interest of the greater good—couldn't possibly sit well. Just tonight she'd killed someone herself, and he suspected that once she had a chance to process everything, she was going to have an avalanche of emotions about that. There was a reason she'd wanted to be a medic in the Army—she could handle losing someone she'd tried and failed to save, but being the one to actively kill hadn't sat well.

So the thought of August and Ricardo engaging in premeditated murder had to be making her stomach turn. And under normal circumstances, he'd never have told her what they were doing, but it was the only way he could get her to understand how serious this situation was, and how it truly was a matter of either her life or Matt's. At least the thought of not having a front row seat to her ex's death might motivate her to take them up on the offer of getting her the hell out of town.

He and August exchanged glances. August looked dubious, but he hadn't said anything, so presumably he was deferring to Ricardo to know how to handle this one. That, or he was going to be *so* fucking smug later on.

Eve inhaled deeply through her nose and set her shoulders back. "If you want to off him, then what better way to flush him out than to use me as bait?"

"What?" Ricardo stared at her. "No! That's out of the question!"

"Why?" She fixed steely eyes on him. "Am I wrong?"

Ricardo opened his mouth to speak, but August was faster.

"Eve." August looked right at her, his expression placid but his voice firm. "I get it. Honestly. And no one is trying to treat you like a damsel in distress or like you won't be able to take care of yourself. But the fact is, this is what Ricardo and I *do*. And quite frankly, it's a hell of a lot easier to focus on putting bullets in buttholes like your ex when we're not looking over our shoulders to make sure no one's putting bullets in *you*."

Eve scowled but didn't protest.

"I'm going to owe Elodie about a million favors," August went on, "but I can have her get you to my family's private jet, and you can go stay with my parents at their chateau in southern France."

"Southern—" Eve blinked. "A private jet to the south of France? Jesus, Ricardo." She flailed a hand at August. "Why didn't you *lead* with that?"

"Yeah, Ricky." August elbowed him. "Don't bury the lede."

Ricardo groaned and rolled his eyes. At least she wasn't fighting them anymore. To August, he said, "Would you please call your sister and get the ball rolling?"

August smiled sweetly at him—God, he was going to be insufferable for the rest of the night—and chirped, "But of course, darling," before sashaying out of the living room with smugness rolling off him in waves.

He was damn lucky he was cute.

Eve suppressed a giggle. "He must really keep you on your toes."

Ricardo faced her. "You have no idea."

She smiled, but it faded. "Are you guys really sure about this plan?"

"Taking out Matt?"

Shuddering, she nodded.

"I don't see any other alternatives where he stops hurting people."

She swallowed. "What about the rest of the people he was working with? They'll just replace him and keep moving, won't they?"

"In theory." Ricardo smiled. "But we have some... I won't say 'friends,' but some contacts who don't tolerate human trafficking and will be more than happy to put the whole ring out of business."

"Through legal means?"

"Through..." He thought about it. "*Effective* means."

Eve pursed her lips, but after a moment, she sighed, shaking her head and laughing softly. "You know, if I had known about this side of you when we were married, I don't think I'd have been able to handle it. But now..." She trailed off as if she wasn't sure how to finish the thought.

Ricardo stepped closer and put his hands on her shoulders. "That's why I didn't tell you. I didn't tell anyone because I didn't want to go to prison, but I especially kept it from you because I..." He hesitated, and he avoided her eyes as he softly added, "I knew it would change how you looked at me. Letting you think I was a cheater was better than the alternative."

She sighed, and to his surprise, she hugged him. "Trust you to always be trying to protect people who don't want to be protected."

He hugged her back. "You just said you wouldn't have wanted to know."

"Right, but that didn't mean I wanted to believe you were a cheater." She let him go and looked up at him. "Maybe I'm just not wired to be with someone who needs to protect me." With a laugh, she gestured in the direction August had gone. "He doesn't seem to mind."

"Pfft. He used me as a human shield once. Literally." Ricardo huffed. "No, he doesn't mind being protected as long as it's on his terms."

"A human—really?"

Ricardo waved a hand. "Long story."

She snickered. "You'll have to tell me that one someday. But, um..." She motioned toward the stairs. "I should go pack my things. Knowing August and Elodie, that flight is probably going to be sooner than later."

"Probably."

They exchanged awkward smiles, and then Ricardo watched his ex-wife head for the stairs. As much as he despised Matt and everything the asshole had done, he was admittedly grateful for a chance to cross paths with Eve again. They'd put some things to bed that had been eating at him more than he'd realized. Maybe when this was over, they could even be friends going forward. It wasn't like anyone would be able to keep her and Elodie separated, so he hoped they could be friendly.

But he'd deal with that once this was all over. Right now, the wheels were turning to get Eve on a plane and out of Matt's reach. Then there would be nothing left to do but lure Matt out of the shadows—something that wouldn't be difficult when he was so dangerously enraged—and do the world a favor by knocking him off this mortal coil.

That would take some planning. Matt may have been reckless at times, but he wasn't stupid, and he did have as much spec ops training as Ricardo. He probably had a cache of highly illegal and incredibly effective weapons at his disposal as well.

Fortunately, so did Ricardo.

So while August arranged for Eve's expatriation, Ricardo went upstairs to pick out just the right gun for this occasion.

CHAPTER 18

"How can you watch him go off like this and stay so calm?"

August glanced over at Eve, who had her arms crossed over her chest as Ricardo headed down the steep driveway to the front gate in August's custom-armored Range Rover. "Why shouldn't I be calm?" he asked—calmly, because quirky bitch was his resting state.

"Because!" she exclaimed, those arms coming apart so she could throw them up in the air. It had been about twenty-four hours since the showdown at the Coleman, and it was evening now, the sun completely down, and as her adrenaline worked its way out of her system, the fatigue and irritation of a hell of a day was really setting in. That, coupled with packing for a trip to the French Riviera that she wasn't really excited about all so that Ricardo and August could take out her ex-boyfriend, had left her a little tetchy.

She'd made them promise, at least, that if they took Matt out before she left, she wouldn't have to go at all. Ricardo wasn't happy with that, but it seemed fair to

August. "Because what?" he asked, teasing out whatever it was that she didn't want to confront.

"Because he's off to set up a *murder!* And if he doesn't do it right, or things get bad, or you get into trouble doing your part—"

"Hey!" August interrupted in faux-outrage. "My parts always go exactly right, I'll have you know."

If she cocked her head any harder, she'd be a rooster. "That's not what I've heard."

"Ricky is a lying liar who lies," August said blithely. "Trust me, this is the simple part. It's getting here that's hard, and to be perfectly honest—which I hate, so I hope you appreciate this—Ricardo is better at the planning stuff than I am. He's absolutely meticulous, and we've already used this gambit successfully against Matt once, so—"

"But that's part of why I'm worried," Eve said. "You're planning to meet him in an hour in a remote location so you can 'talk it out,' but doing that last time went badly for him, didn't it? And now he knows you're working with Ricardo, so why would he feel comfortable doing it again?"

"Because he doesn't have a choice." August had been quite clear about that in his Agent Thomas persona. "As angry as Matt is, as vengeful as he might be, the one thing that's even more pressing right now is his need for safety. Because shit is heating up out there between the Vaccaros and Cavalcantes, and the Madame is in *actual* federal custody, and you'd better believe she's singing like a bird in interrogation to save her own skin. There's no chance of salvaging his relationship with the Vaccaros, so his best option is to work with me."

"He must be thrilled," she mused.

"Oh, he is." He'd left no doubt in August's mind, certainly, if the number of swear words flung his way—in three languages, no less—was any indication. "I'd be more surprised if he wasn't viciously upset at me and Ricardo and life in general, but he's not suicidal. He can't go home and he can't seek help through his regular avenues, so he's got to work with me."

Eve sighed. She looked tired, the way she had when she first got here—dark circles under her eyes, tightness in the line of her mouth, none of the relaxed and fun-loving lady that had emerged as she'd started to feel safe. August hated it—it made him feel like they were going backward, and that wasn't the way you wanted to go when you were this close to the finish line.

"I hope you're right," she said.

"Self-interest wins ninety-nine times out of a hundred." He squeezed her shoulder gently. "I promise you. And nobody knows how to get the job done better than Ricardo. He's going to be fine."

"I feel a little like an idiot," she confessed. "That he managed to hide such a big part of himself from me. I bought that he was a *cheater*, for fuck's sake, when he'd never given me any real reason to believe he was unfaithful. And then I went and fell for a man I *knew* was bad news, but I didn't want to believe that either."

"Ricardo is a surprisingly good actor when he bothers to put in an effort," August said. "Believe me, I know."

"I'm sure you do."

August decided it was time to redirect the conversation. "So, I'll give him half an hour's head start, then I'll head out. Elodie and her people should be here half an hour after that to take you to the airport, and she's got all the codes, so you don't have to worry about letting her in, but let's go over the safety protocols one more time just in case."

Eve took a deep breath, then nodded briskly. "All right."

"First off, no one should make it through the gate who doesn't have the proper code and isn't in the facial recognition system. If they keep trying despite that, the alarm goes off. If they try to bypass the gate and get caught on camera —" which they would, because August had a movie studio's worth of cameras out there "—the alarm goes off. If the alarm goes off, you..."

"Get into your suite and lock it down."

"Perfect." August had already added her palmprint to the security system, so it shouldn't be a problem, but she knew the backup codes for the inside of the house if it didn't work for some reason. "If someone shoots at the house, you don't even have to worry, because anything that isn't a rocket launcher won't make it through the glass. The alarm will go off, then same scenario."

"Right."

"If someone tries to jump your car once you're off the premises with my sister and her bodyguards, well." August grinned. "I feel really, really sorry for them, because Elodie has some of the best personal security operatives in the western hemisphere, and they are very, very angry at us right now." The head of his sister's bodyguards had spent a good fifteen minutes haranguing August after he learned about the stunt they'd pulled at the hotel. He'd told the man to talk to Elodie about it instead, and his exact words had been: *"She can fire me. You can't. Stop being a goddamn dumbass, you little shit."*

"And angry is good?" Eve was trying to sound skeptical, he could tell, but she mostly just sounded amused now. *Score.*

"Yes, because it sharpens their edges. Some people get sloppy—these people just get better." Honestly, if Ricardo didn't already have that sexy intimidation factor going,

August would consider seducing the head of his sister's security just to get being manhandled by someone out of his system. "It's all going to be fine," he promised. "Really. By this time tomorrow, you'll be sipping your cocktail of choice in the south of France, and Ricardo and I will be—"

"TMI, I don't need to hear the rest," Eve said with a grin. "I think I can imagine it if I need to, thanks."

"You can imagine me watching trashy reality television shows and binging on gourmet popcorn?" Because that was *one* of his comedown rituals from jobs, the most G-rated one and, in some ways, the most fun. A lot of the other did involve, well, *coming* as part of the comedown, but Eve didn't need to know that.

"Popcorn, really?"

"Really! It's so good, let me get you some." All the better to keep her distracted for another twenty-five minutes before he was due to leave.

When August finally got into the Beamer—his "Agent Thomas" car—he was feeling pretty good about himself. He'd chatted Eve into a downright bubbly state before he left, his sister would be here to get her in an hour, and an hour after that at most and the world would be a better place for everyone in it. Ricardo had texted that he was in position, and as soon as August and Matt got to the location, well...it would be game over.

Not a second too soon, as far as he was concerned.

August opened the garage door and drove out into the light of the setting sun, silently promising his Jaguar that he would take it for a spin as soon as this job was over. He sang along softly to Huey Lewis's *Working For A Living* as he headed down the hill toward his gate. Just as he got to the part about being damned—

Glass. Glass surrounding him, flying into his face, a

hundred cuts opening up in less than a second. August swung the wheel hard to the left as he squeezed his eyes shut, but it was too late to protect himself completely—his eyelids felt gritty as he closed them.

Bump, bump—smash! The car ran into the decorative, three-foot tall marble wall he'd had installed to provide visitors with a nice spot to sit and admire the landscaping from. Not that he could do any admiring right now, since he had fucking *glass* in his fucking *eyes*.

Fucking great.

Eyes still closed, August unbuckled his seat belt, slid the chair back as far as it would go, and hunkered down behind the engine block. Not a second too soon—the driver's side headrest seemed to explode a moment later, rattling the entire seat.

Water, water, where's the water? He kept water in all of his cars in case he had to rinse off certain kinds of irritant (*not* pepper spray, he'd learned the hard way) or... His fumbling fingers found the thick plastic bottle, and after forcing his shaking fingers to cooperate, because screw adrenaline dumps, he poured it over his face, rinsing off as many of the shards as he could.

August blinked his eyes open carefully, but closed them again almost as fast. There was definitely more than one piece in there, and the more he moved his eyelids, the worse it felt. Hopefully none of them did permanent damage.

A pain in his right foot was suddenly catching up to him, too. He reached down to feel his foot, then swore as they encountered a bulge in the leather vamp that was positively agonizing. At least one of the pins holding it together had likely been dislodged when he hit the wall.

"It's fine." Hearing his own voice was as reassuring as things could get when he couldn't have Ricardo do the reassuring. "You're fine. Got the engine block and the wall between you and a shooter, so all you have to do is call for backup and you'll be able to wait them out." *Them*, ha-fucking-ha; this was Matt. August was sure of it. There was no one else he'd pissed off this badly in the past few weeks.

"Okay, call. Call him. Phone, phone, where's my—"

August's world was suddenly rocked with sound as a chunk of the marble wall in front of him shattered into dust. The shots came fast and fierce, and all August could do was crouch there and listen to the destruction until his marble wall was gone and the bullets were hitting his engine block. They were doing a decent job of penetrating it too, if the shrieking metal and shuddering frame were anything to go by.

Matt didn't need to come any closer to shell him like a pea. He had to be using armor-piercing rounds. No wonder he'd gotten through the reinforced windshield like it was nothing.

"Fuck." If August got out of the car, he'd be shot and, well, basically exploded at this range. If he stayed in the car, he'd be shot and peppered with a bunch of engine fragments for good measure, just in case he had delusions of leaving behind a good-looking corpse. "Fuck, *fuck*."

No, there had to be a way out of this. Some way to distract Matt, get him looking somewhere else, while August crawled to safety—thank God he hadn't armed the landmines, given his current mobility. If he could just find his goddamn *phone*, he could probably muddle his way through getting into the security settings and activating the floodlights, which would blind Matt for long enough to—

A sudden onslaught of light filled his car, visible even through his closed eyes. That much light ought to come with a complimentary traumatic brain injury, it hurt so much to look at.

Ah. Eve already found the floodlights. Awesome.

August had installed them with the idea that they'd be an effective deterrent for an attacker, illuminating the grounds and making it impossible to focus on anything inside the house.

Check-goddamn-check.

Now to make use of the distraction and get to the nearest entrance to the tunnels beneath the house, because there was no way he was going to make it up the hill with his foot all fucked up. August wrenched his door open, shifted to the left, and—

Blam-blam-blam!

The car rocked with the impact of multiple shots. They weren't as carefully aimed as the first ones had been, but Matt definitely still knew where he was. The light was a help, but August was still no better than a sitting duck out here. Matt would get lucky sooner or later, and then—

Blam!

One of the rounds finally got through the engine, sending a shower of foam into the air as it tore the passenger seat apart.

Make that sooner.

August crawled out of the car and onto the ground. He was still protected by the wall this way, and less than five hundred feet from a way into the tunnels. It was a long way in his current state, especially since he was literally going to have to make his way blind. He wasn't going to be getting any help, so he'd better get his ass in gear.

He crawled about five feet, using the wall as a guide, before he heard a telltale whistle, and then—

Cracking, breaking. The smell of fire. It had to be an

explosion, followed by the groan of a falling tree and someone shouting bloody murder. August flattened out and covered his head as debris from his front fence rained down around him.

Auditory hallucinations, maybe? Or I really did get a concussion, because that had to be an RPG to the rescue. Is it my birthday? Have I died and gone to heaven?

"Get the fuck up!"

Nope, that wasn't the voice of an angel. "Get up!" Eve shook his shoulder. "I didn't manage a direct hit on Matt, so if he still has two feet, he'll be here soon."

This was bad. "You aren't supposed to be outside."

"Oh, you would rather I stand around inside and watch my ex murder you in your own front yard? When you had a goddamn RPG right there in your fucking death closet?"

"Ricardo will be angry." Eve was supposed to stay protected. She didn't like violence, even though she seemed pretty damn good at it—she was supposed to stay *inside*, God damn it.

"Fuck that! You don't tell me what to do, and he can be angry all he wants later!"

"Oh shit, did I say that out loud?" *Definitely* a head injury. Screw it—she was here now, he might as well make the most of it. "Help me up." He held out his arm and let her pull him to his feet. When she tried to tow him along behind her, though, he let out a manly shout of pain.

Eve was back by his side in a second, slinging his arm around her shoulders. "Status," she barked as she guided them both back to the ground.

"Useless right foot, possible concussion, and I also can't see anything," August admitted.

"Shit."

"Yeah." He pointed in what he hoped was the right

direction. "At the end of the wall is a gardener's shed. Inside the shed is a trapdoor that leads into the house's tunnel network."

"Okay." He could feel her nodding. "Okay, yeah, doable. Can we get into the shed?"

"Easily."

"Great. Can we get into the tunnels?"

Ah. "Um, it's biometrically locked."

Eve made an impatient noise. "Okay, well, you've still got two hands, so—"

"It's got a retinal scan, too."

She went still for a moment, then groaned. "August, seriously?"

"It's a solid security measure!" he protested, shifting his weight farther from his right side. His ankle was aching now too. Brilliant.

"All right, well, since you keyed me into the house security system, can we use my retina?"

"Afraid not." Once someone was already in his house, making them use a retinal scan just seemed over-the-top.

Never again. Everybody is scanning in after this.

Eve very gently touched his face, wiping away the liquid warmth gathering in the corner of his eyes. Not water, not tears. He could smell the difference between tears and blood. "Do you think you could even use it?"

"I won't know until I try." It seemed like the only option at this point.

"Okay." She blew out a heavy breath. "Give me your gun."

He handed over his Glock with the best smile he could muster. "What, you didn't want to feel me up to get it?"

"I'm not an asshole who gets off by hitting on my ex's boyfriend, so no. Now, we should—"

"YOU MOTHERFUCKERS!"

"Shit." All of a sudden, Eve had August upright again, one arm firmly around his waist as she towed them toward the shed. "He can't see us yet, I don't think, but we need to go faster."

August nodded and gritted his teeth. He had an impulse—a terrible, ridiculous impulse—to tell her to go, to leave him and run. He'd made an art out of self-centeredness, but he wasn't about to sacrifice the well-being of someone he cared about by acting like an anchor. Eve fell into that "caring" category, and now that he was useless, it felt wrong to make her risk herself for his sake. She might kill him herself if he said it out loud, though, so he kept his mouth shut and tried to hop along as fast as he could.

"Eve! *Agent!* Ha, you think you can kill me? Think I'm gonna go down like a helpless little civilian?"

"Sounds like he would know," August muttered. They had to have gone halfway by now. Five hundred feet wasn't *that* far.

"Probably. Come on, we've got to move faster." She picked up the pace and he did his best to match her, to help her as much as he could. He didn't know exactly where Matt was, but he was undoubtedly armed, and the second he caught sight of them, they were dead.

"Almost there," she gasped. "Almost there..." They finally came to a stop.

"Great!" God, who knew holding still could feel so good? "Now shoot the lock."

"I thought you said this would be easy to get into!"

"That is easy!"

"Oh, for Christ's sake." She adjusted her grip on him to get a better grip on the gun, then—

Blam!

That...was not their gun. That was Matt's gun, and he'd just fired dangerously close to them. "Now, Eve!"

She let off one round. Metal clanked, a hinge creaked, and then they were inside the shed. She slammed the door shut.

Matt proceeded to blow half the roof off, from the sound of it. They both ducked down instinctively, and August nearly choked keeping himself from screaming as his right foot tried to bear weight.

Eve settled August against the ground. "Where's the door, where's the door..."

"Move the weed whacker," he advised. "It's okay, we have some time."

"How do you figure that, genius?" she snapped. "And why do you even *have* a weed whacker? You don't do any of this maintenance yourself!"

August wasn't about to get into the complexities of his lawn care program right now. "We have time because he hasn't shot the shed to pieces yet. He must be low on ammunition."

He heard her mutter something about "small fucking favors" before she said, "Ha!" She swept something aside, then took August's hand and led him over to the door. "Okay, here's the scanner for your palm print." She set his right hand on a piece of cool, smooth glass. The computer acknowledged him with a small beep. "Now the retinal scan...right here." She positioned his face right above what he assumed was the camera. "Quick, okay?"

"Okay." August bit his lip to help distract him from the pain in his eyes as he slowly pried his left eyelid open. His vision was practically nonexistent, blood and tears obscuring everything, but he thought he saw the green light of the retinal scan.

The computer declined.

"Try again," Eve urged. He tried again. Same result. "Try the other side!"

Ugh, his right eye felt worse than his left. Still, it was their only shot. He forced his eye to open, stared blearily in the right direction and hoped for a damn miracle, because—

The computer accepted him. The interior locks came undone. "Oh, thank God," Eve said, twisting the handle and flinging open the door. "Come on, you go—"

"You first." August wasn't going to budge on that. "You can help me down after."

"*Fine.*" She lowered herself into the tunnel, and he carefully crawled after her, limping down each step with his good foot. It wasn't until he got to the bottom that he realized he'd forgotten to shut the door.

"Shit, I have to—"

"No, no, I'll get it," Eve said. She started up the ladder, then froze.

The door to the shed was opening.

Matt was here.

CHAPTER 19

It was just Ricardo's luck that he didn't attract a single cop's attention. For all those times he'd been mistaken for an illegal immigrant, a Middle Eastern terrorist, or whatever else a white supremacist with a badge could dream up... For all those times he'd been pulled over just for being foreign while driving...

No one noticed him this time.

Maybe it was because he was in a fancy-ass Range Rover with tinted windows, and since the cops couldn't see who was driving, they just assumed he was a rich and undoubtedly white guy on his way to something important.

The one goddamned time he could have benefitted from a few cops on his tail, because God knew they could use all the reinforcements they could get against Matt, there wasn't a blue light in sight. Not that there was any guarantee the cops would suddenly join his side when they reached what was undoubtedly the warzone, but it was a risk he was willing to take if it meant keeping August and Eve safe.

He gripped the wheel tighter with sweaty hands. Eve's uncharacteristically panicked words kept echoing in his head: *"Matt's here, and August is down. Shit, I have to get him inside."* Then the phone had gone dead.

He had no idea what "August is down" meant. The fact that she'd needed to get him inside said he was probably alive, but for how long? "Down" could mean anything from a turned ankle to multiple gunshots wounds, and Ricardo knew Eve too well to think she'd freak out like this over a turned ankle. She was, after all, a trained combat medic. And he knew Matt too well to think a turned ankle was the extent of what he'd do to August.

There was no telling what he was driving into, only that it was bad. Really, really bad. And two of the people he cared about most in the world were right in the middle of it.

Ricardo's heart pounded harder and harder, and literally the only thing stopping him from pulling over and getting violently ill was that he didn't dare do anything that would keep him away from his boyfriend and ex-wife. If he had anything to say about it, he'd hold out long enough to puke all over Matt's cooling corpse. It would be a fitting sendoff for that son of a bitch.

By the time he pulled onto the street where he and August lived, the acid was burning in his throat and the fear was coursing through him like ice water. In the past ten minutes, he'd tried to call Eve. No answer. A second time. No answer.

Sandman, you'd better hope those two are still alive, or I will drag you to hell myself.

The front gate was open. That wasn't a good sign.

Though he'd been a lapsed Catholic for a long time, Ricardo was taking no chances, and he crossed himself as he pulled through the gate.

The Range Rover had barely started up the driveway before a hail of gunfire peppered the windshield. Fortunately, August had insisted that Ricardo take his most reinforced and bulletproof vehicle, and the bullets only succeeded in startling the shit out of Ricardo and leaving harmless little pockmarks in the Plexiglas.

He kept driving.

A gunman stepped out and fired at the grill. Then at the tires.

Ricardo accelerated and swerved.

The Range Rover—including its tires—was built to withstand gunfire. The gunman, however, was not built to withstand a speeding Range Rover. Neither was his buddy.

Ricardo was flying toward the house before either of them had finished crumpling against the landscaping. Even if they were alive—and that was highly unlikely—*neither* was getting up any time soon.

The Range Rover crested the top of the driveway, and renewed horror drove a string of both Catalan profanity and Catholic pleas for divine intervention from Ricardo's lips.

The Beamer was destroyed, its smoldering corpse eerily reminiscent of when Matt had laid waste to an "insurgent's" Jeep, leaving its occupants in a similar state.

"August is down," Eve had said. *"Shit, I have to get him inside."*

Ricardo's stomach turned.

Whatever condition August was in, it wasn't a turned ankle that had taken him down.

Ricardo stopped beside the car and cracked the window so he could hear any activity. The property was eerily silent aside from what sounded like some distant moaning. That came from behind him. Probably one of the men he'd hit with the Range Rover.

Otherwise...nothing.

On his phone, he pulled up the various cameras and checked the house. Nothing. No one. Still nothing. Nope. Undisturbed.

But when he tried to look at the next camera, the app lagged. In fact, it stalled completely. He tried reloading, but now none of the cameras would show.

Damn it. Matt or one of his goons must have found a way to jam them or... Or something. Whatever the case, Ricardo didn't have camera access now. He was flying blind, and he had to work with it.

He quickly ran through his options. There was no telling where Matt, Eve, or August were, or how many more goons Matt had brought along for the occasion. Ricardo knew for a fact that Matt had learned a thing or two after being buddy-buddy with the team's demolitions expert for a while before the demo guy had realized that maybe teaching Sandman how to build IEDs and pipe bombs was a bad idea. So anything could be rigged with explosives, from the garage doors to August's motorcycles.

If he stepped out of the car out here, he could easily be taken out by a waiting sniper. That was what Ricardo would have done if he'd been in Matt's position—find a perch and wait. It was what he'd *been* doing when Matt had apparently showed up here and—

Focus. Beat yourself up later.

Ricardo took a deep breath, and he shifted his gaze to the garage, which looked unnervingly empty without the Range Rover or the now-destroyed Beamer. If he pulled in there and shut the door, he risked drawing attention to himself, not to mention setting off charges, but the Range Rover would provide some protection from a blast. It was his best bet right now. Then he'd get in the house, and he'd assess his options as he went. Either hunt down Matt or help Eve and August—whichever he could get to first. If August and Eve were smart (and they were), they were in the tunnels August had installed to escape if his house were ever attacked. Hopefully they'd sealed themselves inside, keeping Matt out with the biometric entry points, and then he and Ricardo could face off.

He glanced around, then eased into the garage.

It was empty aside from August's various vehicles. In the vacant spot where August's car had been, there was what looked like a manhole cover, except it was welded in place now. August had decided after their narrow escape a lifetime ago that the entry point in the garage was too easy for a hostile to enter and not at all safe as an exit point, since it could be easily surrounded. He'd sealed it off and had the tunnel extended to the shed behind the house.

Goddammit. Ricardo could have used that entry right now.

Well, he couldn't change what he had to work with. He parked the Range Rover, shut off the engine, and unbuckled his seat belt. Then he pressed the button on the visor for the garage door, and he instinctively flinched, expecting something to explode.

It didn't. The door came down. In under twenty seconds, it stopped, cutting off the outside world.

The door, much like the Range Rover and most of the house, was reinforced to hell and back. Nobody was slamming a car through it like August had when they'd escaped Victor's compound.

Ricardo waited for a few seconds, listening through the cracked window, but there was just silence apart from the steady hum of the air conditioner doing its thing in the background as if the house hadn't become a warzone. Again.

He opened the driver side door. Waited. Nothing. No one.

For long seconds, he watched the side mirror, waiting for a stealthy hostile to sneak up on his quarter panel.

Still nothing. Still no one.

And the longer he waited here, the more time someone had to notice him and do something about it, so it was time to move. He moved into the backseat. There, he slung his rifle onto his back and double-checked his pistols were securely holstered—one on his thigh and the other under his arm. He needed to be able to hear, so he pushed in a pair of earplugs. Though they'd muffle his hearing, they'd protect him from the deafening gunfire, and he could take a plug out and listen without waiting for his ears to stop ringing. It wasn't ideal, but nothing about this was.

Still safely in the Range Rover, he texted Eve again: *I'm here. Where are you?*

Then he pocketed his phone and stepped out through the passenger side backseat door.

In a low crouch, he quickly and silently jogged to the door leading into the kitchen. It was locked, and if he knew August, the whole house was on emergency lockdown—every closed door and window was secured and could only be opened using his elaborate system of biometrics. Fortunately, he'd dragged Ricardo through the tedious process of adding his information, and all it took was a thumbprint on the keypad to unlatch the door.

Ricardo paused to wipe off the keypad, and then he ducked into the kitchen.

He took out one earplug so he could listen as he scanned the room. Nothing in here had been disturbed. There was a cup of coffee on the counter—the blue cup Eve had been using most mornings—with a few drops next to it, as if she'd set it down too hard and some had splashed onto the granite. That raised the hair on Ricardo's neck.

"Oh my God," she'd growled at him a decade ago after he'd left a similar splash on the counter. *"Would it kill you to take two nanoseconds to wipe up a couple of drops?"* He'd had his hands full, and he'd had every intention of coming back after he'd put down the plates and mug he'd been carrying, but she'd swooped in and wiped it up before he'd had a chance to.

He swallowed. Eve had been in here. She'd left in a hurry. Probably when the Beamer had been destroyed outside.

But where the hell were she and August?

A phone buzzed. He instinctively reached for his, but then he realized...it wasn't his.

He looked around.

There.

On the counter nearest the door he'd come through.

His heart dropped. Oh, shit. No wonder she hadn't been picking up.

Did August still have his phone?

And if he texted August, would he give away their position to Matt? At this point, it was a risk he'd have to take. With his heart in his throat, he texted August: *Where are you?*

Then he took stock of his surroundings again. Aside from Eve's phone and coffee, nothing was amiss in here. Standing away from the window, he looked outside.

The shed door was open, the roof partly blown off.

Oh, shit.

On the one hand, that could mean August and Eve were safely in the tunnels. On the other, it could mean they weren't alone.

Putting the earplug back in, he silently cursed whatever Matt had done to the cameras, which kept him from checking on the shed or the tunnels. How the hell was he supposed to get to them?

Then something thumped. Something deep and low, the sound strafing his senses like distant mortar fire. It tripped something instinctive in him—something that understood danger and wanted to engage flight, because fuck fight—and it tried to yank his PTSD up from the depths for good measure.

Ricardo forced himself to focus. He knew there were explosives as part of August's security measures. He'd seen, heard, and felt their effectiveness once before.

The question was, where had it come from, and had it been friendly fire?

On the other side of the yard, smoke started curling out of the shed's open door. Then two men emerged, both coughing and one bleeding from the shoulder.

Ricardo's heart jumped. The first of the two was definitely Matt.

Thinking fast, Ricardo swung his rifle around and lined up a shot. His old spotter had just slipped out of range, but Ricardo dropped the other man, shattering the kitchen window in the process.

Then he hurried out of the kitchen and into the living room, where he pressed himself up against a wall and again took out an earplug to listen. Silence. Fuck.

It had appeared Matt and his goon had taken a hit

during that explosion, so hopefully that meant the source of the blast had been one of August's security measures. That would mean August and Eve had moved to someplace safer. Or, well, they'd made their current location safer by collapsing part of the tunnel or, if nothing else, stunning the shit out of Matt with noise and shrapnel.

The problem was that the tunnel system was so elaborate, Ricardo wasn't sure he could find them if he got into them. The even bigger problem was that the cameras were all dead. There was no guarantee August would be able to see biometric logins on his phone. If he saw someone heavily armed and moving through a tunnel, he might set off a security protocol and make Ricardo one with the dirt and concrete.

He couldn't risk going into one of the tunnels.

Fuck. He couldn't get to Eve and August, wherever they were.

And Matt was still on the move. Possibly making a hasty retreat like the coward he was, but unlikely. Oh, he was a coward, but right now he was a coward scorned, and his ego was way too big for him to back down from taking out those who'd scorned him. Didn't matter if he was outmanned, outgunned, and outmaneuvered. This was the idiot who'd gotten into a fistfight with not one but *three* Spetsnaz guys one night because they'd all been a little drunk and one had made some comments about Matt's mom. Ricardo had later blown one of them in exchange for that serrated knife he still carried, and the man had commented afterward, *"Your idiot friend—he thinks he is invincible giant, yes?"*

Oh, he hadn't been wrong. When someone crossed Matt, there was no reining him back or making him see reason.

Which meant he was rallying. Somewhere on the property right now, either by himself or with whatever men he still had left standing, he was doing the opposite of giving up. Ricardo knew it. He could *feel* it.

And since he couldn't get to August and Eve, his best bet was to neutralize the threat.

A threat that likely couldn't be neutralized by anything short of a bullet to his head.

Ricardo thumbed the trigger guard on his rifle. He'd never felt more compelled to actually write someone's name on a bullet than he did just now, but there wasn't time for that.

All right. Matt had left the shed and headed toward the north end of—

Ricardo's phone vibrated in his pocket. He pulled it out, and August's name lit up the screen. "August? Are you all right? Where are—"

"It's me," Eve said quickly, her voice hushed as if she were trying not to be heard. "Listen, we're in the tunnels. We're... I'm not sure where."

"Can August tell you? Oh, fuck, is he all right? Is he conscious?"

"He's..." She hesitated, which instantly had icicles forming in his blood. "He's conscious, but he can't see."

"He can't..." Ricardo blinked. "Why not? What happened?"

"Glass. From—look, he's got glass shards in his eyes."

Ricardo shuddered. "Holy shit."

"Yeah. He's just trying to keep his eyes closed, but we need to get him out of here and to a hospital ASAP so he doesn't go blind. Plus I think he's got a concussion, and his foot's fucked up."

Ricardo swallowed. Maybe he hadn't been so far off about the turned ankle after all. Except... Oh, no. August's feet weren't like other people's feet. He wasn't going to walk off an injury or limp through it, and if one was messed up, it wouldn't take much to jack up the other while favoring.

"The explosion," he said. "Did you and August go in through the shed?"

"Yes. Matt was following us in, so we went farther into the tunnel and August... I don't know, he told me to push some buttons, and when I did, something blew up and the tunnel caved in." She paused. "What the fuck is up with this house, Ricardo?"

He indulged in a quiet laugh. "You have no idea. But how far did you go from the shed?"

"I... I'm not sure. We took off a little ways, and August had me toss a flash-bang toward Matt, and then I was disoriented myself and I was trying to keep August upright and moving, and we took a couple of turns." She exhaled hard. "I don't know. We're down here somewhere. August needs a doctor. I'm fucking scared. What do we do?"

He'd never heard her this raw and terrified before, and he didn't like it at all. And knowing they had very little time to get August to a hospital before he lost his sight...

Shit. This was bad.

It was bad, and it wasn't going to get un-bad until Ricardo pulled himself together and did something about it.

Until he did something about *Matt*.

"All right. Listen to me." Ricardo took a deep breath. "Stay where you are. Call 911 and tell them we need an ambulance, but tell them we'll meet them at Stratford and Conway. Tell them anything they need to know about August's injuries, but maybe don't get us all arrested."

"Okay. Okay, I can do that. What are you going to do?"

"I'm going to get eyes on Matt and make sure he's not a threat anymore."

"You're going to kill him." It wasn't a question, and she didn't sound even a little bit upset about it.

"That's the plan, yes. Just stay where you are if you can. And remember—we'll meet the ambulance at Stratford and Conway."

"Got it." She paused. "Be careful, okay?"

"I'm always careful."

They ended the call, and Ricardo pocketed his phone. He considered putting in the second earplug, but thought better of it. If he was going to play cat and mouse with Matt, Matt would be running quiet, and Ricardo needed to be able to hear him.

He ducked into the hallway between the kitchen and living room. The house was open plan in places with some strange walls and a spiral staircase, but all its weird angles and curves hadn't been designed with eclectic aesthetics in mind. Ricardo had quickly learned that everything in this building had been strategically placed in the name of home defense. Someone coming into the house was wildly exposed while anyone coming out of the center of the building had barriers in the form of walls, columns, and the staircase itself.

The problem right now was that Matt was outside, and the entire house was locked down. Leaving the house would mean losing the advantage; Ricardo needed Matt to come to him.

Safely hidden in a strangely curved alcove between a replica of Michelangelo's *David* and a painting of a man's taint and asshole, Ricardo took out his phone again.

Tell August to disengage the house locks, he wrote. *Trust me.*

The response came a moment later:

Are you fucking insane? This house has safeguards for a reason. Oh my God.

He rolled his eyes. Thank you, voice-to-text, for ensuring that August could still send messages even while blind and concussed.

Disengage the locks, he wrote back, *or I will shoot the butthole painting. Don't test me.*

There was no response for a solid minute.

Then, *Locks are disengaged, and August said to tell you "I hate you."*

Good, he replied. *Send me Matt's contact.*

No hesitation this time. In seconds, he had Matt's cell phone number. Adrenaline shot through him as he wrote:

I'm in the house, Sandman. Come and get it. – Hurricane

He hated his Green Beret nickname, but it would get Matt's attention.

It worked, too—within minutes, a door somewhere in the house clicked, and it creaked open on its hinges like something out of an old haunted house. That was, like the creaky steps on the stairs, another safety protocol. The sound was annoying in day to day life, but in a situation like this, it allowed Ricardo to zero in on exactly where the hostile was coming from.

Not that his target was going for quiet or subtle, apparently.

"All right, Hurricane." Matt's voice sounded odd, as if he had on a helmet or a gas mask or something. Probably something he'd put on after the explosion that had driven him out of the shed. "You want to do this? Let's do this."

Ricardo crept along the wall, rifle poised and ready.

Boots stepped sharply on the kitchen floor. No, Matt was definitely not going for stealth, was he?

"Where are you, Ricardo?" Matt taunted. "Come on out."

Ricardo halted, furrowing his brow behind his rifle. Something wasn't right. The voice wasn't muffled like it came from a mask. It was wrong somehow.

He backtracked two silent steps.

"You want to do this?" Matt called out. "Let's do this."

Why did he sound exactly like he had when he'd said that a moment ago.

Heart pounding, Ricardo retreated another step. He glanced around, searching for movement. Shadows. Anything.

"Where are you, Ricardo? Come on out."

His blood ran colder.

The boots came closer.

Ricardo turned and went back the way he'd come, moving as stealthily as he possibly could. He ducked around a corner and—

Ran right into Matt.

In a heartbeat, Matt had raised a pistol and swung it, intending to pistol whip Ricardo, but Ricardo was faster. He sidestepped, then grabbed Matt's hand and twisted, driving a cry of fury and pain out of him as the gun tumbled to the floor. Ricardo kicked it away, but instantly regretted it because there was at least one other hostile in the house. Someone who'd been playing a recorded version of Matt's voice.

Well, it couldn't be helped now.

He twisted Matt's arm harder, then used his body weight to slam him into a wall. Matt managed to hit the back of Ricardo's knee with his own, and in Ricardo's split second of distraction, Matt wrenched his arm free. He made a play for Ricardo's rifle, but Ricardo was faster, and the butt of the gun made a satisfying crunch as it demolished the bone and cartilage of Matt's nose.

Matt cried out and staggered back as blood poured down his face and onto his tactical vest. "Fuck!" he sputtered, trying to slow the bleeding with his hand. "Son of a..."

Ricardo leveled the rifle at him, curled his finger around the trigger, and—

Bang!

A punch to his side made him grunt. He squeezed the trigger, but the shot went wide. Matt hit the deck. Ricardo staggered a step, recovered, and spun around to drop the goon who'd shot him. He quickly checked his side. No blood. None of that all too familiar deep, horrible pain. Unlike last time, the bullet hadn't gone *between* the trauma plates. Good.

In the seconds it took for Ricardo to shoot his assailant and check for a wound, though, Matt scrambled to his feet and lunged at him. They both went down, hitting the hardwood floor with a grunt from Ricardo as Matt's weight landed on top of him, and they grappled for the rifle. Matt got his hands on the barrel and managed shove the butt into Ricardo's gut. The trauma plate helped, but it still fucking hurt, which mostly served to piss off Ricardo. He threw a fist into Matt's bloody face, and from the cry of pain, he'd hit some of those newly tender spots.

Matt faltered, and Ricardo seized the opportunity to throw him off. Matt tumbled against the coffee table, but he rolled into a crouch, and when he came up, he had a crazed expression... and an incredibly nasty-looking knife in his hand.

Ricardo swallowed. Everyone said never take a knife to a gunfight, but in a close-quarters brawl, a knife could be far deadlier than a gun. And he knew for a fact that Matt had killed an enemy combatant—an actual one this time—in just such a fight.

Before Ricardo could get his hand on his own knife, Matt lunged. Ricardo grabbed his wrist, but inertia sent them both crashing into the coffee table. Ugh, fuck August and his insistence on a *metal* coffee table. The impact hurt like hell, stunning Ricardo for a split second, but he didn't let go of Matt's arm. They wrestled some more, but Matt had always been better at hand-to-hand combat than Ricardo, and he got Ricardo pinned to the floor with the rifle under his back. Ricardo still had a hold of Matt's wrist, but his other arm was pinned between Matt's knee and his own side. Every time he moved, the rifle or a trauma plate dug in painfully. He could grit his teeth through that, but he couldn't get free because he had no leverage, and he wouldn't unless he released that arm, which would earn himself a knife across the throat.

"I can't believe you, Torralba," Matt growled, spitting blood in Ricardo's face as he spoke. "You cheated on her, and now you're working with her to fuck me over? Where's the loyalty?"

"Eat a dick, Sandman," Ricardo snarled back.

Matt glared at him, lips peeling back across blood-stained teeth. "You're not winning her back, you moron. You can fight her battles all you want, but she's not yours any—"

"I don't give a fuck," Ricardo snapped, straining to keep a grip on Matt's arm. "She can fight her own battles. You're a piece of shit human trafficker, and I'm—"

Matt laughed coldly. "Christ. You're *still* a bleeding heart? No wonder you let that bitch cuck you into—"

Ricardo jerked his own arm free and grabbed Matt's

throat. Matt roared with fury and flailed, and the two of them were again wrestling on the floor.

This couldn't go on long. If Matt's stamina was anything like it had been back in the day, he'd keep fighting until Ricardo was too exhausted to go on, and then he'd go for the killing blow. Ricardo had to get and keep the advantage—and end this—first.

It was a risky move, but he didn't have much choice. He went for the pistol on his thigh.

In that same moment, Matt jerked his arm free.

The blade glinted in the light and arced downward. Expecting Matt go for his throat, Ricardo tried to block it, but instead he went for his gut.

The blade caught on a buckle of his tactical vest. The trauma plate kept it from going any further.

Matt reared back to try again.

Bang!

His whole body jerked, and for good measure, Ricardo squeezed off a second shot in the same spot—just under the bottom lip of Matt's vest so the bullet had unobstructed access to all those squishy vital organs the Kevlar and plates were meant to protect.

Matt slumped, and Ricardo shoved him off, sending him toppling to the side as blood poured out.

Ricardo stumbled to his feet and looked down at his ex-spotter, who was still alive but not for long. He just stared at the ceiling, moaning pitifully and painfully as he ruined the brand new floor.

Ricardo wasn't an animal, and outside of squeezing answers out of people, he didn't abide by suffering. He stopped Matt's moaning with two shots to the forehead.

Between the rapidly spreading pool of blood and the bullet holes, the floor was definitely wrecked. It was almost amusing to imagine how bitchy and furious August would be when he saw it.

But if Eve and Ricardo didn't hurry, August wouldn't see *anything*.

With a renewed surge of adrenaline, Ricardo took out his phone. He wiped blood on his pants, then sent a text:

Matt is gone. Where are you?

CHAPTER 20

It was embarrassing to admit it, but August didn't remember much after Ricardo found him and Eve.

It wasn't only embarrassing, it was reckless. It was the sort of thing he never would have allowed himself even a year ago. The sort of thing he hadn't let himself do since before he was kidnapped the first time.

Be aware of your surroundings. Make your own exit. Always have a Plan B, and C, and Z.

Even after Eve had told him, trembling with exhaustion and relief, that Matt was dead and Ricardo was on his way, August hadn't let himself go. Bleeding from his eyes and trying not to think about the way he desperately wanted to blink and couldn't, he'd still been able to help guide Ricardo to them. And then, when Ricardo arrived…

It was like August's whole world went soft around the edges. The pain eased, somehow, and his heartrate slowed down, and when Ricardo leaned in and kissed him despite the blood and the tears and the fact that August had to look like a horror show, well. How could he not give himself over to that?

In retrospect, he never stood a chance.

Getting to the ambulance took an unaccountably long period of time, getting to the hospital felt like it took an eternity, and then there was a brisk interview period and, right after that, sweet oblivion at last. August went unconscious holding on to Ricardo's hand, and he'd woken up still holding on to it.

That had been the nicest part about waking up. The only nice part, really.

"Corneal abrasions, huh." It was a nice way of saying *You scratched the shit out of your eyes and eyelids and you're lucky as fuck you didn't slice anything off.* "How long do I have to wear the eye patches?"

"Just a few days," Ricardo said. "And you'll be asleep for some of that anyway, since you're going in for surgery in four hours."

"Great." *Fucking great.* It turned out he'd broken not one, but two of the pins in his foot, along with a number of small and already fragile bones. His orthopedic surgeon was flying in for the procedure, but just the thought of more people seeing his feet, *touching* his feet, made August want to draw them up beneath his body. He hated hospitals, and not being able to see made it ten times worse. It felt like when he was a kid again, when his feet had been broken for the first time, and all he'd been able to do was bury his face against his brother's body, close his eyes, and wish he'd been the one to take a hammer to the head.

Oh, shit. He was spiraling.

"Hey." He turned toward where he expected Ricardo's face to be and smiled winningly. "I'll give you a million bucks if you spring me from this joint."

"Not happening."

The skin on the back of August's neck began to prickle with sweat. His hands became clammy. "Two million."

"August..."

"Three. Five. Ten." He was on the verge of hyperventilating, and fuck, he hated this part. August was so good at tamping down his anxiety most of the time; he was amazing at avoiding his triggers. But he was in a hospital, and he couldn't walk, and he couldn't see, and his eyes hurt even though he was on the good stuff and he was worried he'd never be able to see well enough to work again, and that might be a good thing for the poor suckers whose contracts he would have taken but it was bad news for him, bad, because that meant he'd be stuck inside of himself more and he hated being alone in here, he couldn't stand himself for that long, and why the fuck hadn't he been more careful, now he was—

"Hey. No."

"Fuck...you," August rasped, and then Ricardo was on the bed with him, the grip on August's hand transferred to his shoulders, and August couldn't help himself. He leaned in and pressed his face against the side of Ricardo's neck, avoiding his eyes because he wasn't a total idiot but trying to breathe, thickly, wetly. "Fuck."

"Breathe with me."

"No."

"August." Ricardo set one of August's hands on his chest. "Stop being a stubborn ass and do this."

"Just go." *Please don't go.*

"No."

"Go!"

"No." Ricardo was implacable. "And you can't make me, so stop trying and breathe with me."

Caught between desperately wanting to sulk and really

not wanting to give in to his anxieties, August made a half-hearted attempt to breathe with Ricardo. Even his shitty effort paid off, too—his head cleared after a few minutes, and the pain across his chest lessened. Of course it did. Ricardo was going to be such a bitch about being right, too.

"I'm all...fucked up right now," August confessed.

"I know." Ricardo pressed a kiss to the top of his head. "It's all right. I won't tell anyone."

Huh. Or maybe he wouldn't be a bitch about it. Would wonders never cease? Speaking of wondering... "Where's Elodie?"

"She's taking care of Eve. They were here for hours, but Eve needed to rest and I promised your sister I'd take care of you until she gets back."

August smiled despite the shitty way he felt. "Just that long?"

"As long as you want me," Ricardo amended. August felt his head shift as he looked toward the door. Then Ricardo muttered, "Shit."

August recognized that particular tone of voice. "Cops?"

"Worse. Pedro Silva."

Wait a second...Wait, what? "Do I have a concussion? Because I thought you just said Pedro fucking Silva was outside my hospital room."

"You do have a concussion, and yes, Silva is here. Hang on." He stroked the back of August's neck before gently detaching him and leaning him back against the bed. "I'll see what kind of shit we're in."

Probably the kind I can pay someone to shovel us out of.

The thought of it just made August feel even more tired. He didn't want to deal with the police right now, didn't want to put on his spoiled billionaire face and throw around threats and charm with equal abandon. He didn't want for Ricardo to have to slip away, which he would if the cops got involved because he didn't want the heat it brought down on him. August just wanted it all to go away.

"Since when do you work with the cops?" Ricardo asked someone, presumably Silva, loud enough that August could hear him.

"Since I knew I needed to have enough of them on my side to provide cover in case a business deal went south," Silva replied. "Like this one. Jesus Christ, we're going to be mopping up the blood for days. Do you have any idea how many bodies are lying in the street right now thanks to the war you instigated?"

"I didn't instigate anything."

Silva snorted derisively. "Yeah, sure. Next time, just keep your goddamn mouth shut, all right? What the people at the top don't know won't hurt them."

"I take it you're in the 'live and let human traffickers live' camp, then." Ricardo's voice had gone deadly soft. It took Silva a moment to reply.

"No," he said at last. "But I would have done things differently. Slower, more carefully. Less mess spread around, less scrutiny to have to deal with. Speaking of which, the bodies at your boytoy's house are gone."

"How did you know about those?"

"I'm sorry, do you not see my friends in blue over there? They checked, of course. But the police have better things to do than navigate the botched kidnapping of a billionaire right now."

Oh. Huh, that was a good play. That was actually a very good play. An oldie but a goodie. August was a little surprised that Silva had come up with it himself.

"And will those bodies *stay* gone?" Ricardo pressed.

"Shit, I'm not digging them out of the concrete," Silva said with a snort. "But I want you to know, you're going to owe me for this. Owe me big."

This time it was Ricardo who took a moment to answer. "We'll see," he said at last. "I won't be your pet killer."

"I wouldn't trust you not to turn around and bite the hand that feeds you anyway," Silva retorted.

"It wouldn't be you, regardless."

"Nah, it would probably be your pretty boy in there, huh?"

August tried to look like he wasn't listening with all his energy.

"Maybe not so pretty any more, though," Silva mused. "Are his eyes going to be all right?"

"Yes."

"Are you just saying that, or—"

"Thanks for stopping by, time for you to go."

"A favor, Garcia!" Silva called out again as he walked away. "Count on it!"

Ricardo muttered something August couldn't really hear, something with "puta" and "mierda" in it, then came back into the room and firmly shut the door.

"Whoever would have pictured Pedro Silva as our fairy godmother?" August asked, reaching a hand out blindly. Ricardo took it a second later. "How many bodies did he have to clean up?"

"Two." He said it so glibly that August was sure it was an underestimate. He didn't feel like pushing, though.

"Was it hard to kill Matt?" he asked instead.

"No." Ricardo's answer was solid, immediate, and incredibly soothing. August had been almost sure that Ricardo would think of it as a good thing—hell, he'd been prepared to do it before they'd been ambushed, but it was one thing to kill your former spotter from a thousand yards away and another to shoot him at close range. "I only wish I did it a long time ago. He didn't deserve all the chances he got, all the time to damage other people. If I'd taken that step before I left the service, he wouldn't have been able to hurt Eve. To hurt you." Ricardo's fingertips brushed against August's scratched and bruised cheek, then trailed down his neck and shoulder. "It's no use feeling guilty about it, but I do anyway. A little."

"I think it shows that you're a good person, deep down," August said. "That you didn't kill him when it would have been easy for you. You were hoping he'd turn himself around."

"Or I was feeling lazy and didn't want to have to get rid of the body on my own."

"Or that," August agreed. "That's also a definite possibility." He felt like laughing but also felt too woozy to pull it off. He let his head fall back against the pillow instead. "So. Am I really not pretty anymore?"

"Nope. You're hideous. I can hardly bear to look at you."

August smacked where he figured Ricardo's shoulder was and got a satisfying impact. "Hey! I could be legitimately fucked up about my appearance here!"

"You're not, though. You know you're still gorgeous."

Hearing his boyfriend describe him as "gorgeous" really *was* almost enough to fuck August up, because that wasn't the sort of thing they said to each other often...or ever, really. It was a good thing he was high, because he didn't want to think too hard about how much he must be blushing. "Smooth talker." He shifted uncomfortably in the bed. "I'm not really worried about my eyes either. Glasses are sexy."

Ricardo successfully read between the lines. "Your feet will be fine. Your sister told me your surgeon is the best on the East Coast."

"She is." Dr. Hawthorn was just the right blend of authoritative and mothering for August not to get snippy with her, and her technique was stellar. "I won't be good for much if I can't run, though."

Ricardo was silent for a moment. "Give yourself a chance to try before you start considering yourself a failure," he finally said.

"I'm just saying, if you don't want to be with someone who can't keep up with you, I'd understand that."

"Are you actually saying that it would make sense for me to break up with you because you might not get to be an assassin anymore?" Ricardo sounded *angry*, of all things.

"Yes? No? Maybe?" August sat up and flung his hands into the air. "I don't know! It made sense in my head! I just...want you to be happy, I guess. Shit."

Ricardo sighed the sigh of the incredibly put-upon. "Leaving you won't make me happy."

Well, that was nice and to the point. "Fine, then stay," August snapped.

"Fine, I will."

"*Fine.*"

"Good."

"Great."

Ricardo leaned in and sweetly kissed his lips, then pushed one of his iron-hard fingers into the center of August's forehead until he laid down again. "Now go the fuck to sleep. You're irritating when you're mopey."

"You're one to talk," August griped, but now that he was horizontal again, he could concede that Ricardo might have a point. "Wake me up when I'm fixed."

"Enjoy your eternal rest then, Sleeping Beauty."

August chuckled. "Fucker." God, he was tired, and the drugs were pulling him deeper, helping him forget his itching eyes and his aching feet and think only about how good it was going to feel to be unconscious.

And how safe he felt with Ricardo by his side. And he was going to stay, too.

Forever, if August had anything to say about it.

CHAPTER 21

Ricardo didn't want to be anywhere but by August's side, even though his battered boyfriend was out of the woods. He finally believed that, too, after the doctor had patiently explained four times that, no, those weird light and dark spots on the CT scan were not time bombs waiting for August to roll his eyes too hard and cause a brain bleed. Not that he'd be rolling his eyes any time soon unless he wanted to regret it; all the glass had been recovered, and now it was just a matter of being vigilant about signs of infection or other complications.

Barring any problems with anesthesia or anything else during the surgery later today, August would be discharged tomorrow. He'd begin the process of steadily recovering while no doubt being a demanding, whining pain in Ricardo's ass until Ricardo seriously considered smothering him with a pillow. He'd be fine. As terrifying as it had been to see him bleeding from the eyes and drifting in and out of consciousness, August was going to be *fine*.

But Ricardo still didn't want to be away from him.

He did, however, need some coffee, and when Elodie

and Eve came back, they encouraged him to take a break while they stayed with August.

So... Ricardo had gone. The coffee did him some good. So did the chicken salad sandwich, a small bag of Lays, and an M&M cookie, because why the hell not?

Once he'd finished eating, he headed back upstairs. He'd only been away for maybe twenty minutes, and that already seemed like too long. He needed to keep eyes on both Eve and August for a while until his brain stopped freaking out the moment one or both of them was out of earshot.

Halfway back to August's room, though, Ricardo paused to collect himself. As much as he wanted to be with August, he needed a moment, so he took it.

Matt was dead. The girls who'd been en route to a terrible fate were going to be returned safely to their families. The trafficking empire was coming down. The cops were duly bribed and otherwise compelled to not worry about the carnage at August's house.

Eve was safe. So was August. For all too long today, Ricardo hadn't known for sure if he'd ever be able to say that again. There'd been so many variables. So many possibilities. So many ways two of the people he loved the most could have been gone forever.

But they were okay. There would be some recovery time, and he knew for sure he'd be entertaining the idea of killing August himself over the coming weeks or months, but Eve and August were alive and likely to stay that way.

"Feel better?" Eve's voice startled him out of his thoughts, and he spun around to find her there with a coffee cup in her hand.

"A lot better, yeah."

She glanced back at August's room, then turned to him. "He said someone came by. Someone, uh… Powerful?"

Ricardo doubted August had disclosed much. He was probably on enough drugs to be more talkative than usual. That, or he'd given Elodie a heads up, speaking in French as they often did when they wanted to be discreet. Ricardo wondered when they'd figure out that Eve was also fluent in French.

Still, they wouldn't have spilled too much, and they must not have if she didn't know too many details. Ricardo sighed, shaking his head. "They're in the same business as your ex."

Her eyes widened. "Oh."

"It's nothing to worry about. That was the gangster August and I talked to when this all started." Ricardo gestured toward the elevator. "He was just letting me know that he and his men are going to make sure the organization isn't hurting anyone anymore." Close enough. She didn't need to know the rest.

"Ooh." Eve released a long breath, her shoulders sinking. "That's good. Jesus, I didn't even know that was what Matt was involved in. This rabbit hole has been…an experience."

"I'm sure it has. But it's over."

She nodded slowly. "Yeah. It is. And, um…" She stared into her coffee for a moment before she looked in his eyes again, and now the fatigue was coming off her in waves. "Thank you. I honestly had no idea who else to turn to for this, and I'm sorry for dragging you and August into… God, especially now that August is hurt, and…"

"Eve." He put his hands on her shoulders. "He'll be fine. He knew the risks when he went into it, and once he knew there were kids being kidnapped, we couldn't have stopped him if we tried. And things like this—it's what he and I do."

"Yeah, so I've learned." Her brow pinched. "I, um, should talk to Andi about your alimony. You really shouldn't have to keep paying when it turns out you didn't cheat on me."

Ricardo shook his head, releasing her shoulders. "I'm living with a billionaire, and the money will help you get on your feet after all of this. And I did lie to you, even if it wasn't what you thought."

"Okay, but I get why you did."

"Still. Get your feet under you, and then maybe we can talk money once everything settles."

She exhaled slowly. "All right. But sooner than later. And I mean it—thank you. Both of you. For everything. I was a fucking idiot for getting involved with that dolt, but thank God I had you—and your boyfriend, as it turned out—to help me get away from him. And to stop him from hurting all those kids."

He chuckled. "You did say I was good for some things now and then."

Eve blushed as she laughed. "You're good for a lot of things. Stop it." Then she put her coffee cup down by her feet, stepped closer, and hugged him. "Thank you, and I'm glad you and August are okay."

He returned her embrace. "You're welcome. I'm glad you're okay too." He paused. "And that Matt's dead."

She laughed, letting him go. "I never thought I'd say this about anyone, but I'm glad that fucker is dead too."

A pair of nurses walking by did horrified double takes but kept going. Ricardo and Eve just shook their heads and chuckled.

As she picked up her coffee, he gestured past her. "I should go see how August is doing."

"Right." She paused. "Do you mind if I join you?"

"Don't you need to go home and rest?"

"I'd rather stay here and make sure he's okay." With a soft smile, she added, "And maybe you could use some support while your man's on the table."

To his surprise, he couldn't find the stubbornness to insist he'd be fine. Maybe it wouldn't be so bad, having someone here until August was safely out of surgery and in recovery.

"All right. Thanks."

"Don't mention it." She paused. "And Elodie's my ride anyway, so it's not like I was going anywhere."

Ricardo laughed. "*There's* the truth."

She just snickered, and together, they headed into August's room.

Elodie was already there, and someone had brought in a couple more chairs, so Eve and Ricardo sat down.

"Now that you're here, Ricky..." August's voice was earnest enough to make Ricardo raise a suspicious eyebrow. "They're taking me into surgery soon. You know that, right?"

"Yes. I told you that."

"Right. Right. But..." He squeezed Ricardo's hand. "I mean, there's anesthesia involved. I could die."

"August. Don't talk like—"

"No. *Listen* to me."

Ricardo eyed him, kind of grateful August was blind right now and couldn't see his deepening suspicion. Elodie was clearly trying to smother a soundless laugh. Eve looked puzzled but amused.

Yeah, this was going to be good.

August took a deep breath. "I could die, so I need you to tell me something before I go in."

"You know I'm not the only one in here, right?"

"I know." The twitch of August's lip confirmed that wherever he was going with this, it was going to make Ricardo want to smack him. "But, baby, since this *may* be my dying wish, I need you to tell me—why did Matt call you Hurricane?"

Eve burst out laughing, which almost masked the sound of Ricardo's groan. He glared at her, and she clapped a hand over her mouth but didn't look the least bit repentant.

"Hurricane?" Elodie asked. "Do I want to know?"

"Ooh, yes." Eve was still giggling uncontrollably. "Yes, you definitely do."

They both watched Ricardo expectantly.

Ricardo glared at them.

"Come on, darling," August taunted. "My time is growing short. Tell me, so if the anesthesia gods take me, I can die in peace."

"You can die right now if you keep it up," Ricardo grumbled.

"Uh."

Ricardo's head snapped toward the door, and a bemused nurse watched them.

"Should I...?" She gestured over her shoulder. "I can come back."

"No!" August beckoned her over with his free hand. "Ricky was just about to tell us why his old Army buddies called him Hurricane."

Elodie at least made a valiant effort to contain her amusement, but Eve was going to pass out if she kept laughing like that.

The nurse looked around the room, then shrugged. "Eh,

I've heard it all before." Toeing the door shut behind her, she gave Ricardo a pointed look. "But if you're planning on committing murder, I don't want to do the paperwork, so leave me out of it."

"He won't murder me," August said, full of cockiness as ever. "I'm an amazing piece of ass, and I gave him a *closet*."

"Oh my." The nurse smirked. "That's commitment." She started checking over August's monitors. "So... Hurricane?"

Ricardo groaned. At this rate, if he kept avoiding the answer, August was going to get half the hospital in here. This was the smallest his audience was going to be.

With a defeated sigh, he sat back against his chair. "Because I sometimes brought people home to the barracks or my apartment. And when we were done..." His face was so hot now. So. Hot. God, did he have to? Did he really?

"Wait, are you shitting me?" August's expression was completely serious. "This had to do with your *hookups?* With you being a Green Beret *man slut?*"

Even Eve sobered, glancing back and forth between Ricardo and August like she was as caught off guard as he was by August's stunned anger. The nurse looked like she was ready to bail, and Elodie was probably going to be right behind her.

Ricardo cleared his throat. "It was a long time ago."

"And, what?" August demanded. "You'd bring people home and destroy your room or something? Fuck them and leave the place looking like a tornado went through?"

Ricardo hesitated, but then quietly admitted, "Well. More like a *hurricane* went through. Hence the nickname."

The room fell so silent, Ricardo could hear monitors beeping across the hall. Everyone without bandages over their eyes exchanged uneasy looks.

And then August burst out laughing so hard he was wheezing. "Oh my God. Oh God. That's... Oh, that's priceless."

Everyone else stared at him.

"I've been trying to figure it out," August said through his cackling. "Because why the fuck would someone call you... Oh, my God, that's amazing. That's hilarious. I'm calling you Hurricane forever. *Forever*, Ricky."

Ricardo watched him through narrowed eyes. "I'm going to smother you with a pillow. You know that, right?"

"Or you could just blow me." August snickered. "Like a hurricane."

Ricardo let his face fall into his hands, and when he heard Eve and Elodie laughing, he gave them the finger.

The nurse patted his shoulder. "You know, I can put in a good word with the nurses in the OR. They can give him something that'll make him real stupid for a few hours."

He looked up at her. "What difference would *that* make?"

"Well, he won't remember your nickname, and he'll just babble about the patterns in the ceiling and whatever he's hallucinating."

"Mmhmm." Ricardo arched an eyebrow. "Like I said, what difference would that make?"

The nurse just laughed and left the room.

As exasperated as he was, Ricardo had to admit it was reassuring to see August acting like his usual obnoxious self. He was facing down a period of blindness, not to mention surgery on his feet, which was a psychological minefield for him.

But, even if it was at Ricardo's expense, he was laughing. And he was, even if Ricardo still struggled to believe it, out of the woods.

Tomorrow, they would go home. August would get back on his feet. Eve would, metaphorically, do the same.

There would be contracts in the future. More danger. More chaos, because God knew there would be chaos wherever August went.

And wherever August went, Ricardo would go too.

THE END

DON'T MISS THESE OTHER TITLES BY CARI Z & L.A. WITT!

The Bad Behavior Series
Risky Behavior
Suspicious Behavior
Reckless Behavior
Romantic Behavior
Protective Behavior

The Double Trouble Duology
Double or Nothing
Doubling Down

You Had One Job

The Hitman vs Hitman series
Hitman vs Hitman
Sniper vs Spotter
Killer vs Kingpin (coming soon)

ABOUT THE AUTHORS

Cari Z. is a Colorado girl who loves snow and sunshine. She writes award-winning LGBTQ fiction featuring aliens, supervillains, soothsayers, and even normal people sometimes

Cari has published short stories, novellas and novels with numerous print and e-presses, and she also offers up a tremendous amount of free content on Literotica.com, under the name Carizabeth. Follow her blog to read her serial stories, with new chapters posting every week.

Want to follow along or get in touch? No problem!
Website: http://cari-z.net
Email: carizabeth@hotmail.com
Twitter: @author_cariz

L.A. Witt and her husband have been exiled from Spain and sent to live in Maine because rhymes are fun. She now divides her time between writing, assuring people she is aware that Maine is cold, wondering where to put her next tattoo, and trying to reason with a surly Maine coon. Rumor has it her arch nemesis, Lauren Gallagher, is also somewhere in the wilds of New England, which is why L.A. is also spending a portion of her time training a team of spec ops lobsters. Authors Ann Gallagher and Lori A. Witt have been asked to assist in lobster training, but they "have books to write" and "need to focus on our careers" and "don't you think this rivalry has gotten a little out of hand?" They're probably just helping Lauren raise her army of squirrels trained to ride moose into battle.

   Website: www.gallagherwitt.com
   Email: gallagherwitt@gmail.com
   Twitter: @GallagherWitt